"I'm so damned scared, Danny."

Mary Elise's thready words barely whispered against his neck until he might have questioned his hearing. But he felt each word and all her fear soak into him along with the heat of her rapid breaths.

"Tell me," he coaxed. "Tell me what to do for you."

She inched back, her hand sliding up his face again. "Oh, Danny, can't you see that you and all this—" she slipped her hand around his neck in a sensual glide "—this tension between us that we can't ignore is a big part of the problem? You need to believe me when I say I just can't risk staying here with you."

His arms around her twitched, muscles convulsively tensing to hold her closer, safer. As much as he wanted to reassure her, he couldn't. He knew himself too well.

Dear Reader,

This year may be winding down, but the excitement's as high as ever here at Silhouette Intimate Moments. National bestselling author Merline Lovelace starts the month off with a bang with *A Question of Intent,* the first of a wonderful new miniseries called TO PROTECT AND DEFEND. Look for the next book, *Full Throttle,* in Silhouette Desire in January 2004.

Because you've told us you like miniseries, we've got three more for you this month. Marie Ferrarella continues her family-based CAVANAUGH JUSTICE miniseries with *Crime and Passion.* Then we have two military options: *Strategic Engagement* features another of Catherine Mann's WINGMEN WARRIORS, while Ingrid Weaver shows she can *Aim for the Heart* with her newest EAGLE SQUADRON tale. We've got a couple of superb stand-alone novels for you, too: *Midnight Run,* in which a wrongly accused cop has only one option— the heroine!—to save his freedom, by reader favorite Linda Castillo, and Laura Gale's deeply moving debut, *The Tie That Binds,* about a reunited couple's fight to save their daughter's life.

Enjoy them all—and we'll see you again next month, for six more of the best and most exciting romances around.

Yours,

Leslie Wainger

Leslie J. Wainger
Executive Editor

Please address questions and book requests to:
Silhouette Reader Service
U.S.: 3010 Walden Ave., P.O. Box 1325, Buffalo, NY 14269
Canadian: P.O. Box 609, Fort Erie, Ont. L2A 5X3

Strategic Engagement
CATHERINE MANN

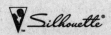

INTIMATE MOMENTS™

Published by Silhouette Books

America's Publisher of Contemporary Romance

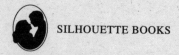 SILHOUETTE BOOKS

ISBN 0-373-27327-4

STRATEGIC ENGAGEMENT

Copyright © 2003 by Catherine Mann

This edition published by arrangement with Harlequin Books S.A.

® and TM are trademarks of Harlequin Books S.A., used under license.
Trademarks indicated with ® are registered in the United States Patent
and Trademark Office, the Canadian Trade Marks Office and in other
countries.

Visit Silhouette at www.eHarlequin.com

Printed in U.S.A.

Books by Catherine Mann

Silhouette Intimate Moments

Wedding at White Sands #1158
*Grayson's Surrender #1175
*Taking Cover #1187
*Under Siege #1198
The Cinderella Mission #1202
*Private Maneuvers #1226
*Strategic Engagement #1257

*Wingmen Warriors

CATHERINE MANN

writes contemporary military romances, a natural fit since she's married to her very own USAF research source. Prior to publication, Catherine graduated with a B.A. in fine arts: theater from the College of Charleston and received her master's degree in theater from UNC Greensboro. Now a RITA® Award winner, Catherine finds following her aviator husband around the world with four children, a beagle and a tabby in tow offers her endless inspiration for new plots. Learn more about her work, as well as her adventures in military life, by visiting her Web site: http://catherinemann.com. Or contact her at P.O. Box 41433, Dayton, OH 45441.

Dedication:
To military families everywhere.

Acknowledgments:

To Homer and Karen Tucker, treasured friends who are
family in my heart if not by blood relation. Thank you
for your never-faltering faith in my stories.

To Major Kevin "Bjorn" Brown and his wonderful wife,
Leah. Thank you, Kevin, for your generous insights into
the C-17 world. (Any mistakes are strictly my own!)
Many thanks also to Leah, a talented author
and dear friend, for cheering me on
and keeping me up to date on Charleston AFB.

And as always, thank you to my very own hero, Rob,
for making our happily-ever-after a beautiful adventure.

Chapter 1

Eleven years ago Mary Elise McRae had expected to fill a hope chest for Daniel Baker. But she'd never thought she would fill it quite so literally.

Her body currently folded inside a five-by-five-foot wooden crate, Mary Elise hugged the two small boys closer. The rough-hewn box jostled on the back of the flatbed truck, jarring bony little elbows and knees against her. Hard. Not that anyone dared do more than breathe in the cedar-scented darkness.

A lone horn honked along the stretch of desert road in their escape route from Rubistan. The truck jerked to a stop. A goat blocking the way? Or a cow? Either animal slow when Mary Elise needed fast. Headlights from the truck behind them shone through the tiny slits between the boards.

A Rubistanian guard from the embassy tracking them.

She'd heard his voice during the loading onto the truck. Procedure didn't allow him on the U.S. government's vehicle, but those ominous beams sparked fear inside her as surely as if he'd been sitting alongside puffing away on one of those cigars he favored. Would he use this delay as an excuse to ambush them? Cause an "accident?"

The diesel engine's growl increased and the truck lurched to life. Mary Elise exhaled her relief in the stifling enclosure. Only another half hour, max, until she delivered Trey and Austin safely aboard a U.S. military cargo plane. Then she would say her tearful farewells to the two children being smuggled out of this Middle-Eastern hell in the back of Captain Daniel Baker's C-17.

Danny.

His name echoed in her mind amid the grind of changing gears. What would Daniel say when he saw her for the first time in eleven years? If only he had advance warning she would be with the boys, but she'd expected to stay at the embassy, not be in this sweltering crate.

With any luck, they'd be too rushed to talk. She would pass over her young charges. Thank Daniel for answering the emergency SOS she'd anonymously routed through the economic attaché. Then haul butt off the airstrip, back to her tiny apartment in Rubistan's capital, back to her teaching post at the American embassy school.

Back to her solitary life.

She wouldn't let memories of Daniel make her yearn for anything more. She'd worked damned hard for her pocket of peace away from Savannah. Peace bought with the help of Daniel's father. Trey and Austin's father, too. And today she would repay that debt.

"Mary 'Lise?" Austin whispered from under her chin. "Wanna get out. Gotta go."

"Shh," she urged as loudly as she dared. "Soon, sweetie. Soon." She hoped.

Sweat trickled down her neck, caking sand to her skin

as Mary Elise willed Austin silent. A crate of computers didn't whisper for a bathroom, after all. Sure, a diplomatic pouch was immune from inspection—a pouch being U.S. government property of any size from the embassy. Totally immune. Unless that "pouch" starting talking.

Her arms locked tighter around thin, preschooler shoulders on her left and the more substantial nine-year-old frame on her right. At least Trey was old enough to follow instructions, his shoulders pumping under her arm with each heavy breath. Little Austin was a wild card.

Bracing her feet against the other side to combat jolts, she suppressed the illogical bubble of laughter. Definitely a card. Wild. Precious. And looked so much like his adult half brother Daniel.

So much like the baby she and Daniel might have had if not for the miscarriage.

Of course she hadn't been able to turn away when Austin had pumped out tears at the sight of the crate. He'd begged for Mary 'Lise to crawl inside with him instead of his twenty-one-year-old nanny, a pale nanny who'd seemed all too willing to bow out.

The truck squealed to a stop. A tiny hand tucked into hers and clutched tight with chubby stickiness. She pressed a silent kiss to Austin's brow.

"Well, hello there, gentlemen," the masculine bass rumbled.

Danny.

Even with eleven years more testosterone infused into deepening his voice, she would recognize that hint of a drawl anywhere. No rushing. Even in the middle of an unstable country, on a darkened runway where threats lurked in countless shadows…Danny didn't hurry for anyone. Life followed him. He never followed life.

His ambling lope thudded closer. Could they hear her heart thump outside the box?

A second set of footsteps sounded. Faster. Cigar smoke wafted through the thin slits between boards. The distinctive scent of imported Cubans favored by the Rubistanian guard from the embassy snaked around her.

The slower bootsteps, Daniel's, stopped. "How downright neighborly of you to offer an escort, but my folks here can handle things now."

"We have procedure to follow in my country, Cap-i-tain," the guard clipped out in heavily accented English.

"Lighten up there, Sparky. I know all about your procedure. The paperwork's pristine…well, except for some ketchup on the edge there from my fries. Now back on up so my loadmaster can finish the transfer."

Daniel's affected flippancy reached into the box with calming comfort. And unwelcome arousal. His voice shouldn't still have the power to strum her numbed senses to life, especially not now. She wasn't a teenager anymore. She was a mature woman with control over her life. She'd moved on after the debacle with Danny. Married someone else.

Bad example.

Lighten up, 'Lise. Danny's mantra echoed in her head through the years. *Life's just not that complicated.*

She wished.

"Time to head on out, Sparky," Daniel called, casual and irreverent as ever. "The sooner Tag over there can load up and lock down, the sooner we'll get off your runway and out of this…garden spot."

A trail of tangy smoke slithered into the box. "What is your hurry, Cap-i-tain?"

"Hurry?" Daniel's bass rumbled closer, louder. The truck shifted with the weight of another body. "I need to head home for my annual pilgrimage to the Frito-Lay factory. Besides, my copilot's just a kid and it's past her bedtime.''

''Hey, now,'' a female voice called from below. ''Frito-Lay? I thought you were going to Hershey, Pennsylvania.''

''That was last month, Wren.''

''And you didn't bring me any chocolate? I'm crushed.''

''I thought about you. But what can I say? I got hungry on the way home.''

Their lighthearted voices filled the box, and Mary Elise resented the twinge of envy over his easy rapport with the copilot. She'd once shared that same relationship with Daniel until the summer their friendship had spiraled into something more. So much more.

Memories swirled in the murky box with oppressive weight. So Daniel still loved his junk food. They'd met twenty-two years ago over a chocolate Ho-Ho. She'd pulled the treat from her Holly Hobby lunch box to thank him for bloodying Buddy Davis's nose after the bully made fun of her Yankee accent.

Did Daniel still like video games, too? Hide his genius brain behind jokes?

Kiss with an intense thoroughness that turned a woman's insides to warmed syrup?

A hand patted the box once, again, and again, with slow reassurance. Daniel. ''And speaking of hungry,'' he said, his hand thumping a lulling lazy beat. ''There's a flight lunch and a bag of licorice with my name written all over it waiting in the cockpit. Let's step this up.''

Smoke spiraled inside, mingling with the ripe scent of fresh-cut boards. A low wheeze hissed from Trey. His head fell back against her arm as he sucked in air.

Tension stretched inside her. Mary Elise rubbed a soothing hand along his back, a poor substitute for his inhaler, but all she could risk. The smoke, cedar and fear were too much for anyone, much less a child with asthma. As if these kids hadn't already been through enough with their parents' "accidental" deaths and a Rubistanian uncle trying to claim them...and their inheritance.

All the more reason to get the children to their half brother on American soil. Screw official diplomatic channels where the boys could be in college before Rubistan coughed them up.

Mary Elise hugged the boys closer, her hair snagging along the wood. Pulling. Stinging her scalp. Hard. Her eyes watered.

Oh, God. Come on, Daniel. They needed to get rid of that guard so someone could crack open the box, let Trey breathe.

And let her out.

Another puff of cigar smoke tendriled inside. "How interesting that your name tag reads Baker, Cap-i-tain. That is the last name of your ambassador who so recently died."

The thudding stopped. Silence echoed for three wheezing breaths from Trey before the rhythmic tap resumed. "Baker's a common last name over in America, Sparky."

"Of course. If you were related you would be in mourning, not working."

The vehicle dipped with added weight, then footsteps shuddered the truck bed. Not Daniel's lope. The clipped pace of the guard. "Is that a loose board I see right—"

"Don't even think about it." Daniel's steely voice iced the humid air. The click of a cocked gun echoed. "If you lay so much as one finger on that box, I'll blow your damned hand off. A diplomatic pouch is sovereign United

States government territory. Move back and get off this truck. Now.''

Bugs droned in response along with the low hum of the idling plane engines. Please, please, please, be careful, Danny. She hadn't wanted to see him and now she couldn't bear the thought of never laying eyes on him again. She'd brought him here, hadn't had a choice for the boys. But if things went to hell, she would never forgive herself.

An exhale sounded along with the retreat of boots and smoke. The gun snicked as it was uncocked.

The crate rolled forward.

Air rushed from her lungs. Not that she should be surprised at Daniel's victory. The teenager she'd known carried an untamed look in his eyes, the veneer of ten generations of Savannah wealth having worn thin for him. So often he'd flung himself into brawls like a scrappy street fighter in defiance of his pedigree. In defense of her. He'd always won, too. Except once.

I'm sorry. She winged her apology for then as well as now.

He'd taken a punch from his father when she'd been as much at fault for the unplanned pregnancy. Of course Daniel had never raised a hand to defend himself.

God, she wished she had the option of fighting back against her ex-husband, fists and brawn and bluster, instead of shadow dancing with insidious threats. He'd never actually struck her, just controlled her, betrayed her body in a way so soul rending she wondered if she could ever recover. And then when she'd dared leave him, he'd hired a hit man to take her out.

Not that the police would help her, thanks to her ex's far-reaching influence.

She wasn't a wilting flower, but she also wasn't stupid.

So she'd run. She'd even been willing to move to a hotbed of political unrest in the Middle-Eastern country of Rubistan to stay alive. At least in Rubistan no one thought it might be a nifty idea to kill her simply because she couldn't bear him children.

Visions of her Georgia home chilled the sweat sealing her silk shirt to her skin. Come on, come on, come on. Open the damned box.

The sides closed in with claustrophobic pressure. She shoved away the need to run. For the boys. The precious warm weights beside her who smelled of chocolate and sunshine and dreams she would never have.

The crate tipped. Mary Elise and the children slid, wedging into the corner with the minimal padding of a couple of blankets.

"Tag, go easy there," Daniel called. "Wouldn't want to crack a keyboard now, would we?"

"No worries, sir." A voice sounded beside them as the box jerked to a stop. "I'll treat it like one of my own."

A mechanical drone built. The dim streaks of light faded. The load-ramp shutting? The world faded around her to near black until the ramp clanked closed.

She forced her breathing to regulate. Maybe they needed privacy to open the crate. That made sense. Then they could slip her back off the plane under the cover of darkness. Not ideal. But doable.

Lazy footsteps picked up speed along the metal floor. A final thump sounded on the planked top. "Lock it down tight, Tag."

"Roger that, Captain."

The thud of boots faded. Chains jangled in the time fugue of waiting. Was it safe to talk? Engines roared and grew louder. Forget waiting.

Mary Elise opened her mouth and shouted. And couldn't hear herself over the engines.

Her heart hammered her chest. The boys wriggled closer. She screamed. A soundless shriek swallowed by the din.

The crate vibrated, joggled as the plane moved. Faster. Forward. Picking up speed. The roar built, swelled. Tension clenched her chest until each breath became a struggle like Trey with his asthma.

The box tilted back. Gravity slid her with the boys until she landed against the wooden wall as the plane…

Went…

Up.

Oh, God. They were airborne.

Airborne. And not a damned moment too soon.

Captain Daniel ''Crusty'' Baker maxed the throttle. Level at twenty-eight thousand feet. Time to plow through the night sky out of Rubistianian airspace so they could crack open the crate. He'd tried to keep the takeoff as smooth as possible for the boys and their nanny, but he couldn't risk letting them out.

Not while a pair of enemy MiG-21s flew an ominous escort in the star-studded sky.

Swiping aside the unopened bag of licorice, Crusty switched to closed interphone frequency. ''Hold tough in back, we're almost over the border.''

Where he hoped the MiGs would peel away.

''Roger, sir,'' answered Senior Master Sergeant J. T. ''Tag'' Price, loadmaster for the mission. ''We're hanging in there.''

Relief pilot, 1st Lt. Bo Rokowsky, loomed, strapped in behind Daniel, restless energy filling the cockpit.

Copilot, 1st Lt. Darcy ''Wren'' Renshaw, worked from

the right seat, punching numbers into the navigational system. "Five minutes and counting down."

No room for error with those MiGs hungry for an excuse to pop them with an infrared missile. Damn, but he owed this crew. Sure the mission had been CIA sanctioned—barely. Approved in a sped-through process that would likely leave heads rolling later when their new squadron commander returned from TDY—temporary duty.

Renshaw had signed on out of friendship. Tag out of honor. Rokowsky out of craziness. The wild-eyed lieutenant constantly gave new meaning to their squadron motto of Anything, Anywhere, Anytime.

Daniel adjusted airspeed, keeping his eyes trained on the holographic HUD—heads up display—perched at the bottom of his windscreen. He owed Renshaw double. Her boyfriend, who worked for the Air Force's Office of Special Investigations, had used his old CIA contacts to push through paperwork for this embassy run in less than forty-eight hours after the call from the economic attaché. The final mission orders had even included a couple of the Air Force's elite security forces, Ravens, to accompany them.

Who couldn't offer protection against the MiGs keeping pace alongside.

Daniel's gun weighed like lead in his pocket. The Rubistanians knew. Of course they knew. But their government couldn't search without concrete evidence the boys were in that crate.

His half brothers. A couple of kids he'd only seen a handful of times. Sure, he could blame that on being oceans apart, but he knew damned well it had nothing to do with distance in miles. It had everything to do with the distance between his father and him that had started eleven years ago. His father had been a senator in those days. Full of himself and his power, the old man had dumped his wife for a hot young translator from Rubistan and started a new family.

Later his father had assumed the position of ambassador to Rubistan so his wife could be near her family. Of course, then the old man had decided to dump her for a newer hottie model—until a blown-up embassy Mercedes had preempted the divorce.

Yeah, the old guy sure as hell had been a poster boy for the wisdom of bachelorhood. And damned if he didn't feel guilty as hell for the crappy, disloyal thought. If only they'd had a chance to come close to understanding each other.

Daniel's hand clenched around the throttle. Steady. They were almost to the border. The box was locked down tight, with the nanny inside to keep the kids calm and safe. The transfer had gone as smoothly as could be expected.

Except when he'd almost had a freaking heart attack over seeing a long wisp of red hair trailing from a crease in the crate. One glimpse of that strand glinting in the tarmac lights and he'd hauled ass onto the truck to put himself between the auburn thread and the guard. Hand behind his back, he'd given the telltale strand a quick yank—and prayed the nanny would stay quiet.

Daniel flicked at a lone red hair clinging to his sleeve. Again. He'd flung it away more than once, but the thing kept sticking to his flight suit. He shook his hand to dislodge it from his glove and tried not to think about another person with hair that shade of auburn. Why the hell was she right there in his mind today?

Mary Elise.

He damned well didn't believe in the mystical. He preferred the mathematical precision of his world of dark ops testing. But he'd never been able to explain the connection between himself and Mary Elise that had started over a shared Ho-Ho after he'd beaten the crap out of Buddy Davis for picking on the new kid about her accent.

Years later the connection had frayed because of a night of impulsive sex. Great sex. Impossible-to-forget sex with his best friend.

Then not friends. Not anymore. No friendship. No baby. No connection with Mary Elise. Until today.

The hair drifted across his control panel.

Renshaw keyed up the mike. "Ten seconds and counting down."

Daniel steadied his breath with each count. Focus. Fly. It must just be his father's death two weeks ago knocking him off balance. Since he'd been so deep in-country on an assignment by the time the message reached him about his father, Daniel had even missed the memorial service. A miscommunication snafu left out his stepmother's death, so he'd assumed the boys were fine.

Definitely a hellacious couple of weeks of surprises. At least he was in the homestretch.

"Three. Two," Wren chanted. "One. Over the Rubistanian border."

Daniel twisted to check-visual out the window. Like clockwork, the MiGs peeled away.

A collective sigh echoed through the headset.

In the clear. "Okay, Tag, go ahead and break open that crate now."

He would worry later about what to do with his brothers. Between their nanny and the brand-new pair of Game Boys in his flight bag, he might not even have to figure that one out until morning.

Daniel reached to punch in the radio frequency to notify Ankara center in Turkey that they'd crossed over into their airspace. The charge of having bested the enemy stirred an adrenaline buzz.

"Captain Baker?" Tag clipped through the headset.

"Yeah, Tag?" Daniel's hand fell away from the radio controls. "Problem?"

"As a matter of fact, there is. I think you're going to want to come down here and check this out for yourself."

Tension snapped through the crew compartment.

"Roger. I'm on my way." Daniel waggled the stick, the fighterlike stick in the C-17 a sleek upgrade from the steering yoke of older cargo planes. "Wren, you got the jet?"

The stick wiggled in his grip in tandem response as she signaled her control. Sweat dotted her brow, dampening her short brown hair to her head, but no hint of stress showed through her concentration. "Roger, Crusty, I have the jet."

Daniel unplugged his headset and charged down the narrow stairwell into the belly of the plane. Victory-sparked adrenaline ignited into a darker dread.

He may not know these brothers of his, but they were counting on him, damn it. They didn't have anyone else other than a megalomaniac uncle in Rubistan who wanted their inheritance to funnel into terrorist training camps.

No way in hell would that slime get his hands on Trey and Austin.

Daniel cleared the stairs and entered the cargo hold. His eyes adjusted to the dim glow of lights tracking the roof and illuminating the metal cave. The crate gaped open. Tag stood with boots braced, the bear of a man cradling a tousle-headed three-year-old like a seasoned parental veteran.

Austin.

Relief pounded through Daniel. His eyes jerked to the

grouping by the row of seats where Trey sat with his elbows on bony knees. Everyone alive.

Cricking his neck from side to side, Daniel strode toward the cluster hovering around Trey. The two Ravens stood guard in full battle dress camouflage, machine guns slung over their shoulders. Body armor padding their chests, both men scowled down at the willowy woman kneeling in front of Trey.

Red hair trailed down her back.

Daniel shut down thoughts of another woman. Everyone seemed okay and that's what mattered most. Some a helluva lot more than *okay*. The woman's brown silk shirt clung to her slim shoulders, to her elegant arms. And legs. Man, she had long legs, legs encased in tan pants smudged with dirt. Hugging a sweetly rounded bottom that begged admiration.

Daniel scrubbed a hand over his gritty—and damned wayward—eyes. Adrenaline played hell with a man's libido, especially after two days of no sleep. He did not need to be seducing the nanny, no matter how intriguing the idea of swiping aside all that silk and hair sounded.

He had other, more practical needs for her, rather than testing the waters to see if she might be interested in some uncomplicated sex. Uncomplicated sex was easy to find with any of the string of women who wanted to "fix" him—iron his wrinkled flight suits, make him eat right. Dealing with his brothers, however, would be complicated as hell.

Daniel shifted his attention to his nine-year-old brother. Trey hunched over, hands hooked behind his head on his buzz-cut brown hair as he sucked in gasps of air.

Crap. Daniel strode forward. "What's going on here?"

Trey jerked upright. "No-thing," he gasped out.

The nanny's shoulders rippled under silk. Still kneeling, she straightened her back but didn't turn.

His hand fell to her shoulder, wavy red hair snagging on his flight glove. A jolt shot up his arm.

Don't be a sap. There were at least a million women with hair that color. "Ma'am? Is there something we can do for him?"

Slowly her head turned, her fiery hair tugging under his fingers. She looked up at him, and Daniel stared down into the greenest eyes he'd ever seen.

Holy hell.

There might be a million women with hair that color of auburn. But there was only one woman with eyes that particular shade of fresh-mown spring grass.

Mary Elise braced her shoulders with the same defensive bravado she'd worn when telling him the rabbit died.

"Hello, Danny."

Chapter 2

Mary Elise decided the inside of that box might not be too bad after all. At least in there she could only hear Danny. Now she could hear and *see* him. All of him. Every damned fine inch of him.

Dim lights filled the gray cavern, glinting off Daniel's dark hair, casting shadows along the angles of his face. His lanky good looks had hardened into a lean body cut with whipcord strength that stretched just shy of six feet tall.

If only she could distance herself from his appeal, but the day-from-hell wreaked havoc on her normally rigid self-control. Instead, she could only stare at him and soak up the differences wrought by age.

One gloved hand flattened against the side of the plane, he lounged with that same loose-hipped carelessness he'd worn when she'd told him she was pregnant. As if her announcement hadn't meant the end of his Air Force

Academy dream since cadets can't marry until after graduation.

Except his dream hadn't ended. He'd won the Academy ring and wore the flight suit now, wrinkled though it might be at the moment.

Attraction be damned, she wanted to flatten him right onto his awesome butt. Care about *something*. Let it be important to see the woman you almost married. She'd never been head-over-heels *in* love with him, but she *had* loved him. Once. He'd been her friend, and the betrayal of how easily he'd let go after she lost the baby had hurt.

His indifference hurt now.

He shouldn't still have the power to wound her. Her ex had done so much worse to her and she'd held strong. She'd be damned if she'd let Daniel trample her heart with one distant look.

Mary Elise gripped the barred edge of the seat to steady her hands. She might not be able to regulate her pulse or her feelings, but she could control what she did about them. Bigger worries loomed, anyway, far more important than discovering if Daniel Baker still administered the most thorough, long and intense kisses she'd ever known.

"Danny, could you pass me the smaller bag inside the crate, please? The black canvas one. Trey needs his inhaler."

"Don't...want it," Trey insisted.

Daniel's forehead trenched. "The kid has asthma? Why didn't someone tell me?" He shifted away, mumbling, "And why didn't someone mention who the hell would be accompanying them?"

So it bothered him after all. Mary Elise stifled the urge to do an impromptu victory dance and rubbed soothing circles along Trey's back while Daniel reached into the crate.

His flight suit stretched across narrow hips that veed up his back into broad shoulders. Muscles rippled under taut green fabric with restrained strength. He pivoted around with athletic fluidity, pitching the bag toward her.

"Thank you," she said, avoiding eyes that told her too well she wouldn't be able to dodge talking soon.

Mary Elise yanked the zipper open and rifled inside the pouch until her fingers closed around the inhaler. She snapped off the cap and thrust her hand toward Trey.

He brought the medicine to his mouth and pumped once, twice, again.

She prayed they wouldn't be stranded in the air with Trey in a full-blown attack. "Come on, hon, take one more hit off the inhaler, okay?"

His shoulders heaved with a shuddering inhale.

Mary Elise waited for signs of relief. Years spent tending her chronically ill mother had left her with more knowledge about lung disease than some doctors. Her mother's illness had also left her unsupervised, free to tromp alongside the neighbor boy. Never once had Danny complained about a pesky tagalong two years his junior. He'd shrugged off any teasing—when had Danny cared what others thought anyway—and labeled her his mascot.

Daniel knelt beside her. The scent of bay rum mingled with the pervasive air of hydraulic fluid. "What else can you do for him?"

Mary Elise focused on the hydraulic fluid. Fat lot of good it did her with the warmth of Danny's arm inches away from her breast. "His nebulizer's in the other bag. We can set that up if the Albuterol inhaler doesn't do the trick."

Trey's heaving shoulders slowed.

She swept a hand over his pale brow. "Better, hon?"

The boy nodded.

Daniel held out his hand for the inhaler. ''Hey, buddy, let me take that for you.''

''You're not…my buddy. Don't even…know you.''

Mary Elise stiffened.

Daniel stilled, then slowly retracted his hand. ''That's right.'' His arms fell to rest on his knee. ''We don't know each other. And we'll duke that one out later on terra firma back in the States. Right now you just take care of yourself.''

Trey clamped his mouth shut and fixed his gaze somewhere over his brother's head.

Shoving to his feet by Tag, Daniel ruffled Austin's sweaty curls. ''Hey there, sport.''

Austin studied him with wary eyes, but at least not openly hostile. Daniel tugged off his flight gloves and reached into his thigh pocket. His hand whipped back out with a chocolate bar. ''Snickers?''

Austin's brown eyes sparkled.

Mary Elise rose, Daniel topping her by only a few inches. A perfect fit. Double damn. ''He's allergic to nuts.''

''How about licorice?''

''He might choke.''

Daniel's jaw flexed. ''Three Musketeers bar?''

Mary Elise refrained from asking for an apple, a senseless request after the kid had already been offered candy. ''That would be fine.''

Daniel fished the treat out of his seemingly bottomless pocket for Austin, then turned back to his other brother.

Trey hunched back in the seat, arms tight across his chest. ''I'm not hungry.''

Uh-oh. The kid loved licorice. Mary Elise waited for Daniel's reaction. Prayed somewhere inside this harder new Daniel there still lived the Danny who'd sat with her during her bout with chicken pox, teaching her to play poker, tutoring her in math, making her laugh so she wouldn't scratch.

Shrugging, Daniel zipped his thigh pocket closed. "Fair enough. I have to head back up to the crew compartment. If you decide you're hungry later on, Tag here can give you a hand."

Mary Elise winged a silent thanks for the easy out Daniel offered Trey. Maybe they would be okay after all.

"Mary Elise?" Daniel called. "Got a second?"

Big-time uh-oh. She didn't want this talk right now, not when the old Danny still hovered in her memory.

Better pitch those sympathetic leanings back in the crate and maintain her distance. Keep it light. Do the *old friends* routine.

Old friends who happened to know every inch of each other's body.

Daniel cupped her elbow, his grip hot, firm—familiar. And it had been so long since a man had touched her. Her body absorbed the sensation. Stupid. Wrong.

But pulling away would lend too much importance to a simple gesture. She kept her eyes forward and suppressed a shiver. He was a good-looking guy, no question, in a rumpled way that defied her need for order.

Hormones, pure and simple.

The day's danger and stress left her vulnerable. That must be the reason she wanted to tuck against his broad chest, the only reason she yearned to savor the comfort of bay rum and chocolate.

Her eyes landed on the little round scar beside his brow. Two weeks after her recovery, Daniel's chicken pox had spread fast and furious. She'd brought a deck of cards to his house and reamed him out for not telling her he hadn't been exposed before. He'd just shrugged, scratching the corner of his eyebrow.

How could he be such a stranger and so familiar all at once?

His boots thudded along the metal tracks lining the belly of the plane as he put space between them and the boys. Tucked in a corner, he stopped, releasing her elbow. "Do I need to call ahead for an emergency landing?"

Mary Elise fingered the parachutes dangling from the wall for distraction. "I don't think so. Where would we land, anyway?"

"We can chance it in Turkey. Germany would be better."

"But?"

"It's safer if we press through straight for the States. Except of course Trey's health has to come first."

Intimacy wrapped around her, different from the sensual atmosphere of a few moments ago. Rather a more comfortable aura of two parents discussing their children. Each parent-style word sliced her insides with endless tiny paper cuts.

She forced herself to think of Trey. "I'll keep a close watch on him, especially for the next hour, but I think the worst has passed, now that he's away from the guard's smoke. Once we land, you could take him by the E.R. just to be certain."

"I'll have a flight surgeon waiting for us." Daniel lifted his headset from around his neck and readjusted the fit before plugging into the mounted outlet. "Wren, patch a call through to Charleston and have Doc Bennett meet us when we land. One of the boys has asthma and I want him checked out. Make sure Kathleen knows I'm the one asking."

Kathleen? An irrational jealousy stirred. Of course Daniel had women in his life, professionally and personally. Not that she cared.

Yeah, right.

Daniel flipped the mouthpiece away. "All set. Anything else we can do?"

She was finished playing out this bizarre pseudoparenting game. She'd made her restitution to Daniel's father. No more guilt. The boys had their brother Danny now. He could feed them junk food until they spun out on sugar if he wished.

They weren't her children. Even considering assuming that role poured straight alcohol on every one of her internal paper cuts.

Mary Elise retreated deeper inside herself and away from Daniel's too familiar smile. "We'll be okay, except he's usually physically drained after an attack. Please pull the blankets out of the crate for me to spread out here so he can sleep."

Daniel watched her face tighten into the prim lines meant to distance him but instead made him want to gather up a fistful of her hair and kiss the look away. All the same, her autocratic coolness evicted their brief moment of connection.

For the best while he was trying like hell to find solid ground after being knocked on his ass over finding her in his plane. He wanted nothing more than to take an hour or ten to study this new Mary Elise in front of him. To understand her. But she wasn't a scientific equation.

A poised elegant woman stood in place of his freckled coltish friend. He'd be a fool not to notice her appeal. He'd be an even bigger fool to act on it.

Those two boys needed him. Austin would likely be a snap to figure out. The imp had a gleam in his eyes Daniel recognized well. Trey, however, looked so much like their imperious old man, he could already predict the head butting.

Time to get his mind the hell off unforgettable red hair and gentle curves.

Daniel dropped his hand from the side of the plane and allowed extra air to slide between them before he fell victim to the temptation to untangle a strand of her hair from her gold hoop earring. "There are two crew-rest bunks. We can put the boys there."

"Does that break some kind of regulation? What about the crew's sleep?" She straightened both of the rings on her right hand—a ruby dinner ring on her middle finger and on her thumb, a large gold band worn only half way down.

Too large to have been her wedding ring.

What had she done with her band after her divorce? She'd mailed his engagement solitaire to him once he'd returned to the Academy, in spite of his insistence that she keep it.

The diamond ring burned a hole in his sleeve pocket even now, a constant reminder to learn from past mistakes. "This whole mission breaks regs. I'm not overly concerned about a little technicality such as where they sleep. The crew can rack back here if they need to catch a nap."

The plane jostled on an air pocket. His hand shot up instinctively to brace her waist. Her familiar scent of honeysuckle teased his nose.

His hand cupped her ribs, the underside of her breast heating his skin. Small, soft. Perfect.

Were her breasts as sensitive as they'd been in the early weeks of her pregnancy? They'd spent every one of those postpregnancy test days exploring each other's bodies without fear of consequence since the consequences had already occurred.

The heat of her now fired memories. Fired him. If he moved his thumb...

His headset crackled in his ears.

"Crusty?" Renshaw called. "Wanna finish that update, please?"

He jerked his hand away and flipped the mouthpiece in place. "The nanny opted not to join us and sent a substitute. We have a stowaway."

"Stowaway?" Bo Rokowsky piped up. "Man or woman?"

Daniel's hand clenched around the memory of warm silk and soft Mary Elise against his hand. "Woman."

"Is she hot?"

Yes. Hell, yes. "Not germane to the mission, Rokowsky."

"'Cause if she is, I'll take over down there and you can come up here."

"Can it, Bo."

"Touchy, touchy. Or maybe not enough touching lately in spite of all those women wanting to cook you dinner and iron your flight suits."

So what if he enjoyed a few casserole gifts now and again? Big freaking deal, and nothing compared to Rokowsky's history with women.

He wouldn't discuss Mary Elise over interphone with the squadron Casanova. A man who sure as hell wasn't getting anywhere near her during this flight. "Keep this up and I'll tell her what your call sign stands for, 'Bo.'" The guy's real name had long ago faded from memories as he'd gone by Bo since training days. "Meanwhile, how about working on flying the plane or something?"

Daniel flipped the mouthpiece aside again. ''We need to talk.''

''We are talking.'' Her spine pulled straighter—which exposed a tempting patch of graceful neck.

He nodded toward his brothers. ''Away from them so they can't read your body language. I need to know more about what happened in Rubistan if I'm going to keep them safe.''

Tension rippled through her.

He resisted the urge to stroke her arm, cup her shoulder and pull her to him. Worse than wanting to palm her breast, he wanted Mary Elise to fling her arms around his neck like so many times before.

Damn, he'd missed her. Missed their easy friendship. No surprise he'd screwed it up. A slew of failed relationships since with casserole-cooking and uniform-ironing women hammered home his shortcomings in the relationship department. The latest to walk had deemed him ''emotionally unavailable.''

Whatever the hell that meant.

Sure, he was sorry when each relationship self-destructed. But not one of them had left a hole in his life. Except Mary Elise.

His grip tightened as if he could somehow reinvent the past by holding tighter. She winced.

He raised his hands, backing away. ''Sorry.''

For so many damned things he wouldn't do any differently now. *Emotionally unavailable* worked well for him.

''Let me get the boys settled, Danny. We can talk once they're asleep.''

At least she didn't argue or pretend they could ignore the fact that she stood in his plane in place of the boys' nanny from Florida.

He didn't know why she was here. Didn't know why

it mattered so damned much to him. But he did owe her. "Thanks for getting them out of there."

"I'd do it for anyone."

Yes, she would. But she hadn't done it for anyone. She'd done it for him. And just as when she'd passed him that Ho-Ho twenty-two years ago, he couldn't walk away.

Mary Elise sagged into the seat across from the two crew bunks in the Spartan sleeping cubicle behind the cockpit. Trey tangled in the covers on the top, slack-jawed with exhaustion. On the bottom, Austin clutched his ragged sailboat quilt, sucking on a corner as if he could somehow taste home.

How much would the little guy remember of the ordeal, the crate, the escape?

Would he remember his parents?

Franklin Baker hadn't been the best of fathers to Daniel, but he'd been trying to compensate with Trey and Austin. Their mother may have been a dim bulb, but she'd loved her boys. They'd loved her.

Trey and Austin had been shuffled so much in their short lives—born in the States, moving a couple of years ago, now back again. And the turmoil wasn't over yet. A new home. A guardian they didn't even know.

Their brother.

Danny.

The mammoth aircraft seemed to shrink, the gray beams and bolts closing in on her. Such a large plane shouldn't feel so very small, nowhere to turn without bumping into him. They must be plowing through the most turbulent stretch of airspace in the sky. One more pitch against Daniel's rock-solid chest and she would lose her mind.

Toying with her earring, she untangled threads of hair

from the hoop. He should *not* have the ability to unsettle her so much. She wanted to exchange a nostalgic smile and hug while they both acknowledged their lives had moved on for the best.

Except she hadn't. What about him?

A tingle started up her spine. She could feel *him,* standing behind her. Danny. Mary Elise glanced up and over her shoulder, already accepting she would find him.

Not Danny, but rather the stranger, Daniel, lounged in the doorway, rumpled flight suit making her long to swipe her hands over the wrinkles.

The muscles.

Silently he stared back at her. No doubt churning the whole mess around in his analytical brain, searching for a way to make sense of it all. Then opting to cover his confusion with a joke.

She didn't want that joke. She wanted a piece of the past to replace the awkwardness. ''Remember the time you painted your face and decked out in cammo to see if you could break into the Savannah River Site plant?''

The C-17 droned for what seemed like an hour, probably closer to seconds, before a slow smile dimpled Danny's cheeks. He canted closer to be heard over the plane's roar, the privacy curtain swaying closed behind him. ''Well, hell, Mary Elise, I was doing a public service. Anyplace constructing and testing the parts for nukes needed to have stronger security if a twelve-year-old could bust inside.''

''No respect for danger, ever.'' Her eyes fell to rest on the children, checking the steady rise and fall of their chests, any snuffling breaths masked by the rumble of engines vibrating the plane. With each exhalation she thanked God for their sturdy little bodies, so resilient.

Five miscarriages had taught her well how fragile young life could be.

Although, Danny had seemed to possess a godlike invincibility in his youth. Or perhaps that had more to do with how he'd never groused over a tagalong tired of tiptoeing so as not to disrupt her bed-bound mother. "You wouldn't have been caught if I hadn't snuck along."

"You always did worry too much." His shoulders filled the portal and her eyes.

Mary Elise welcomed the escape into happier times with smaller childhood worries. "You could have left me behind when the alarm went off. I wouldn't have ratted you out."

"Which is why I couldn't leave you."

But he had. Eventually. After her miscarriage, she'd seen the caged look in his eyes, the need to run once he was free of obligations. She hadn't expected they would still get married—right away. She understood his need to finish school. But she *had* expected something more from him after all the times they'd made love following her pregnancy test. They'd moved past being friends, she'd thought. His need to escape her had hurt.

She'd hurt him right back. God, had she ever let her temper have its way with her as she'd sent him away.

Life had since taught her to contain more volatile emotions. "You always did have a soft spot for causes."

One hint of what waited for her back in Savannah and he would grease up in cammo to take on her ex in some commando raid. All the more reason to park her butt back in Rubistan. She'd quickly discovered how little help the police could be against Kent with his wealth and power. Even her parents hadn't believed her, instead buying into Kent's less messy explanation of postpartum depression.

The icy press of an assassin's gun to her temple had

not been a delusion. Only quick reflexes and an escape to Rubistan had saved her life.

Danny sank into the seat beside her. "I assume you were the one who nudged the economic attaché to call me."

His firm thigh molded to hers. She nodded, swallowed. "Uh-huh."

"Thank you."

"You're welcome." She pushed the words free from her cotton mouth.

He stretched his leg in front of him, rubbing a too long caress against her. "How the hell did you end up in that box in place of the nanny? Or are you their new nanny?"

She suppressed the urge to inch away. Not that she could go anywhere without slamming the wall. "I work at the embassy school, teaching English. I'm just close to the boys since they attend the school."

"How did you go from being editor of a newspaper in Savannah to teaching in Rubistan?"

"Excuse me?" she bristled. "I don't consider it a step down, thank you very much."

He elbowed her gently. "Cool your jets, 'Lise. I was talking basic geography."

She measured her words. "I wanted a change of scenery. Your father helped."

"My father." Muscles bunched visibly under the creased flight suit.

He'd never allowed himself to vent or rant, always taking on everyone else's battles and ignoring his own. Who would be there to help him through the grief over his father's death?

The Kathleen person he'd called for?

She couldn't begrudge him that. Especially when the boys would need a woman's influence more than ever.

They also needed their brother steady. Daniel's hero worship for his father had died in a rift they'd never bridged, which would only make the coming weeks tougher for him.

Mary Elise let herself touch him. Just his arm. Lightly. "I'm so sorry."

He didn't answer for an extended moment before he stood to leave, pulling away emotionally as well as physically. As she'd known he would. He had always been more at ease with simple. Uncomplicated.

Daniel paused in the doorway. "I'll take you up front to patch through a call."

She struggled to understand his words in the wake of the liquid heat pulsing through her veins. "Patch a call?"

"Home."

She frowned. "My apartment's empty right now."

"I meant Savannah. I don't have your parents' number or I'd do it for you. Unless there's someone else you'd prefer to contact." His eyes chilled. "Like your husband."

"My *ex*-husband."

"Right." His emotionless gaze pinned her. "Do you want me to call Kent McRae?"

Hearing her ex-husband's name sent a tremor through her. Followed by a completely different shiver over realizing Daniel had cared enough to track her transition from Mary Elise Fitzgerald to Mary Elise McRae. From a single college journalism student to the wife of a major newspaper publisher.

And who was she now?

Alive. Just how she damn well intended to stay. "I'm not planning to go home. I'll turn right around and return to Rubistan and my job."

"Think again." Familiar chocolate-brown eyes hardened into the different, darker Danny.

What in the world had he seen and experienced during their years apart? "Excuse me?"

"We may have escaped Rubistan without being searched. But they knew. Once you and the boys come up missing at the same time, it won't take longer than a puff on that guard's cigar to link you to this. If you go back, you'll be jailed—or dead—an hour after you touch down."

All those thousands of emotional paper cuts flamed to life in full-blown dread. The implications of the past hours swelled into certainty. She hated the helplessness. Most of all hated that she would have to turn to Danny for answers after a year of hoping never to need anyone again. "What happens after we land in Charleston?"

"What kind of ID do you have?"

"I didn't have time to grab my purse before I got in the crate," she answered automatically, pushing the words through numb lips. "But I always keep my passport on me."

"Good, then you'll be processed through the base. In the meantime, you have to stay somewhere. With your parents or me?" Daniel leaned closer, bay rum obliterating hydraulic fluid in a sensory tidal wave. "It's your call to make, and quite frankly, I need you more right now."

Chapter 3

"You need me?" Mary Elise enunciated slowly.

Daniel watched her brows pull together over confused green eyes. He wasn't feeling much steadier himself.

He braced a hand against the bulkhead and planted both boots for balance. Where the hell had his words come from?

There were probably a hundred different services he could call to help at a moment's notice. He knew at least a dozen women who would enjoy nothing more than mothering the boys as a way to entice him into being "emotionally available."

And none of them were Mary Elise.

He tried to tell himself his motives for keeping her close were rooted in protectiveness. That long-ago connection had kicked into overdrive in the past few minutes. Right about the time he'd mentioned calling Savannah.

He didn't consider himself an intuitive guy, a fact reinforced by his double-digit tally of breakups. But even he could sense something was wrong here. Her edginess should be easing with every mile they put between themselves and Rubistan.

Should be.

But wasn't.

Eleven years of distance between them didn't matter. He owed this woman, and until her frown smoothed, he wouldn't back off.

He was doing this for her. And for the boys. Not because he wanted to find out if the freckles dotting her smooth creamy skin had faded with age. "I need your help with stuff like asthma meds and nut allergies. At this rate, the boys won't make it through the week with me."

Mary Elise straightened in her seat. Daniel looked deeper into those lush green eyes that had once been so expressive and wondered when she'd learned to close herself off.

"I'll make a list." Her cool efficiency almost covered her underlying edginess. Almost. "Starting with Austin's EpiPen."

"Eppie what?"

"Epinephrine injection pen. Medicine in case he accidentally eats something with nuts or peanut oil or—"

"Stop." He made a giant *T* with his hands. "Time out. You can compile lists all day long and it won't change the fact that I have no experience with kids. I need help settling the boys."

She pleated her pants between fidgety fingers. "You haven't made any accommodations for them?"

"Hell, Mary Elise, I was a little busy planning how to smuggle them out of Rubistan without getting our asses shot off."

"Oh."

"Apology accepted."

Her hands flattened on her trim thighs, a smile playing with her lips. ''Uh, sorry?''

He winked. ''No problem.''

A smile and a wink linked them more than all his earlier speeches.

The deafening din of engines and the closed curtain offered a bubble of privacy and protection from being overheard. Not that he had thoughts of unrolling the past with her. He hadn't been much for emotional sharefests then, either.

Besides, he didn't want to trek back to the past. Too many memories waited there of a time he'd been less of a man. Too much his father's son—seducing an innocent, betraying a friendship. His father's wedding had marked a time of rotten decisions for everyone.

Halfway into a bottle of champagne, Daniel had found himself watching nineteen-year-old Mary Elise with new eyes. Another shared bottle and some consolation later, Daniel had found himself looking at all of Mary Elise with new eyes.

''What happens now?''

She'd asked him that then as well. *What do I do now, Danny?*

God help him, he'd shown her.

He'd been so pissed at his old man for going the whole trophy wife route. He didn't deal well with emotions on a good day, and a bad day had a way of playing hell with a man's self-control. Today marked another one of his worst days on record, but he wouldn't screw up this time. No matter how enticing the image of draping that red hair over his chest. Mary Elise over him.

Mary Elise sighing.

''Danny?'' She flung her hair over her shoulder in a

crimson waterfall. "If you haven't made arrangements for the boys, what do you propose we do once we land?"

"Hell if I know." Then or now. "And it doesn't look as if Trey knows what to do about me any more than I know what to do about him."

Her brows pulled tighter, deepening her perpetual frown. "You aren't going to give them up. Are you?"

"No. Absolutely not. I'll figure it out. Soon."

"Once you're through worrying about our asses."

He did *not* want to think about her ass. "Right." Daniel scrubbed a hand over his bristly chin. "I have leave time built up. I'll take it now until the boys and I can work out a plan. But I sure would appreciate your help for the next few days. Since you're an American Express card short of being able to check into a Motel 6, I'm thinking we can make a trade."

She shot him a disapproving look that had likely commanded boardrooms, then later classrooms. "Or you could do the gentlemanly thing and loan me a couple hundred bucks."

Already he could feel her slipping away. Damn it, the boys needed her. And while he might not be Captain Communication, he wasn't walking away without finding out what had her forehead trenched deeper than a fresh-plowed field. "Sure, I *could* loan you the money."

"But you don't want to." Mary Elise willed away the rogue twinge of excitement. She wanted to say her good-byes. Right? Danny had been a generous friend. An exciting lover.

And a lousy boyfriend.

Once that boyfriend/lover line had been crossed, recapturing the friendship became impossible. She knew keeping her distance now lent more credence to her feelings all those years ago. But her heart bore too many scars to risk opening it again.

All the same, guilt nudged her to say, "The boys *do* need me."

"Yes, ma'am, they do," he continued with a sincerity too reminiscent of past times conning his way out of trouble. "This is about more than asthma and EpiPens. Trey and Austin are alone and scared. They don't know me from Adam."

She didn't buy into the Danny-perfected con tones for even a minute, but his logic had merit. Turning away from Austin crying in the crate hadn't been an option. Why did she think now would be any different?

Scar tissue also made a person tough. She would hang on to that for the next few days with Danny and the boys. "Okay, okay! I actually agreed two arguments ago. You always were persistent."

"And you were always too nice."

Watching the dimples creep into Daniel's cheeks and past her defenses, Mary Elise decided "nice" didn't factor anywhere into her swirl of emotions. "Nice? Careful, Danny, or I'll change my mind."

"So you'll help me for a couple of weeks?"

"A couple of days." Hopefully enough time to formulate a new plan.

"Until I find another nanny."

Which would take at least a week. "For the boys."

"I never thought otherwise."

He ducked back into the crew compartment, leaving her alone with her thoughts and two sleeping children. The cubicle echoed without him, the repercussions of her decision crowding the confined space. Since Kent didn't know her location, a week should be safe before she risked alerting him by withdrawing money from her account. She could use the time to decide where to go and what to do with her life.

A week to stay with those two boys who'd first tugged her heart because of Daniel and then stolen her heart by being themselves. She wouldn't even let herself think about being a surrogate-mother figure to them. Her dreams of family were dead, thanks to Kent.

Mary Elise leaned forward and tucked the sailboat blanket around Austin, his puffy breaths whispering over her wrist. She started to pull away, but he grappled for her hand without waking.

Stroking a thumb over butter-soft skin, she studied the miracle of five tiny fingers and couldn't stem memories of all the babies she'd miscarried. She'd wanted to adopt, but Kent had insisted they keep trying for a biological child. She'd gone on the pill, anyway. For all the good it had done her. Then the surprise pregnancy had lasted longer than any of her other four first-trimester miscarriages.

She'd finally dared to hope.

Losing her son at twenty-four weeks had almost destroyed her. Discovering Kent had replaced her birth control pills with placebos months earlier finished the job.

Weariness swamped her along with the memories. She surrendered to the need for sleep and the tug of a chubby little hand. Mary Elise slid into the bottom bunk, curving herself protectively around Austin.

No, Kent had never raised a hand to her, which somehow made his menacing plans after she left all the more chilling. Hindsight told her she should have seen the warning signs. He'd been abusing her and controlling her in other ways for years, culminating in that final violation of her body and trust.

Now she had one week to find a new safe haven. And

pray seven days of playing house with Danny and two precious boys wouldn't slice past her scar tissue into what little soul she had left.

One booted foot resting on the bottom crew bunk across from him, Daniel sprawled in the unrelenting seat. Well, as much as a guy could sprawl in the tight space. Another half hour and he would take over flying while Wren sacked out.

He should be sleeping, but couldn't. Too wired. Seeing Mary Elise now when he was still reeling from his father's death rattled him. No question.

Daniel studied the three sleeping figures that had thrown his life into chaos. Sure he didn't give a damn about ironing his uniform or eating on a schedule, but he was in charge of his world and his emotions.

Or he had been until Mary Elise and the boys.

In the past hour he'd made strides in regaining control. She was staying. The boys would level out. And somehow that still didn't unkink the knot in his neck that had started right about the minute she'd turned those deep-green eyes his way for the first time in eleven years.

No risk of seeing her eyes now. She lay sleeping on the bottom bunk, her back to him, her body curved around Austin. Her hair tangled around the child and over the edge of the bed. The little guy snoozed on with his knees tucked to his chest, his blanket gripped in a white-knuckled fist.

Leaning, Daniel captured a lock of her hair and tested the silky texture between two fingers. He'd done the right thing asking her to stay. The boys had already lost their parents. They needed a familiar person to ease them through the transition.

On the top bunk, Trey rolled and shifted until he settled onto his back. All three, dead to the world.

Thank God they weren't dead period, only exhausted from the long hours and ordeal. A few more minutes of staring at them and he would have his balance back.

A shadow slid through the doorway. Daniel glanced up to find Tag waiting silently.

The Senior Master Sergeant nodded toward the bunks. ''I'll watch over them if you need to catch some sleep.''

''I'm set until we land. No worries.''

Tag studied him silently, gaze falling to the lock of hair still twined around Daniel's fingers.

Well, hell.

Daniel dropped the strand. A lone determined hair clung to the wrist of his flight suit like before. He didn't waste energy refuting Tag's all-knowing expression. Why bother when he actually appreciated the older man's no-bull approach to life? The man appreciated facts and the uncomplicated.

Years of working top-secret test projects at Edwards AFB in California had honed Daniel's instincts. He didn't think of those instincts as anything of a woo-hoo nature. Rather, he made observations and processed them quickly. Efficiently. Two weeks into his transfer to Charleston AFB in South Carolina, Daniel had realized Tag was a troop to trust.

Even with something as important as Mary Elise.

''You know, Tag, I believe I'll take you up on that offer in another half hour.'' Daniel flicked aside the hair on his wrist. ''I don't need sleep, but I have to head back up front soon and I'd rather not wake Mary Elise. So, yeah, I would appreciate it if you kept an eye on them in case one of the boys rouses before her.''

Tag lumbered in through the door, curtain closing behind him, and lowered himself into the other seat. "Small world, her showing up on this flight."

And an even smaller world on base. No doubt, gossip would make the rounds three times over by the next nightfall. Not from Tag, but Bo would have a helluva time sharing the inside scoop at the club.

"Family connection. We knew each other a long time ago." Daniel shot him a half smile. "That 'Danny' of hers probably gave us away."

"Ah, so you're old friends."

Daniel hesitated a second too long.

Tag's quirked brow shot up toward the older man's salt-and-pepper hairline.

Finally, Daniel settled for, "We have…history."

Tag nodded again. Waited. Studied the sleeping trio. Finally shifted his attention back to Daniel. "Is the older kid yours?"

The notion blazed across Daniel's mind in a flash of horror. Had she faked a miscarriage? He'd never seen Trey's mother pregnant. He could imagine selfless Mary Elise cutting him free so he could complete his senior year at the Academy.

Simple math severed the irrational thought. Trey was over a year too young. "No. Trey's not mine." Daniel's head thunked back against the bulkhead. Damn it, why couldn't Tag have shown up fifteen minutes later once the world had stopped rocking under his boots? "Ours would have been ten now."

Hell, he hadn't told anyone about that time with Mary Elise. Something about the way Tag didn't push made it easier to talk during a day when the past crowded his brain.

Daniel hooked a hand on his knee, boot propped beside the trailing hair, and lost himself in the hypnotic sway of red. "She miscarried early, before we had a chance to get married. I would have married her though. No way would I have let her down."

But he had, in so many other ways, both of them too damned young. He'd been knocked on his ass by how much a few short weeks of making love to her had shaken him. So he'd run like hell the minute she'd given him the green light.

"And here you two are again."

"Not for long. She'll settle back in Savannah and I'll be in Charleston."

"All of two and a half hours apart," Tag's dry tones mixed with the rumble of four engines. "Might as well be on different planets."

Daniel snorted. "I think I enjoyed you more when you stayed quiet."

"My wife likely disagrees," he answered, his dry wit more parched than normal. Not that the guy looked open to making the current sharingfest a two-way deal.

Tag canted forward, elbows on his knees. "While I'm on a roll, here's some hard-earned wisdom you can take or leave. So you had a thing going once? But you were too young to hang on to it. Makes sense. That Mars and Venus stuff is hard as hell for an old guy like me to figure out. It can be damned near impossible when you're younger."

Daniel shook his head, half believing, yet knowing he couldn't let himself off the hook that easily. "Where were you eleven years ago when I wanted to hear something like this?"

"Making my own mistakes," Tag answered with fatherly wisdom, even though his forty-one years made any true parental connection impossible.

"She and I are history."

Tag stayed silent.

Crap. Did parents go to a school to develop that look?

Daniel followed Tag's gaze. Straight down to Daniel's hand that had somehow found its way back into Mary Elise's hair.

He untwisted his finger from the strands, not a speedy proposition. The hair unwrapped and unwrapped in a long unraveling stretch.

"History," Daniel repeated as if he could will it so.

"Sure. You can take that route. Let go, quick and easy like. Or you can use the second chance to get your head on straight about this woman. Your choice. Don't screw it up—" he grinned, standing "—*sir*. I'll be back in a half hour."

Tag swept aside the curtain and ducked out of the small quarters, his hard-earned wisdom lingering long after the curtain stopped rippling.

Daniel watched the pendulum swish of Mary Elise's hair and thought of that wary flash in her eyes at the mention of her ex. More cause to be careful around her, and it wasn't as if the woman wanted a commitment from him anymore.

He did "no commitment" damned well.

Tag's talk of second chances had merit. Now was Daniel's chance to right the past. He may have taken the easy route and let her send him packing eleven years ago. But he wasn't running away from her now.

With a cool determination that had carried him through countless secret test missions, Daniel fixed his mind on a dual goal. Nothing would happen to his brothers on his watch. And no one, most especially himself, would ever hurt Mary Elise again.

Kent McRae gripped his steering wheel until it hurt. From the comfort of his Mercedes, he watched the C-17 circle above the thick band of evergreens. Night sounds and darkness wrapped around him while he waited, tucked just outside the main gate of Charleston Air Force Base.

The drive up from Savannah after the call from the economic attaché in Rubistan had given him time to think, to strategize. He didn't like it when plans went off-kilter.

And Mary Elise had skewed his life once too often.

He forced his hold on the steering wheel to relax. No losing control. Stay steady and focused. If only she'd been inside that rigged car with Ambassador Baker as he'd been led to expect. That she'd survived, then turned to another man to help with the boys, stirred a cold wrath.

One explosion and his life could have been back on track, the past cleared away so he could start his future with a new wife. However, the week's events would only prove a minor setback for a persistent man.

Kent raised binoculars for a better view of the circling plane. Persistence paid off, after all. If only Mary Elise could have believed him about that. But her defective body housed a defective mind. She simply didn't comprehend, no matter how often he'd told her to keep trying and eventually they would have their perfect family.

He'd loved her, damn it. So much. And she'd left him. He'd thought he could win her back. Finally accepted otherwise. And if he couldn't have her, at least he would have a clean slate to begin a new life with a more malleable woman.

And Baker? Every crime needed a fall guy. The appearance of a murder/suicide between old lovers should satisfy authorities.

The oversize cargo plane straightened out of the turn, lining up with the runway, lower, closer, roaring overhead. Kent watched and waited. Patient.

Persistent.

Chapter 4

Her patience had worn thin.

Mary Elise wanted to call this day over. Now. The
cargo plane had finally landed in Charleston, and they
were seconds away from exiting the metal cavern that had
grown more claustrophobic with each minute closer to the
States.

Hitching the sleeping Austin higher on her hip, Mary
Elise followed the loadmaster's lead through the belly of
the plane toward the hatch. The remaining hours of the
flight had dragged, drawn tight by anxiety over what
awaited her once she exited the front gate. What would
she do with her life and how would she deal with the
possibility that Kent might find her?

Moreover, how would she handle a week alone with
Daniel?

She tried to shake off the jangle of emotions. The fear
of the unknown had to be worse than reality. Surely once
she had a good night's sleep she could restore her bound-

aries and do away with the awful vulnerability pricking her insides.

The seal popped and swooshed as the hatch swung open. Her brief nap in the airplane barely made a dent in her weariness. Not that landing put her much closer to crawling into bed and sleeping away the exhaustion and frustration of the past hours. Trey still needed to check in with a doctor about his asthma.

The doctor. Kathleen. The woman who would drop everything just for Danny. Of course if he had someone else in his life, that would free her.

Yeah right, like she'd ever been free of this guy's ghost. Surely it had more to do with him being her first lover that earned him a special spot in her memories.

Daniel stepped into sight from the stairwell leading up to the cockpit. She eyed the stretch of his shoulders as she made her way toward the exit hatch. What about *her* spot in *his* memories? How much importance did she want there?

Daniel pivoted to her. "Let me take the little slugger."

Austin clung tighter in his sleep, his grip firm around her neck and growing dangerously tight around her heart. "I can carry him."

"The steps are steep. A tumble will land you both hard." He leaned to whisper against her ear, his warm breath scented with chocolate and the promise of passion. "Temporary truce. Everything doesn't have to be a battle between us."

Score one for Daniel. She passed over the sleeping child and forced herself not to smooth the boy's tousled curls.

Or the stray lock brushing Daniel's brow.

Steadying her hand on the metal rail, she descended the steps and inhaled the familiar Southern aromas in front of her mingling with Daniel's bay rum behind her. The early afternoon sun crested over the band of pine trees and live oaks bordering the stretch of cement. Nostalgia nicked her, the low country of South Carolina so like her Savannah home. A hungry longing filled her to inhale greedy gulps of both the place and the man.

Rubistan's isolation from temptation had merit.

Mary Elise steeled herself to move forward. The hum of engines from a distant bus, truck and ambulance mingled with the symphony of crickets and June bugs. Autumn in South Carolina resembled the summer heat in many Northern climes. Her silk shirt clung to her back by the time she cleared the last step.

A byproduct of the temperature, damn it, not the lure of home. She had to stop the past from dinging her control.

Guiding a groggy Trey to the side, she waited for Daniel and the others to clear the craft. She flipped a mental switch within herself, shifting from a too-vulnerable woman to analytical reporter mode. She would observe the world around her without getting involved.

One of the copilots, the young guy with a devilish twinkle in his eyes, strutted across the cement, guitar case slung over his back. "Need any help there, sir? I've got extra seats in my car."

He tossed a wink her way, his flirting complimentary without a threatening edge. She allowed herself a smile. Detached, but participating, interacting in normal human exchanges. Something she hadn't done in so long.

Daniel stepped closer. "No, thanks, Bo. My truck has an extended cab. We'll be fine."

"Okay, then. Take it easy, sir." Bo backed away, morning sun glinting off the copilot's jet-black hair and perfect features, increasing his fallen-angel air.

Actually more like an impish fallen cherub since the guy was probably all of twenty-five, making Daniel's hundred-percent adult male hard lines vibrate tension through the air.

Jaw set, Danny cupped her elbow as he guided her toward the waiting crew bus. "Did you want to ride with him?"

Jealousy laced his words. Surprising her. Thrilling her.

"Of course I didn't." The answer fell free before she could think to say something that would put more distance between them. Instead she just stared back as the thrill tripped through her, all the while blaming the yearning on a weakness born of exhaustion.

Running footsteps jarred her back to the present. The copilot, Darcy Renshaw, sprinted by toward the waiting military truck. The passenger door opened and a man stepped out, a civilian if his unconventional clothes and spiked hair were anything to go by. His seafoam-colored windbreaker clashed with flowered, knee-length swim trunks. Darcy dropped her flight bag and flung her arms around his neck seconds before he kissed her. *Really* kissed her, like a man who couldn't get enough of that one woman.

Screw distance. Analytical observations went up in flames as embers of long-dead dreams sparked. What would it be like to inspire that kind of passion? She and Daniel had been on fire for each other during those uninhibited weeks of lovemaking. But sometimes she wondered if years apart might have painted her memories a deeper shade of red as her discontent in her marriage grew.

Daniel cleared his throat.

Mary Elise glanced up. "They're married?"

"Nah, still in the newly engaged stage."

A rush of heat swelled through her. Yeah, she and Daniel had fallen well into that can't-get-enough engaged state. "Oh. Uh, they seem well suited."

He patted Austin's head to soothe the yawning child back to sleep and charged forward, the path past the necking couple the only route toward the waiting ambulance. "They met last summer on a joint mission to Guam."

"He's Air Force?" She eyed the man's nonregulation hair with curiosity, hair currently getting a finger comb from an amorous lady copilot who wasn't overly concerned about public displays of affection.

"Was CIA. Now he's a civilian employee with the OSI—Office of Special Investigations. Kind of like the Air Force's own CIA." Daniel cleared his throat and urged her forward, not even breaking stride as they drew alongside the embracing couple. "Thanks for your help, Spike. I owe ya one."

Without slowing the kiss, the man pulled his hand off Darcy Renshaw's waist and held his palm up for a high-five.

As they strode past, realization crept over Mary Elise. Wren's spiky-haired boyfriend who looked more like a beach bum than an OSI Special Agent had played a role in the boys' escape as well.

Had known exactly how much danger his fiancée flew into.

Mary Elise couldn't resist glancing over her shoulder. The air crackled. Desire derived from a day filled with life and death stakes licked the air, scorching her even from a distance.

She turned her back on the image and thoughts of partnerships it inspired. "Spike? A nickname because of his hair, I assume."

"Yeah. Normally OSI guys don't get their own call

sign, but we made Spike an honorary member of the squadron once he and Renshaw hooked up.''

The air whirled with the dynamics of so many relationships, platonic as well as passionate. Her mind and body went into sensory overload after years of deprivation.

Kent had severed ties from people except in the working environment, later taking even that from her, insisting work-related stress caused the miscarriages. The past months in Rubistan she'd soaked up the teaching time with children like a healing balm after enforced distance from little ones. Even so, those relationships were superficial. She hadn't been a real part of any community for years.

And then it hit her what bothered her so much about this homecoming, why she wanted distance as a buffer from pain.

Daniel had moved on, made a life for himself with new friends, new direction, ever changing and growing. But she'd allowed herself to stagnate, frozen in time. How telling that when she'd needed help running from Kent's threat, she'd turned to someone from her past. Daniel's father. Sure, she'd escaped the immediate danger, but she still hadn't been able to lower the walls that sealed her from experiencing emotions. She'd focused on survival for so long, she wasn't sure she really knew how to live anymore.

Entering a world full of feelings, like love—anything—again was a scary-as-hell proposition. And not one she intended to attempt with Daniel anywhere near her.

The man of the hour beside her paused, a new tension radiating from him in waves. She didn't have to look to know. An instinctive understanding of him that had gone dormant over the years roared to life.

Mary Elise searched the windswept stretch of cement

for the source of Danny's tension. She didn't have to look far. From behind the driver's side of the truck, a man in a flight suit slid out with cougarlike stealthiness.

She didn't know much about military rank gracing the shoulders of flight suits, but even she recognized this man's air of authority. The adversarial vibes between them snapped along the air.

A shiver ripped through her. This sort of antagonistic relationship she had experienced and understood well. While she'd learned to haul butt in the other direction for self-preservation, she couldn't squelch a driving desire to fling herself between Daniel and the man stalking toward them.

Time for the crap to hit the fan.

Watching the new Squadron Commander stride forward, Daniel passed Austin to Mary Elise and braced his shoulders. Not that he intended to let things fly now in front of the kids.

He saluted the higher-ranking officer. "Hello, sir."

The last word bit on its way up and out, but he knew protocol. It was just tougher to swallow with some than others.

Damn he missed the boundary-pushing days of flying cutting-edge test missions at Edwards AFB. But he had to exist in a day-to-day flying job to fill time as well as maintain cover between the higher ordered, dark ops missions that periodically came his way. Like the one he'd just completed when the call came through to retrieve his brothers.

Yeah, he missed the freedom of his old job. But even the beginning of his transfer to Charleston AFB as Chief of Training Flight hadn't been too bad. Until the new boss took over. Lt. Col. Lucas Quade was nothing like their old commander, Zach Dawson.

The past summer had marked the end of Dawson's reign as Squadron Commander. While he'd opted to stay on at the base for another year for family reasons, Dawson had shifted to Assistant Deputy of Operations for the Wing. Quade had transferred in from the Pentagon to take his place.

Not a smooth transition in the least for the C-17 squadron. Quade lent a darker shading to the squadron motto, Anything, Anywhere, Anytime. This guy was everywhere, all the time, breathing down their necks. His ever-present scowl could melt the paint off an airplane.

Daniel stepped in front of Mary Elise and the boys, between them and the anger pulsing quietly from the commander. "I didn't expect to see you back from your TDY to England for two more days, sir."

At least he'd hoped not when he'd pushed this mission through in the commander's absence.

"No doubt," Quade answered, his low growl riding wind that didn't dare disturb his close-cropped dark hair. "Lucky I was able to cut it short and meet you on the flight line."

Daniel shot a pointed look toward the bedraggled children then back to his commander. "I'll be in your office first thing tomorrow morning after I settle them in."

"Yes, you will, Captain." Quade nodded to Mary Elise. "Welcome back to the States, ma'am." Spinning on his heel, he slid away as silently as he'd approached.

Mary Elise drew up shoulder to shoulder. Austin stirred, yawning, stuffing a fist against his eye.

"Crap," Daniel mumbled under his breath.

Mary Elise cocked her head to the side. "Problem?"

There'd been a time when he'd shared everything with

Mary Elise. Her insights had kept his wings level on more than one occasion. But opening that door to the past would invite a host of other issues better left alone when he needed objectivity to figure out what the hell was chugging through that brain of hers. "Normal red tape. No big deal."

He should be covered, thanks to Spike's CIA connections. Daniel shrugged off what couldn't be dealt with until the next day. He'd take the fall in a heartbeat if Quade started gunning for anyone else on the crew.

Daniel tapped Trey on the shoulder and pointed to the ambulance. "You ready to get checked out so we can head home?"

Trey jammed his hands in his pockets and shrugged. "Doesn't matter. Just wanna go to bed."

More concerns. Where would he put everyone in his condo? A small condo with only one bed—a big bed that he could too well envision sharing with Mary Elise.

A headache started behind his right eye, like a tiny hammer rapping with irritating persistence. "Not much longer and we'll hit the road. You'll be in b— Uh, you'll be tucked in before you can say Hershey's chocolate."

Austin pulled his thumb out of his mouth. "Crap."

Daniel screeched to a halt. "What?"

Trey smirked. "I think he heard *you* say it."

"Thanks. I figured that."

Mary Elise tapped Austin's mouth. "What's wrong, hon?"

"Got no jammies. Want my sailboat jammies. Crap." His thumb popped back in his mouth.

Daniel flinched over the curse, but couldn't bring himself to reprimand his brother. Poor kid had lost his parents and everything familiar in the span of a couple of weeks.

''You can both wear my T-shirts. I have one with an airplane on it, just for you, pal.''

''Mary 'Lise got no jammies, neither.''

An image he did *not* need, thank you very much. ''She can borrow a T-shirt, too.''

Another image no less tormenting than the last splayed across his mind in a tangle of long red hair and even longer legs. In his bed.

''And a toof brush and shampoo?''

Daniel blinked back to the present and Austin's latest question. ''We'll buy some.''

''For Mary 'Lise, too?''

Already he could see, smell her shampoo in his shower. The little hammer picked up speed and force in his head, pounding in time with each thud of his boots across cement. ''You bet.''

''And toof paste? Bubble-gum kind.''

''Yes,'' he promised, rushing to add before the three-year-old question machine could preempt him, ''for Mary Elise, too.''

Blessed silence echoed for four strides across the tarmac before Austin's thumb popped back out of his mouth again. ''Need my pull-ups.''

He turned to Mary Elise for interpretation. ''Pull-ups?''

Trey snorted. ''Diapers. For babies.''

''Am not a baby!''

''Are so.'' Trey sniffed. ''And no way am I sharing a bed with anybody who still wears a diaper to sleep. Yuck!''

The pounding behind Daniel's eye morphed into a jackhammer.

Mary Elise guided Trey alongside while explaining to Danny, ''They're like underwear.''

Daniel willed Austin silent. Please Lord, no mentions

of Mary Elise's underwear from the peanut gallery. "We'll make a quick stop by the base shoppette for necessities and buy the rest tomorrow. No worries, boys."

End of bedtime ritual discussions. Life back in control, Daniel forged ahead into the late-morning sun.

Yeah, order. Control. Gained from a logical act of the will.

He led them toward the military ambulance, his old Air Force Academy pal Doc Kathleen Bennett waiting as promised. His freshman year at the Academy, he and his classmate Tanner Bennett had both followed her around like lost puppies. Bennett had ultimately won. For the best, since those two were meant to be together, and he sure as hell hadn't harbored any feelings deeper than a teenage case of the hots.

The flight surgeon braced her boot on the bumper, tucking a stray strand of wind-whipped red hair behind her ear. Daniel paused in his tracks. How damned strange he hadn't realized something until just that moment. Every woman he'd ever dated or been attracted to had red hair.

Control spiraled into a nosedive.

Chapter 5

Mary Elise gathered her red hair in one hand and flung the rope over her shoulder. Amid a string of stilted houses, Daniel's condo complex loomed ahead through the windshield of his truck. Their visit with the doc had been followed by a quick-mart trip and a refueling stop at McDonald's, which stretched her never-ending day into late afternoon. Finally she could sleep.

In Daniel's home. Uh-oh.

She eyed the singles-type setup, a sleek soft-gray cement three-story complex complete with a pool, hot tub, tennis courts, set on marshy beachfront property that guaranteed they couldn't let Austin out of their sight for even a second.

At least Trey was healthy according to the flight surgeon, apparently an old classmate of Daniel's, a *married* classmate with a baby. Mary Elise stifled the rogue twinge of relief. No, she didn't need to confuse herself by combating strange twinges of jealousy over women like Kathleen Bennett or the copilot, Darcy Renshaw. Instead, she faced something far more unsettling. More proof of how Daniel had made a new life with new friends—friendship far more important than fleeting flings.

While she guided a bleary-eyed Trey toward the door, Daniel unbuckled the sleeping Austin and grabbed the shopping bag of pull-ups, silent. As he'd been for hours. Not that she intended to risk chitchat before a long sleep.

An hour later Mary Elise stood at the sliding balcony doors in Daniel's bedroom, Austin snoozing in the queen-size bed behind her. She pressed a palm to the screen separating her from the glistening breakers crashing against the shoreline. Egrets bobbed on spindly legs, long beaks pecking the sand while gulls dipped and soared to find a late-afternoon snack.

A prickle of awareness tingled up her spine as she felt *him,* Daniel, enter the room, and she didn't even have the energy to deny she felt him. He cruised to a stop just behind her, his heat warming her back in contrast with the gentle sea breeze caressing her front.

She glanced over her shoulder, the sleek silver and gray decor of his bedroom somehow matching the man's precise mathematical mentality. "Trey's asleep?"

Daniel definitely resembled the part of an overwhelmed father, hair askew, weariness stamping his handsome face. "Yeah, hopefully the dinner kept them up long enough to nudge them toward sacking out through the night. Trey didn't even balk at the prospect of a sleeping bag on the computer room floor once I mentioned the alternative was bunking with Austin in pull-ups."

Mary Elise offered him the obligatory chuckle he obviously expected and shifted her gaze to the artwork gracing his walls rather than the laugh lines crinkling the corners of Danny's eyes. The framed Escher-style print of a winding staircase seemingly leading nowhere pretty much summed up her life.

Daniel leaned a broad shoulder against the molding framing the sliding doors. "You sure you don't mind sharing a bed with the little guy tonight?"

"Not at all. I'm too tired to notice he's there."

Daniel eyed his bed, rumpled gray spread rising with each baby breath from Austin. "That pull-up thing is leak proof, right?"

"Says so on the package." A smile tugged at her lips as she thought of Daniel's boggled expression when they'd bought the sleeper-diapers, a purchase so conspicuously different from that of the airman behind them intent on buying a bottle of wine, a plastic-wrapped rose—and a box of condoms.

Mary Elise banished that memory. Pronto.

Daniel speared a hand through his tousled hair until it stood even more on end, much like his buddy Spike's. "I'll find bunk beds over at the base tomorrow. The BX furniture outlet has a decent enough selection."

"Uh, the boys might want to go with you and choose for themselves."

"Right. Of course." He shot her a wry smile. "Not used to accounting to other people."

He shoved away from the wall and crossed to the bed. Hands so comfortable flying an airplane fumbled a bit in fitting the bulky comforter around tiny shoulders, not that it stalled him in the task. He persevered until the shiny gray bedspread tucked as snuggly around Austin as any cotton sailboat blankie.

Her heart hitched.

Tension rippled up Daniel's back beneath the stretched green fabric. He reached toward Austin.

Swiped a tear off the cherub cheek.

Tears stung her own eyes. "He wants his mother."

A long swallow moved Daniel's throat before he dropped to the foot of the bed. Broad shoulders sagged for the first time in a day that would have leveled most men hours ago. "What the hell am I going to do with two kids, Mary Elise?"

His hoarse question filled the room. She crossed her arms over her chest to keep from gathering both Austin and Danny close. It would be difficult enough for her not to play mama to this motherless child. She damn well couldn't afford to play anything more than friends with Danny. "You'll make adjustments."

"How? My schedule's hellish. I'm gone for weeks at a time. This place is too small." He flicked a hand toward the glass doors revealing the stretch of sandy beach. "Even that's a hazard with Austin around."

His quiet anguish echoed, transporting her back to the time he'd asked her how his father could be so cliché as to opt for a trophy wife in his midlife crisis. Why couldn't the guy have just bought a freaking sports car?

Daniel rested his elbows on his knees while studying the mud-brown carpet as if it bore answers not likely held in the stack of books by his bed. "What kind of screwed-up world is this where those boys don't have anyone but me and a terrorist uncle ready to recruit them for his own special brand of 'summer camp'?"

Austin shuffled under the covers. With undue concentration, she closed the glass door and drew the steel blinds, trying to avoid other memories. Of knowing Daniel was trapped by circumstance now as he'd been years ago with her pregnancy. But even at twenty-one, he'd been a man of honor, putting others first. She'd known he would come through for their baby.

She just hadn't expected the surprise need for him to come through for her, too.

A tiny voice taunted from the far corners of her brain that she'd misjudged Kent. Horribly so.

She'd been looking for something different in those days. Her medical problems had increased, the endometriosis progressing to the point she'd realized bearing children would be doubtful. Her first miscarriage years ago hadn't been some fluke, and with the build-up of internal scar tissue over the years, even conception became difficult. She'd met Kent at a time when she'd expected to focus on her newspaper career since life had shifted her plans.

Kent changed the rules.

She refused to let her ex-husband take anything else from her, and that included what good memories she had of Daniel. Despite the traumatic last hours, she welcomed the distraction of thinking about someone else's problems, tackling concerns that didn't involve a stalker ex-husband.

Moving deeper into the room, she let her hands glide over Daniel's dresser, tap a change cup, an abacus. "The world isn't fair, Danny, and it's wasted energy expecting it to be. We make the best of what we have."

Mary Elise shuffled the abacus beads back and forth and back again. Whimsical memories slipped past her guard. "God knows, you always were one who could build a rocket out of a junior chemistry lab and a piece of your mother's Corning Ware."

A rusty chuckle slipped free. "I blew a hole in the yard big enough for a pig roast. Man, was my father pissed."

Too easily she could see Danny standing in the middle of his parents' landscaped lawn taking a reaming from his father. The son not recognizing his father's fear for his safety. The father not recognizing his son's need for freedom and acceptance.

"But you built a rocket, Danny, when most kids were still struggling to put together store-bought model planes or cars." Forget keeping her distance. She knelt at his feet so she could see his eyes. "You can do this. You'll move to a bigger place. A live-in nanny is probably their best choice, someone they can bond with. They have money, which gives you options."

"The old man's money." He grimaced.

She raised a hand to rest on his knee. He ducked away from her touch. From her offer of comfort.

Daniel strode toward the door. "There are extra towels under the sink. Sweats on the closet shelf, T-shirts in the top dresser drawer."

She trailed him, the two of them meeting in the suddenly too small portal, a pendulum in the hall ticking away the seconds. She should have expected him to duck past. The old Danny had dodged offers of comfort over his parents' split, seeking escape in her body rather than in her arms.

His eyes narrowed, his pupils widening. *Uh-oh.*

She stared into his brown eyes so deep and dark. He'd lost his father in a far more tragic way now than during the rift at his father's wedding. Would Daniel reach for her again? She wanted his kiss as much as—no, more than—before since she knew the promise of what they could experience together. Her body hungered for human touch.

His touch.

Except, she would have to stop as she should have done years ago. Because Danny with his restless feet didn't do forever well. Difficult enough to overcome even before she'd lost her ability to trust in forever.

In a move so quick she didn't see him shift, he pulled her to him. But not for a kiss.

Daniel gathered her against his chest, held her close and a little too tight. She wouldn't allow herself the indulgence of bringing her arms up. She simply absorbed the familiar feel and scent of him, absorbed the differences she'd observed earlier, the harder edges of a man instead of a boy.

Why was he doing this to her? To them?

Daniel pressed a brusque kiss to the top of her head, then softly spoke heated words into her hair. "Crawling into that box was the stupidest thing you could have done. You damn well could have died today."

He held her tighter for one final, eternal moment that ticked by with countless clicks from the pendulum. Then he thrust her away, the door snicking closed behind him.

She stood frozen, an odd contradiction since every nerve within her had flamed to life.

Stupidest thing? Not by a long shot. Crawling *out* of that box and agreeing to stay with Danny beat her other decision by a mile.

Pulling Mary Elise into his arms had to be the stupidest damned thing he'd done since his rocket blasted a hole in the yard and through the neighbor's stained-glass window twenty years ago.

Daniel thudded down the carpeted hall into his living room and dropped to the edge of the leather sofa. One foot at a time, he unlaced his boots and thunked them on the floor. Sleeping would be tough enough with Mary Elise a couple of doors down. Now it would be impossible with the feel of her body imprinted anew in his brain and a persistent auburn hair twined round his wrist.

So what if he preferred redheads? He had a "type."

Big freaking deal. Most guys had a type or a preferred female attribute that attracted them. Made perfect sense and had absolutely nothing to do with Mary Elise.

Slumping back on the sofa, he scooped up a Rubik's Cube from the end table and clicked through rotations while sorting through his life. He normally liked puzzles and the order they restored to his world. He might wear wrinkled flight suits and inside-out T-shirts, but he had reasons. He appreciated order and logic.

Yeah, he had a type—spunky redheads. Except Mary Elise's spunk had been tempered to a quieter, steely will. What had happened to the scrawny girl who followed him into a nuclear plant, jotting notes for a school newspaper exposé? The coltish teen who'd chewed him out for not staying away from her chicken pox?

And what had she been holding back from telling him during the flight?

His hands whipped across the cube, lining up a new row of blues before shuffling yellows. Her voice may have quieted over the years, but the passion in her expression when she'd looked at him hadn't diminished. He'd stood in his bedroom doorway staring into her eyes, green eyes alive with confusion and pain and yes, even a desire so strong an emotional half-wit like him could read it.

Then and now he could only think what it would have been like if the day's outcome had been different. Too easily things could have gone to hell. Tag's call on the headset to alert him of a problem could have been worse. Finding Mary Elise in that crate had shocked a year off his life.

Finding her dead in that crate would have damned near killed him.

He'd forced that image out of his mind all day. During those few quiet moments in the doorway, the scenario had blindsided him like a bogey flying in from a six-o'clock position. This incredible titian-haired crusader who snuck junk food to a kid with a health food fanatic mom and crawled into crates with frightened little boys at the risk of her own life could have died before he had the chance to hold her again.

So he'd pulled her close in honor of those good memories they'd shared. And his logical brain taunted him with an irrefutable fact.

He had to hold her again.

The next morning Daniel measured coffee grounds while listening to three weeks' worth of messages on his voice mail. He'd barely had time to fling his duffel bag on the bed after a covert TDY dropping CIA officers deep into Cantou before the call from the Rubistanian attaché had rung through.

Cordless phone tucked under his chin, Daniel returned the bag of coffee to the steel cabinet in his galley kitchen and tucked the paper filter into the coffeemaker. He figured he would have at least another hour to get his head together before Mary Elise and the boys rolled out of bed. He never needed much sleep at a pop himself, and the bunking conditions hadn't been the best. A fact that had more to do with a raging arousal harder than the sofa.

And a host of memories even more unrelenting. So persistent even his morning ritual of a five-mile run on the beach followed by a workout in the clubhouse gym hadn't helped. By the time he hit the cold shower and changed into a clean flight suit, he accepted the fact that Mary Elise had lodged herself in his brain again.

Daniel jammed the glass pot under the water purifier while listening through the seventy-five accumulated messages.

Two hang-ups.

The dry cleaners calling for him to pick up his service dress uniform. As much as he might wish otherwise, he couldn't get away with wearing everything wrinkled and unstarched.

Next message, an automated telemarketer.

Punching Delete, he shut the water off with his elbow, juggling the coffeepot before finally opting for speakerphone.

"Hey, Dan?" Sultry Southern tones crooned through the speaker, filling the sparse kitchen. "Hannah from upstairs in 18-B. If you get this message, give me a call and let me know when you'll be back. I can ask the superintendent to let me in so you'll have milk and stuff waiting when you get home."

Great. That "and stuff" would no doubt be unfit for kids' eyes, like the time he'd returned to find Hannah waiting with a shrimp casserole and a ribbed tank top that encased gravity-defying double-D's. And Hannah was *smart* as well as hot—a biochemist researcher at the medical university, for crying out loud—what more could a man want? Yet still he wasn't interested in the brainy blonde.

Blonde? Not redhead. Crap.

Two more hang-ups cycled through.

He flipped the coffeemaker on as the next message picked up. "Daniel? Elaine. Uh, just wanted to let you know I'll be in Charleston on business next week and, uh, thought maybe we could, well, have dinner or something. I'll cook. Well, call me."

An image of auburn-haired Elaine taunted him. Daniel glanced heavenward and barked, "Okay, okay, Big Guy. You've made your point."

He'd actually had a semiserious relationship with

Elaine, a chef at a five-star joint. He'd even donned a tie for her once, not that he hesitated in breaking things off six months ago when he'd transferred from California. He'd cited the long-distance-relationship reason, already realizing they wouldn't work out. She'd offered to pack up her ginzu knives and follow him.

Damn, but he felt bad.

Not bad enough to mislead her by letting her food processor back into his life. Like his life wasn't screwed up enough right now anyway. And then he still had to puzzle through whatever had Mary Elise so on edge. Daniel reached on top of the refrigerator for a box of Pop-Tarts.

"Is she a good cook?" Trey's voice drifted from behind him.

Pivoting, Daniel ripped open the pastry box. "Run that by me again?"

His brother stood in the archway, knobby knees showing just below the hem of a Thunderbirds air show T-shirt. Not a hint of bed-head in sight in his dark hair, the kid carried a puffed-chest air and haughty look that would have done their old man proud.

"Is that Elaine lady on the answering machine really a good cook?"

"Yeah, she's a great cook. If you're into stir-fried sprouts and snails." Daniel pulled out a pack of Pop-Tarts and tossed aside the box.

"Actually, I like escargot. Calamari too."

Figures. "Charleston has awesome seafood restaurants. Shrimp trawlers bring stuff in fresh every day."

Trey sniffed. "I've eaten in restaurants around the world. My mom taught us to like anything since we traveled so much. She also said that *healthy* stuff would help us grow."

The boy's condescending glance ran the length of Daniel as if that inch missing from making him six feet tall might have been added with more squid and fewer Moon Pies.

Daniel laughed. The kid was snotty, but gutsy. Gutsy, he could work with. Trey would need that grit to carry him through the transition.

"No worries, kid." He passed the pack of Pop-Tarts to his brother. "We'll find someone to cook for you between restaurant visits. Even I know a growing boy can't live on Twinkies and Mountain Dew."

Trey offered another of his snooty sniffs and shuffled to the refrigerator while days of messages clicked through in the background. Daniel didn't bother shutting off the speakerphone since nothing classified would come through his home phone. And aside from Hannah's message, he didn't expect anything R-rated on his voice mail this time.

Reaching over his brother's head, Daniel pulled a can of orange juice from way back on the top rack, an unconsumed leftover from one of his flight lunches. "Here, kid, vitamin C."

"*My* dad left us lots of money, you know, for shopping and stuff."

Daniel mentally counted to ten. "Thanks, but I can afford a few groceries."

His brothers could keep their damned trust fund. He didn't want a penny of his father's money, and he'd told his old man the same when he'd walked out the door to attend the Air Force Academy. Now he could support the boys fine on his own until they turned twenty-one.

If Trey didn't off him first.

Daniel unhooked a coffee mug from under the cabinet. "You feeling okay today?"

There. That sounded vaguely parental. He paused the

coffeemaker long enough to pour himself some much-needed java.

"I'm not a baby who can't tell you if I'm sick." Trey nibbled the edge of a Pop-Tart with a skeptical scowl.

"Okay. Okay." He'd let the doc handle that one. While Kathleen had given Trey the all's-fine yesterday, she still wanted both of the boys checked out by a pediatrician. After he shopped for bunk beds. And clothes. And food. Healthy food.

Damn.

When the hell was he supposed to go to work? Thank God Mary Elise was with them for a while.

"Mary Elise doesn't want to stay here with us."

Had the kid taken up mind reading? Maybe Trey could figure the woman out. "No sh— Uh, no kidding."

Another thing to change about his life. His language. Just what he needed, Austin swaggering into preschool cursing like a crewdog.

Preschools? Double damn. What did he know about freaking kiddie day cares?

"Hello, Daniel." The deep bass rumbled from the speakerphone. His father's voice.

Shock sucker punched Daniel. His lungs constricted, tight. For a surreal moment he wondered if the past days had been a sick game. His father would come pick up Trey and Austin. Life would go back to normal.

Except for Mary Elise.

Trey's gasp slammed him back to the present. Daniel's gaze locked with his brother's saucer-wide eyes staring back from a pale face as they listened to the voice of the one man who joined them.

And it wasn't a dream or game. The message was more than two weeks old. Daniel listened to the words, the voice, couldn't make himself shut down this last link to a father he hadn't been connected to in years.

"Son, call back as soon as you receive this message. We need to talk about…" He cleared his throat.

Mary Elise? She had said his father arranged the job for her. How long had she been there? Maybe she'd only just arrived.

But why would his dad play Cupid when father-son chitchats were pretty much nothing more than a biannual affair? At best.

Daniel shook free the questions and, for his young brother's sake, reached to lower the volume. Trey sidled closer to the machine, his eyes glinting with a willfulness Daniel recognized well from the mirror.

Their father's voice continued to swell into the room. "I don't want to go into details over an answering machine. It would be better if you placed the call from the base on a secure line."

The message clicked to an end. Trey shifted from his guard post to let Daniel jam the off button.

Secure phones? The limited intelligence that had filtered in about his father and stepmother's deaths rolled through his mind. Their car had been caught in the crossfire between extremist dissidents and local militia. A tragic accident.

Right?

His heart pounded in his ears, each tight breath in sync with Trey's faster gulps of air.

Trey. Crap.

The nine-year-old stood rigid with his small can of orange juice in one white-knuckled fist and his Pop-Tart shaking in his other hand. Glassy brown eyes refused to shed tears. The T-shirt seemed to swallow him whole as his snotty air fell away, leaving behind a grieving little boy.

Daniel thumped his mug on the counter and knelt in front of Trey. "Hey, bud, I hate that this happened to him, too."

He cupped a comforting hand around the boy's shoulder.

Trey shrugged it off, chest filling his T-shirt again. "Like you even care about him." He flung his breakfast pastry toward the sink. Missed. The Pop-Tart slapped the tile floor. "I'll bet you just forgot to mail that 'World's Best Dad' card for Father's Day last year."

Shot well taken, kiddo. "Trey…"

"That's right. I'm Trey. Franklin Baker III. Third. Trey, after my dad. *I* was named for him, not you."

Damn but the kid fought with the gloves off. "I realize you're upset. Hell, I'm upset." Hell? Damn. Damn. Damn. Watch the mouth, Baker. "You don't want to be here. I understand."

"Like *you* want me here."

What could he say to that? His brother needed reassurance, but would recognize a lie in a heartbeat.

Daniel stared at the blueberry Pop-Tart on the gray-flecked tile while the drip, drip, drip of the coffeemaker echoed. Finally he scrounged for words in a situation he'd never imagined facing.

"Trey, you're a smart kid, like the old man. You were well named." No bull in that statement. "So I'm gonna be straight with you. No, this is not what I would have listed on my schedule for the year. Of course I wish you were with your dad and mom right now. That's the way things should be. But life didn't give us a choice, so let's help each other out here."

Trey wavered forward. His bottom lip quivered twice. Daniel squeezed the boy's shoulder.

"No!" Trey jerked back. "I don't know you and I'm

not staying here.'' He spun on his heel and ran down the hall. The slamming door rattled dangling mugs.

"Damn.'' Daniel scooped the Pop-Tart off the floor and into the trash. "Damn. Hell. *And* crap!''

The sight of Mary Elise in the archway halted the flow of bottled curses. Mary Elise in *his* clothes. His gray sweatpants and a T-shirt from a missile-testing project had never looked so good. Fire-red hair streamed over both her shoulders, pert breasts nudging the well-worn cotton to part the curtain of hair.

He needed air. He needed space. Both running low in his small condo.

Daniel turned away and hoped Mary Elise would get the not-so-subtle message that he wasn't in the mood for chitchat. Maybe she would go comfort Trey and leave him the hell alone. He realized his avoidance tactics were juvenile and didn't give a damn.

He jerked open the cabinet to look for…he had no idea what. He just knew he didn't want this attraction, and he definitely didn't want a soul-searching conversation about Trey and their father and the past with Mary Elise. He wanted to smile with her, joke about the incongruous notion of him packing Scooby-Doo lunch boxes and attending school plays. Anything to keep from facing so many truths.

First on the list, his relationship with his father sucked. With that as his only model, he didn't hold out much hope of his ability to parent two needy boys.

Next, and worse, came the gut-scraping knowledge that he hadn't done right by this woman, a person he'd cared about more than anyone then. Not that he had a clue how to tap into the emotional crap he knew she needed. Another blot against his parenting potential.

And damned if he didn't want to plunge right back into

the same mistakes, if it meant a chance to plunge into her one more time.

He let his hand settle on a jar of peanut butter and reached for the silverware drawer.

Apparently Mary Elise didn't take hints. Or plain ignored them as she appeared in the kitchen.

He recognized the tilt of her chin well. She might be a more subdued version of the animated spitfire who'd trailed his tracks and kept him from falling irretrievably into mischief with her dry wit and wisdom. Yet even subdued to half power, this woman had an unmistakable will. The furrow in her brow said it all.

She intended to talk.

Given his self-control lay in the trash right beside that Pop-Tart, he figured the bedroom door and wide expanse of bed waiting a few steps away didn't offer much hope for getting through their conversation with an inch of sanity left.

Chapter 6

Standing beside Daniel in the galley kitchen, Mary Elise forced her brow to smooth and edged aside her urge to offer advice. Danny should hone his own instincts in dealing with the boys. She could already gauge from the way he'd talked to Trey that his intuition was on target. Sure, she might approach things differently, but that didn't make his way wrong.

And therein lay the core truth. He needed to set patterns in place that *he* could maintain, not her way, since she would soon be gone.

She shouldn't tell him what to say to Trey, but she couldn't leave him alone with all that pain pulsing through the small kitchen. The echo of Franklin Baker's voice from the answering machine had shaken her, even if she couldn't hear the words. She could only imagine what Daniel must be feeling.

Given he'd dodged her comfort last night, she didn't expect him to start sobbing on her shoulder by any means.

Still she would be here for him. That much he would have to accept.

Danny folded his arms across his broad chest encased in a clean—albeit wrinkled—flight suit, obviously having finally accepted she wasn't going anywhere. "What? No tips on how I should have handled that?"

She shook her head and padded across gray-speckled tile toward the coffeemaker. Colombian roast and freshly showered Danny scenting the air made an enticing morning blend. "Why would you think that?"

"First day on the parenting job and I already flunked Kids 101." He braced a boot on the cabinet behind him and sagged back with a long exhale. "Do you think I should go after him?"

She forced herself to ask instead of advise. "What do you think?"

"Me? I want to get things settled. Now." He swiped an orange juice can off the counter and crumpled it in his fist before flinging it into a recycling bin with a resounding rattle.

A confrontation when they were both angry and on edge? Ick. She unhooked a dangling black mug to keep from grabbing his arm to stop him. To keep from grabbing him period. "Do what you feel is best."

"The kid's probably in there crying. Alone. I hate that for him." His boot jammed reflexively against the gleaming metal cabinet with a single thud. "But he would resent me more for seeing it."

Bingo, Danny. "I would imagine so."

"So I'll try again later."

"And later again if that's what it takes." She leaned against the counter beside him and sipped the steaming coffee. "He just needs time to assimilate everything."

Daniel nodded.

Of its own will, her hand fell to rest on his upper arm. "I thought you did well in a situation that stinks no matter which way you look at it."

Muscles flexed beneath her touch. Her fingers itched to explore the broadened width of his shoulders. Silence echoed but for the hiss of the coffeemaker and more yearning zipping back and forth. The chill of tile floor seeped into her bare feet while the heat of his arm seared her fingers.

She jerked her hand away. Don't get involved. They needed to make their own way.

And emotions hurt.

Daniel scooped an open Pop-Tart box off the counter. Five seconds later he was slathering peanut butter on top of the purple-and-white-swirled frosting. She quelled a wince.

He chewed through a bite before cutting a glance her way. "Aren't you going to suggest eggs and wheat toast or shove me out of the way so you can whip up something healthy?"

"Daniel, you're thirty-two years old. If you want to eat chocolate frosting on your bagel for breakfast, that's your business."

"So you're not going to try to fix me or bake a casserole."

Confusion cut through the need to lick the peanut butter from the corner of his mouth. "Why would I want to do that?"

"Never mind." He jammed the rest of his breakfast in his mouth and washed it down with a swig of coffee. "I should get moving. Thank you for staying. This morning is crazy enough without worrying about rounding up a baby-sitter."

Guilt swirled through her passion like the mix of that peanut butter through the frosting. She was using him every bit as much as he was using her. Except she wasn't being straight-up honest with him.

For the best, right? Then he wouldn't get hurt trying to sort her mess.

He opened a drawer, withdrawing a notepad and pen. ''I appreciate that you let me reason through how to handle Trey.''

She blinked away her surprise at his perception of her motives.

He thrust the pad and pen toward her. ''But I could still use your input on their routine and those EpiPen things. Could you start a list of the factual stuff?''

She eyed the pen and paper. There'd once been a time she never went anywhere without a notebook handy for capturing the flood of words always ready to pour from her mind through her fingertips.

Written words trickled from her muse in short supply these days.

He waggled the small pad. ''I won't impose on you forever. Just long enough to get through settling the boys.''

A list. He wanted a simple list from her, not a creative writing essay or editorial or, God forbid, a story.

She gripped the edge of the pad without touching him.

''Thank you.'' He held firm, linking them through a silly little pad of paper with Gravity Sucks printed through an image of a crashing plane. ''How weird is it that I have people I spoke to just last week, friends and old girlfriends who I should be calling to pitch in here. But yet here we are.''

''I know the boys.'' She tried to explain away the connection with the logic Danny so valued. Fat lot of good it did her.

The silence swelled between them, filled with the

knowledge that their connection was more. Would it always be like this for them?

She studied the stitches, pockets, zippers along his flight suit as if the different clothing might help convince her this was a different man from the one she'd loved years ago. Her gaze traveled across his chest, to the strong column of his throat.

Her hand inched to the neck of his flight suit where the black T-shirt peeked free. With one finger she traced the raised seam of his inside-out shirt, a sight all too familiar. ''I never thought to ask why you do this?''

Brown eyes deepened from milk chocolate to an intense, darker flavor no less enticing. ''Do what?''

''Wear your T-shirts inside out. You've always done it and I never thought to ask you why before. It was just a part of the Danny picture that I accepted.''

''Maybe I don't notice how I put my shirts on.''

She shook her head. ''I don't think so. If that were the case, you'd have your T-shirts on right side out some of the time. But you don't. You think through and have a reason for everything you do, Danny. You always have.''

A smile crinkled the corners of his eyes. ''Not everyone realizes that. You're scary, you know.''

''Yeah, right. I'm intimidating as hell.''

He chuckled. She joined in with ease, their laughs blending between them until she squeezed his hand.

His hand?

She looked down and found their fingers had entwined over the small pad. When? How?

They both yanked back.

He smacked the pad down on the counter. ''The seams scratch.''

''What?'' She fisted her tingling hand by her side.

Daniel kept his back to her, scribbling notes along the

pad. "The outside of a T-shirt is smoother than the inside with the seams. It's more comfortable to wear the shirt inside out. Damned silly to put the smoother side out just so the world thinks you look better while those seams are chaffing away."

He spun to face her, lighthearted Danny firmly stamped across his features. "Time for me to punch out of here, but I'll try to finish up soon. I have to swing by base legal and start paperwork for the boys before flight debrief, then a meeting with my commander. After that, we can head out to buy whatever you and the boys need."

She watched him move, Danny so at ease in his own skin and with the world when his life had been flipped upside down. How much of it was pretense? "You know, Trey's just like you."

He snorted. "You mean Austin, right?"

"No. You and Trey are both torn up over losing your father, and neither one of you can bear to accept a bit of comfort."

The smile fell away, replaced by the newer Danny, the man who drew a gun in foreign countries with little or no backup. "Like you're any different."

A gasp caught in her throat.

Danny tapped her forehead. "Exchanging troubles is a two-way street, Mary Elise. One neither of us seems comfortable traveling anymore."

He waited, and for a weak minute she actually considered leaning against one broad shoulder and telling him everything. Except she understood Danny too well— rather than just offer help as his father had done, he would take over, guns blazing into the middle of her mess.

Or worse yet, he wouldn't believe her about Kent's threats any more than her parents had. Either way, for the sake of the boys, she needed to keep him as far away from Kent as possible.

She stepped back. Away from Danny and the temptation of broad shoulders.

He nudged the pad toward her, no risky hand-to-hand exchange this time. "Here are numbers where you can reach me. If there's a pressing emergency, call this one. The copilot, Renshaw, lives in this complex with her fiancé."

"Spike?" She followed Daniel across the living room to the door.

"Right. Up on the second floor. He's off today and can be down in seconds." Daniel paused under the porch overhang. "Promise me you'll call if you need anything. Not just for the boys. For you too, okay?"

"Okay." She lied. And suspected he knew it.

Daniel loped toward his shiny blue truck. Apparently he took more care with his vehicle than his flight suits.

She stood in the open door, mug cradled in her hands, and let the heated ceramic warm the chill that increased as Danny backed up and drove away. She stared at his empty spot long after the truck's rumble faded.

Shaking off whimsy, she spun toward the condo. Her feet tangled on the arrangement of flowerpots by the neighbor's door. Mary Elise knelt to right one lopsided pot and scoop stray soil. She patted it back into colored planters filled with ferns, pansies and impatiens. Her hand stilled on a final one tucked in the back in an incongruous bland terra-cotta pot.

False Unicorn. She fingered the small greenish-white flowers, their blooms having held on beyond summer blooming season. She'd been so touched when Kent brought her a small pot similar to this once, the simple romantic gesture more special than the dozen roses he'd given her after the second miscarriage. Or so she'd thought. Then he'd explained how False Unicorn root supposedly increased fertility and prevented miscarriages.

By the end of the year, he'd bought her a window garden full of other such plants like red clover blossoms and blue cohosh. Not that he actually expected her to use them. He'd hired specialists, after all. Eventually, hope had withered along with words and creativity while her window garden blossomed in mocking contrast.

A chill iced up her spine. Rising, she searched the parking lot. Found nothing unusual. Her fingers slid from the tiny flowers and sought the warmth of her coffee mug.

Quit imagining things. The plant had nothing to do with Kent. She hadn't heard even a whisper from him in the year since moving overseas. He'd either lost her trail or the edge to his insane fury had dulled.

But those fears were difficult to shed. Trust was hard to recapture.

Mary Elise bolted inside, locked the door and tried to blot the image of the tiny plant outside. Tried. Failed. Hand gripping the knob, she sagged back.

Her gaze trekked across the living room to the bar separating it from the kitchen. Pop-Tart wrappers lay scattered across the counter with an open jar of peanut butter beside them.

Daniel's life might seem wrinkled and disorganized from the outside, but his disorder was a choice for comfort in a man totally together on the inside. While she knew her dry cleaned and wrinkle-free silks shrouded a woman with a mess of a life.

"Crap." Daniel bit out the crewdog-worthy curse with precision since there wasn't anyone *but* crewdogs to hear him in the squadron corridors.

In seconds he would receive an ass-chewing from the Squadron Commander for skirting rules. Technically Daniel hadn't busted a single regulation. But goodwill protocol on the other hand…

Damn, but he hated playing politics. He left those niceties and games to his old man.

Or rather once had. Daniel ignored the pounding ache in his head and in a place some might call a heart while focusing on the more literal pounding yet to come.

He lengthened his strides along the industrial carpet, past photos of previous commanders, by a planning room filled with crew members at work—the kind of toe-the-line officers who made life easier for men like his father and Lt. Col. Quade. Voices drifted into the hall—Marcus ''Joker'' Cardenas and Jack ''Cobra'' Korba. Solid flyers, intense and by the rules.

Unlike himself.

The Squadron Commander's closed door loomed ahead. Man, the old open-door-policy days of Zach Dawson's command were long gone. Just grit through it. Not the first reaming and sure wouldn't be his last. Daniel rapped his knuckles twice.

''Yes.''

Okay, guess that meant enter. Daniel stepped inside the spacious office, stopping short of an oversize wooden desk looming with flags behind it. ''You wanted to see me, sir?''

Lt. Col. Lucas Quade didn't glance up from the file in front of him, the subtle put-down not lost on Daniel. He waited. Studied the rows of airplane photos, a C-17 framed alongside a print of the C-141 Quade flew earlier. Cornell diploma. With honors. Figures.

His old man had wanted him to go there. Actually, his father had wanted him to attend Harvard or Yale, but they didn't have ROTC programs, so the prestigious schools didn't even make Daniel's list of possibilities.

Quade closed the file with precision before raising his gaze to Daniel without standing. "Is that how you report in a military manner, Baker?"

Ah, so that's how the guy wanted to play it. Quade's turf, they had to play Quade's way. Just like days of old with Franklin Baker.

Daniel drew to attention and snapped a sharp salute. "Captain Baker reporting as ordered, sir."

Quade returned the salute, no invitation to sit on the sofa followed like with the past commander. This guy wouldn't be pulling a secret stash of Little Debbie cakes out of his desk drawer to share either. Yeah, he'd received a few "chats" from Dawson about how to better balance the secrets ops Daniel pulled with the commander's need-to-know basis. Chats, not this standing-at-attention bull.

"Baker, I'm sure you realize why you're in here."

"Yes, sir." He kept his eyes on the flag just behind Quade and consoled himself with the fact that a squadron commander usually only held the position for eighteen months to two years.

About how long it felt like this "chat" would last.

The commander jabbed a finger on the closed file with a red cover sheet declaring "Secret." "You're lucky you covered your ass planning this one."

Daniel didn't bother making excuses. Air Force Academy days had picked up where Mary Elise left off in drilling some caution into him.

Quade continued, "I don't question the mission's importance. And I know damned well there are times you can't be straight-up about where you're going. But, *Captain*, that was my plane and those were my flyers. No matter how much paperwork you filed or how many strings you pulled, their safety is still on my shoulders. You should have placed a courtesy call to me.''

The past blended with the present, too many such confrontations with his father hammering his memory at a time when the last thing he wanted was to think of his old man currently dead in the ground.

Quade blinked slowly. ''Answer me one question. Would you have given Dawson a courtesy call?''

Nailed. The question and its obvious affirmative yanked Daniel right back to the present, a not so comfortable place to be. He kept his eyes forward and mind centered on the shopping trip he and Mary Elise would make with the boys.

The Squadron Commander released him from answering by planting his hands on the edge of his desk and standing. ''You didn't call me because you didn't want to risk my having a different take on your plan.''

Silence seemed the wisest course of action. Bunk beds. They would shop for those first and then pick out sheets. Austin said he wanted sailboats. Fine. Mary Elise would help Trey open up enough for the kid to choose what he wanted, too.

Quade pushed a paper across the desk. Daniel glanced down. The guy couldn't actually intend to write him up without grounds? Daniel looked closer and found…leave papers. The commander was giving him two weeks vacation.

''Get your household in order.''

Confusion shifted the ground under his feet. He'd expected to have to beg for leave. ''Thank you, sir.''

''Don't thank me. This isn't some kind of personal favor. You're no good to my squadron if you're distracted.'' He clipped through the words, snagging a fresh file to open. ''Dismissed, Baker.''

O-kay. Daniel spun on his heel to leave, the prospect of bunk-bed shopping suddenly not so daunting after all.

"Baker?"

Slowly Daniel turned.

Quade stood with his back to the door, shuffling pages in the file as if Daniel only warranted half of his attention. "Boundary pushing is necessary to expand the airframe's capabilities. Confidence in the air is admirable." He tucked another page to the back. "Intellectual arrogance, however, will put you face-to-face with an enemy missile someday."

The words chaffed more than any right-side-out T-shirt.

Quade reached for the file cabinet. "Close the door behind you."

Daniel stepped into the hall, shoulders tensed just as after countless confrontations with his father. Hell, yeah, he had trouble with authority figures. Didn't take a freaking Sigmund Freud to figure that one out. Still, he managed. Pushed his boundaries, stayed alive and kept his career on track, accepting the occasional chewing out as the price to pay for freedom.

What baffled him, however, was how easily he'd fallen into the old habit of keeping his temper in check with the promise of seeing Mary Elise.

Much more "seeing Daniel" and she would lose her mind.

Mary Elise plastered herself against the truck door, the back now full of bunk beds, linens, enough food to feed an army, four bags of kids' clothes and two bags for her.

Never had he grown impatient, even when Austin had screamed himself purple with a temper tantrum in the Base Exchange. Not once had Daniel snapped or glanced at his watch, darker emotions apparently shunted away.

Playful Danny had reemerged with a charm and ease that simultaneously dazzled and tormented her. He slid into the family routine without a misstep, as if he lived to purchase new video games and supersize an order at the golden arches.

Which of course he did.

Palmetto trees whizzed by the window along the barrier-island road. Sailboats, a barge, a shrimp trawler bobbed in the distance until she lost herself in the hypnotic regularity. What if she and Danny had stumbled on each other again through a simple passing on the street, no dangerous ex-husband lurking in her past? Could they meet for coffee and discuss their engagement and lost baby with adult perspective, then slide back into their old friendship? Maybe something more.

But she had met Kent. Married him. And knowing him had marked her—transforming her into a different woman, one as incapable of committing words to paper as she was of committing herself to another person.

Threat or no threat, she'd changed. Not for the better. Even if she scraped deep inside herself for the pieces to try, the risk wouldn't be hers and Danny's alone. Echoes of Austin's screaming fit still reverberated in her head, his anguish because he'd lost sight of her for seven seconds when she stepped around an aisle. She wouldn't mislead those two grieving boys into expecting her to stay. They'd lost enough.

Two grieving boys in the process of beating each other to death with blow-up baseball bats that had been on special with the kids' meals at the Base Exchange food court.

Austin thunked Danny on the back of the head.

Daniel ducked. ''Hey, short stuff, you're gonna land us in a ditch. Hold off another minute while I park the truck and we can cross swords on the beach.''

He wove the truck past an unusual abundance of cars lining the street leading into the complex. He crept past every full visitor spot and finally nosed his Ford into a tight space on the end.

"Someone must be throwing a party," he noted off-handedly as he reached back to unbuckle Austin.

Mary Elise couldn't help but think how a week ago he would have likely been joining the party. Still, he didn't say a word or show even a hint of the frustration he must be feeling.

Don't be so wonderful, Danny. Please.

She stepped out of the truck just as one of the second-floor condo doors flung open to emit music and laughter.

Spike strode onto the balcony, his arm hooked over his fiancée's shoulders. "Come on up, Crusty. Most of the squadron's already here and ready to party."

Daniel pulled Austin out before shouting, "Thanks, man, but I need to unload the truck and start putting together furniture so we're not bunking on the floor again. Besides, uh, I've got the kids."

"No problem," Spike insisted, tucking a bathing-suit-clad Darcy Renshaw closer. "There are plenty more rug rats here."

A carrot-topped little girl crawled between Spike's legs seconds before a linebacker-size man plowed past to scoop her up. Mary Elise forced herself not to wince at the sight of a baby that too easily could have been hers and Daniel's.

Darcy stepped forward to lean over the balcony. "Didn't you hear us, Crusty? Most of the squadron's here. Surprise! We're throwing you a baby shower."

Chapter 7

Three hours later, Mary Elise dangled her feet in the pool and tried to soak away the tension of attending a "baby shower" eleven years after the fact with Daniel. Actually, a truly thoughtful gesture on the part of his squadron friends, and she refused to allow past baggage to taint it.

And man, did these people know how to party.

Chlorine drifted along the salty air while Mary Elise kept guard over Austin splashing nearby in the shallow end with his newly christened pair of inflatable water wings. Tables and loungers filled with adults and kids, the pool packed with squadron guests bearing gifts of toys, clothes, even a surprise extravagant present of two bikes.

Three couples strayed beyond the fence to the marshy coastline, gushing tidewaters surging against the beach with circling gulls and herons overhead. Darcy and Spike's condo had overheated quickly with the press of people inside until they'd moved the party, complete with

Bo's guitar entertainment, to the pool in hopes of cooling off.

Feet swishing through the lukewarm water, Mary Elise watched Danny step under the pool shower. Cutoff jean shorts rode low on his slim hips until she could count every ridge of his six-pack abs. Spray streamed down his face, between his defined pecs in a trail southward that left her swallowing hard.

She jerked her gaze away before it followed that water straight down. Geez, how totally embarrassing, not to mention insulting. She liked to think of herself as a normal woman with healthy urges, but also a thinking woman and not an out-of-control bundle of hormones.

As she'd once been around this man.

Gentle guitar pluckings floated along the ocean breeze in a sensual serenade. Great. Apparently, bad-boy Bo had decided to turn his talented fingers to a sappy love song as he sprawled in a chair at an umbrella table. No doubt playing in hopes of luring the splashing hot tub mermaid back to his place.

Couples. Couples. Couples everywhere. Ugh.

At least she and Daniel wouldn't be swimming together half-naked as they'd done so often in his parents' pool. Darcy had offered to share an extra bathing suit with her, but Mary Elise found lazing by the pool the perfect way to end a draining day.

She accepted that some of her lassitude could be attributed to her lack of medicines since her supply now sat useless in her cabinet back in Rubistan. She would have to check in with a doctor soon about new prescriptions. At least the over-the-counter, iron-fortified vitamins she'd bought would help with the anemia that accompanied endometriosis in full tilt.

Her body chemistry might be out of whack, the building

pain only mildly numbed by extra-strength Motrin. But she'd lived with the fallout of her illness for so long, she refused to let it rule her anymore. She would enjoy the moment before her life shifted into another unknown direction.

Besides, since Austin had a conniption fit any time she stepped too far out of his sight line, napping back at Danny's condo wasn't an option.

Across the stretch of cement, Danny yanked the shower chain, ending the spray in a trickle. Shaking the droplets from his hair, he strode toward Mary Elise, the loose-hipped grace of his walk leaving her longing to trace the band of those low-riding cutoffs.

"Are you okay here while I swim? You know Darcy." He jerked a thumb toward their tomboy bombshell hostess sprawled in a lounge chair with a beer at her ringside seat for Bo's concert. "And you've met Julia Dawson, right?"

"Come on over," Darcy called from beside the woman Crusty had called Julia—wife of the prior Squadron Commander. The earthy blonde—Julia—wriggled her red toenails while her toddler son gripped them and giggled.

More families. More couples.

Mary Elise shook off the senseless frustration. Time to cut the self-pity crap.

Crap?

Geez, already Daniel was sneaking into her life and mind in so many ways. And now he had to soften her heart with sensitivity in making sure she didn't feel abandoned or awkward in the group. Yet, he achieved it without plastering himself to her side possessively as Kent had done.

No thoughts of Kent. Not tonight. Just enjoy the moment. "I'm fine, thanks."

Daniel knelt beside her. "I've got Austin now. Go visit or whatever."

Music and swirling water whispered a wake-up to her dormant creative muse. "In a minute."

He canted closer. "Are you okay? Everyone's being nice, right?"

Mary Elise struggled to keep her eyes on his face. She surely didn't want the sensual domino effect that would come from roving eyes, anyway. She'd seen his chest quite well a few seconds ago.

Now to try and forget those muscles. Just a body right? And she knew well what he looked like *without* the jean cutoffs. How really good he looked without them. Her heart rate kicked up a notch.

She willed her eyes to stay locked with his. "Everyone's been great."

And they had, welcoming her, yet not asking the umpteen questions that scrolled across their eyes every time she slipped and called him Danny instead of Daniel.

"Yeah, they have been awesome." He glanced back at his guitar-plucking buddy. "I'm still wondering how Bo financed both those bikes on his salary. I'm thinking lieutenants must be making more these days."

She couldn't help but marvel at the surprise thoughtfulness of the young bachelor, the pair of shiny mountain bikes a fun gift these world-weary kids would probably never forget.

Bo's speeding fingers slowed on the strings. "Every kid should have his own bike. Better for the little fellas to cruise the local sandbox for hot chicks," he said, dismissing his own generosity while he packed away his guitar.

Darcy wadded up a napkin and pelted him. "You're

just trying to score points with unsuspecting women like Hot Tub Hannah over there.''

A wicked twinkle lit Bo's baby blues. ''Do you think it's working?'' He directed the power of that lady-killer gaze toward the blonde in the steaming oasis at the end of the pool and received an encouraging grin in return. Bo stood. ''My cue to soak away my troubles. Thanks again, Crusty, for introducing me to Hannah. I owe ya one. Don't hesitate to call me if you need a sitter.''

Daniel pushed to his feet. ''So you can hit on my neighbor, then take my brothers cruising sandboxes?''

''The park's a great place to meet women. Joggers and dog walkers and babes lounging on picnic blankets.'' His twinkling eyes took on a rapturous gleam before he landed back in the present. ''Not that you need any of that now. Have fun you two.''

Winking, Bo pivoted away to jog toward the hot tub, lowering himself into the frothing bubbles beside Hannah.

With everyone assuming she and Danny were a couple in the making, it would be simple to let herself slip into that notion, as well. But while she might be willing to take pleasure from living where she could, not at so high a price. If she allowed herself to soften around Danny any more, she would crack and spill all.

The temptation was rapidly growing as strong as the desire to press her lips to his warm skin with beads of water begging to be sipped. ''Go. Swim. Play. Whatever.''

Please. Now.

He searched her eyes for an extended second before backing a step. ''All right.'' He turned to Trey, the boy scowling in a pool chair with his knees hugged to his chest. ''Hey, kid? Can you swim?''

Trey sniffed. ''Of course I can.''

"Good. Hold your breath." He scooped his brother up and launched him airborne toward the center of the pool.

Trey shrieked, closing his mouth with a gasp seconds before he landed in the water. Daniel cannon-balled a foot away from him. Spray sluiced a giant wave over the side.

Years slid away to the countless times they'd played in his parents' pool. God, she'd hated it when he'd dunked her. Until she'd learned to dunk him right back.

Daniel exploded to the surface beside Austin and shook the water out of his face.

Austin paddled, his water wings bobbing, and shouted between huffing breaths, "Mary Elise, come in. We're gonna play baseball."

Trey splashed him. "Volleyball, you dweeb."

"Yeah. That."

Mary Elise pulled her feet out of the water. "I'm not swimming today, sweetie. You just have fun with your brothers."

She backed away, mentally recording the image of Danny swimming with Austin's spindly arms locked around the strong column of big brother's neck. Daniel, a man so different from the steely warrior who'd drawn down an enemy guard in a foreign country to save his brothers less than forty-eight hours before. The dual image left her dry-mouthed. Rattled.

Intrigued.

She could watch. And she would enjoy. But she needed to keep enough distance so she could still leave.

Daniel spiked the ball back toward Tag. For all the good it did him. The loadmaster tapped it in the air with ease, setting up the next shot as he passed the volleyball to his teenage son.

Who missed it—hallelujah—since the boy was too busy

ogling the high schooler springing off the diving board, Zach Dawson's daughter, Shelby.

Teenage hormones packed a ferocious punch.

Daniel's gaze drifted back to Mary Elise. He looked beyond the new lines of worry and fatigue around her eyes to the clear green gaze he'd fallen hard for in his youth. Remembered how they'd known everything about each other. Shared every thought, no matter how personal.

Maybe it was the swimming scenario hammering him since they'd enjoyed countless hours in his parents' landscaped backyard and kidney-shaped pool growing up. He'd shut down those memories after they split, but now he'd have to learn to live with them bombarding him from more directions than antiaircraft fire.

"Crusty?" Tag shouted. "You with us, man?"

Daniel nodded, rejoining the game, his mind lofting back to the past as surely as the ball sailing through the air.

"I'm not swimming today, Danny."

Daniel stroked his way through the numbingly cold pool. His teenage body hungered for exercise outside the stifling formality of his parents' house. Early spring weather in Savannah made for chilly water, not that he cared. And usually Mary Elise didn't care, either.

"Why not?" He stopped inches from the cement edge where Mary Elise perched gripping her knees. "Scared of a little freezing water?" He flicked drops in her face.

"Yeah, right."

He hauled himself out to sit beside her. "What's the matter? Really? Come on, spill, because I'm not buying the scared-of-cold-water crap for even a second."

She scooped her hand through the pool and flicked his face right back. "Your dad hears you say crap again and you'll be needing that cold water to rinse out the soap."

"Yeah, yeah, whatever. He hasn't tried that since I was in junior high. Now come on. Swim with me. There's an extra suit in the pool house."

He reached to tug the rope of red hair trailing over her shoulder, then paused. When the hell had Mary Elise gotten breasts? Not much to them, but they sure as hell were there. He jerked his hand away.

"I can't, Danny. Can't. Okay? I'm a girl and there are days it's just easier for a girl if she doesn't swim."

He felt the color drain from his face and knew it didn't have anything to do with the freezing water. Some stuff a guy just didn't want to know. "Oh."

"Yeah, oh. Now go swim and enjoy the fact that you're a boy and can swim all thirty-one days of this month. I'll soak my feet here while we talk about something else."

And he wanted to do just that. Well, until he saw the downward tilt to her mouth, the minifurrow on her serious brow.

Who needed to swim laps, anyway?

Standing, he extended his hand without a word while he waited. He could handle this. Sure, he wanted to dive to the bottom of the pool where he wouldn't have to even think about this discussion. But he was a practical guy and, hell, this was Mary Elise after all. They could talk about anything.

Even if she had developed breasts overnight.

He shoved his hand closer.

She eyed his outstretched arm. "What?"

"Chocolate."

"Huh?"

"Let's go get some chocolate. I hear chicks like to eat a boatload of the stuff when they're, uh—" he stifled his wince for Mary Elise's sake "—not swimming."

A smile so perfect crept across her face and right up

to her eyes that a charge of victory shot through him until Daniel forgot about the pool behind him and the swim he'd waited all winter to take.

Mary Elise fitted her hand in his and stood. "Yeah, right, now I get it. You've just got your eye on that box of Hostess Ho-Hos in my mom's pantry."

"Busted."

Her laugh swelled then faded as they pushed their way through the ivy-covered gate separating their yards. "You're not totally grossed out?"

"Maybe a little."

She punched his arm.

"Hey, joking!" He rubbed his arm, relaxed. He could always do that with Mary Elise, relax, be himself with nothing to prove. Daniel slung an arm around his best friend's shoulders. "This just means you're gonna be able to have kids someday. Right? Nothing gross about that."

She tipped her face up to his. "Thank you, Danny."

Mary Elise arched onto her toes, a soft breast pressed to his side as she grazed a kiss against his cheek right at the corner of his mouth. If he moved his head even…

"Hey! Heads up, Baker."

Daniel blinked. The volleyball whizzed through the air, straight toward his face.

"Crap." He launched to the side and swung his cupped hands up into the ball with a microsecond to spare.

And damned if his gaze didn't land right back on Mary Elise to see if she'd been watching. He wasn't any better than Tag's son, Chris, drooling over a girl until he lost focus on the rest of the freaking world.

Chris punched the air with a victory shout. "Point, game and match for the visiting team."

Tag eased out of formation over to the side of the pool. "Perfect timing. We need to hit the road. My daughter's driving home from college for the weekend, and I promised Rena I'd move boxes out of Nikki's room before she gets here."

Daniel waded closer to Tag as Darcy launched out of her chair to join in the game. No doubt those boxes had been pulled down on his account as the loadmaster and his wife sorted through their son's old clothes to help fill Austin and Trey's empty closet. He stifled another wince at everything he owed his friends. He was a hell of a lot more comfortable being on the giving end. Did Mary Elise feel the same way?

And when the hell had he started analyzing *feelings?*

He shook off the thought faster than beading water in his hair. "Hey, make sure you pass along my thanks to Rena for the kids' clothes." Since the other marrieds had attended together, he couldn't help but notice Rena's absence in light of the conversation with Tag on the flight. "Let Rena know I'll send 'em back your way once these guys get through with them."

Tag shook his head with a look of horror. "Don't come near my house with those things, man. We've almost got our nest empty. Our baby-making days are over." He hauled himself out of the water. "You ready Chris? Chris?"

Christos Price jerked his gaze off Shelby Dawson's belly button ring and back to his father. A dazed look in his eyes glinted like the water streaming down the olive complexion inherited from his mother's Greek roots. "Yeah, Pop. I guess so."

The teen hefted himself from the pool. Right by Mary Elise. Which offered Daniel a convenient excuse to check on her. Just making sure she was comfortable with everyone, of course.

Yeah, right.

She'd settled in with his friends as he'd known she would, already absorbed in conversation with Julia Dawson while they both held sleeping children. Austin snoozed away on Mary Elise's lap, his soggy body soaking her silk shorts set. Not that she seemed to care or look in the least ruffled. Just natural. She should have kids of her own with some lucky bastard who would get to touch her incredible red hair.

Crap.

Daniel backed into the resuming game as they swapped sides, which gave him a perfect view of Mary Elise's night-lit lounge chair. When she'd told him about being pregnant with his child, he hadn't given much thought to the baby itself, or life after the wedding. He'd focused on shutting down thoughts of the future because they contrasted too much with what he'd dreamed for so long.

Yet once she'd lost the baby, once he'd lost Mary Elise in his life, he'd spent the next year thinking about what their baby would have looked like. What she would have looked like holding it.

And that image mirrored the one he was seeing too damned closely for his peace of mind.

He considered waking Austin up for another round of chicken just so he wouldn't have to keep staring at Mary Elise holding the little guy. But the boy's needs came first and God the kid pitched holy hell when taken away from Mary Elise. The boy was breaking his freaking heart with the tight-fisted clinginess to the only mother figure in his world right now. Maybe he could convince Mary Elise to stay in the area.

And then she'd be too busy to meet that lucky bastard who would father her children.

The rogue notion chugged through him as he pumped another serve into the air. She had to settle somewhere, and apparently their Savannah hometown no longer held any allure for her. The idea took flight, leveled out like the ball lofting over the net.

He staunchly ignored the insistent voice telling him he was doing this for himself. So what? Yeah, he wanted her around, but because he needed her to stay put. Made logical sense that she should stay in Charleston. Two plus two equaled four.

His gaze zoned back in on Mary Elise smoothing a hand along the sleeping child's back while her laugh carried on the ocean wind.

The next ball whizzed right by Daniel's head.

Kent McRae closed the Mercedes door—forced to park out on the street where some damned fool might scratch the paint. A nuisance, but an overabundance of vehicles packed the condo lot.

He wove his way through the maze of trucks and SUVs with military ID stickers on the windshield. Adrenaline snapped through him until he wondered why he'd ever bothered to pay someone to take on these tasks before. And to think he never would have known this quiet thrill if necessity hadn't forced him. Help wouldn't be arriving for another four to five days, and he'd sworn not to act decisively until then.

Striding along the lengthy row of Palmetto trees, he checked again to ensure Mary Elise was still engrossed with the pool party and her old lover. Her lover now?

Kent kept his strides even, loose, his hands unclenched. He wouldn't allow her the power over his emotions. He was in control.

He neared the line of mailboxes. As much as he might enjoy ending it now, he couldn't. The boys were off-limits, as per his accomplice's demands. He owed his accomplice too much in tracking Mary Elise's every move to step off their designated course now. And he always paid his debts.

As if he would hurt innocent children like some monster, anyway. He focused his revenge on the deserving.

Meanwhile, he needed Mary Elise off-kilter so she wouldn't become overconfident and opt to disclose her tale of woe to an old boyfriend. Having been married to the woman for three years, he knew which buttons to push. Watching her hand tremble as she'd touched that False Unicorn plant had been…satisfying.

Locating the correct box number, Kent straightened the knot on his favorite tie, silk with pelicans patterned in diagonal lines. A gift from Mary Elise two years ago and now a reminder of unfinished business. A final swipe to smooth his tie crinkled papers inside his suit coat pocket. He tugged out the folded pamphlets guaranteed to make more than her hand tremble. Innocuous fertility clinic literature to most. Pointed for her since she'd visited the same chain of clinics more than once.

A quick glance over his shoulder assured him no one watched. Kent slid out his lock pick and set to work on Baker's mailbox. Given how involved they were in their pool play, he should be well in and out before anyone noticed him. He wouldn't want to upset the boys. No, he wasn't a monster.

Just a man in control of his destiny with a debt to repay.

Chapter 8

Danny blasted out of the water like a sea monster, swiping his arm across the pool to spray Trey before he ducked behind Darcy. Mary Elise watched, smiled, couldn't help herself. Even allowed herself the pleasure of following his leap from the pool, his loose-hipped stride to the ice chest illuminated by a halogen lamp and crescent moon.

Oh, God. Danny was so cute, the boyishness somehow all the more charming coming from a muscle-bound man. Evenings like this made it easy to forget the ways she and Danny had annoyed the hell out of each other.

Distance, she reminded herself. Make lists and keep her distance from the enticing, playful Danny. For starters, her list making used to bug him. Go with the flow, he would tell her. Explore. Find adventure.

She'd found more than enough adventure with Daniel Baker and a bottle of champagne, thank you very much.

The party had wound down to half speed, quiet laughter no longer overriding the shush of gentle ocean waves. As much as she'd enjoyed conversation, she didn't mind the moment of peace.

Rubbing Austin's back, she tried to ease his fitful sleep, letting him snooze on until she could tuck him in his own bed. She could only risk four more days to smooth the transition and then she would have to leave.

Survival instincts screamed at her to run. Now. Long-denied maternal instincts, however, insisted she protect this precious little boy's wounded heart by staying as long as she could risk.

Enough cash waited in her account to carry her for a month, even finance a visit to a clinic to update her meds. Franklin Baker had managed to reroute her transactions while she was overseas so Kent couldn't trace them. She had no way of knowing if Franklin's accounting cover stayed in place. Once she presented ID to withdraw money, she would have to go.

Damn, she was tired of living like this, but what else could she do if even her own parents didn't believe her? Postpartum delusions, Kent had told them when she'd had no choice but to break her long silence over the growing problems in their marriage. Depression from the final late-pregnancy miscarriage.

Yeah, she sure as hell was depressed over losing her child and her marriage. But no way had she imagined the cold steel of a gun barrel pressed to her head as an assassin tried to coerce her into the car so he could launch her vehicle off a bridge in a fake suicide.

All on Kent's payroll.

She'd fought. Escaped. And no one had believed her. The more she'd insisted, the stronger the accusations of paranoia became. One mention of putting her in an institution from Kent with his monied influence and she'd hauled ass out of the country.

Unease tickled along her spine, like a caterpillar making its way ever so slowly up her back. The sense of being watched. Mary Elise held herself still, refusing to cave and look. Much more of this and she would be acting as crazy as Kent convinced her parents she was.

"Mary Elise?"

She jolted. Looked up and found Darcy Renshaw climbing up the pool ladder.

Relief shuddered through her, shaking the caterpillar sensation free. She *was* being watched, by one of Daniel's fellow flyers.

Dripping wet, Darcy sank to the middle of the lounger and sat cross-legged with a long-legged grace that had her fiancé eyeing her with smoky appreciation from across the pool. "Can I get you something to drink?" She stretched to offer up a bag of sunflower seeds from the smorgasbord on the table. "Or anything to eat?"

"You've already done so much. All of you have. I'm a little overwhelmed by it all, so many gifts and so many people. Please say you wrote everything down, like the clothes Tag brought, or was his name Jim or J.T.?" The loadmaster with shoulders as broad as Danny's. God, she hoped his wife knew what a lucky woman she was. "See, already I can't remember half the names, and men can be dense about things like thank-you notes."

"Don't worry about it. No one expects thanks. This is what we do for each other."

"Still…"

Darcy's finger sawed along her dog tag chain pensively. "I'll bet you're tough to help."

She shrugged. Help meant dependency and debts, and she was through with that.

Darcy's laser gaze eased. "There are a lot of us to meet at once, with call signs and real names doubling up what you're trying to learn. You're probably best off just re-membering the call signs.'' She gestured with her fistful of sunflower seeds. "Over there, the big blond guy with the baby who brought the football, that's Bronco. He's married to the flight surgeon Kathleen—or Athena, if we're using nicknames—who took care of Trey when you landed.''

"Bronco?'' She glanced over at the man with his wife, packing up their baby daughter to leave. "Because he looks like a bull?''

"No,'' she said with a wicked glint lighting her eyes. "Although I'll have to use that on him next time he rolls out a crewdog prank. Actually, he turned down a pro ball contract with the Broncos to stay in the military.''

"Wow. Mind-boggling that he would give up that much.'' Of course Daniel had also given up his family money to pursue his own dream. A calling more than a job, he'd once explained to her as he filled out his appli-cation to attend the Air Force Academy. "So there are stories behind some of the names. I guess I just thought they usually linked to someone's personality or the last names, like yours, Wren Renshaw. Or like Danny's, Crusty Baker.''

"Sure it goes with his last name, but also with the fact that he's a bit of a mess.'' Darcy grimaced. "Uh, I don't mean that as an insult. His scruffiness is kind of cute.''

And yet there was so much more to this man who flew military planes and commanded respect from a crew with as much ease as he unraveled equations—or dunked Trey.

God, if only she could view Daniel as simply scruffy or cute it would certainly save her a lot of yearning she had no choice but to ignore. "No offense taken. I've known Daniel a long time.''

Curiosity flared in Darcy's eyes again. "Then, like

Bronco, other names are tied into a watershed event.''
Darcy pointed to the Nordic-looking guy moving in on
Hannah while Bo's back was turned. ''Scorch set his mus-
tache on fire once in the Officer's Club bar with a drink
called a Flaming Dr Pepper.'' Her finger shifted toward a
laughing hulk of a man digging into the ice chest to fish
out two beers, passing one to Crusty. ''There's a great
story about Cobra over there, but it's best not to share the
details with kids around.''

Slowly the men and women became more than a few
names and loud revelers for Mary Elise. They took on
personalities in a tight community she'd invaded.

Absorbing the pieces of Daniel's world, she realized
distance didn't seem to be helping anymore. He'd exploded back into her life and mind. She wouldn't be able
to stop envisioning him in his new environment, wondering about him, how he was handling the changes. Even
with a live-in nanny, he would be thrown feetfirst into
parenting those boys. At least, she hoped he would.

Her hand gravitated to cup the back of Austin's head,
protectiveness twining through her as surely as the boy's
silky soft curls wrapping around her fingers.

Would Daniel find some hot-tub Hannah woman to
share his life with and ease his load? Would the woman
love these two precious little boys?

And one very grown man.

''Okay, fair's fair.'' Darcy's voice sliced through the
green haze of jealousy. ''I've ponied up some gossip, now
how about trade some in return. Starting with how you
met Danny.''

Mary Elise yanked her gaze off broad bare shoulders
and over to the hostess snacking on sunflower seeds with
undisguised curiosity. What would it hurt to share a few
harmless stories? She could leave something of herself

behind in his world from her younger days, the part of her that had been fearless, strong. Willing to risk the occasional broken bone or heart.

"We grew up together." Mary Elise searched for words to explain a relationship she wasn't certain she understood anymore. She stared out over the beachy expanse, the winding island coastline glittering with lights.

When Darcy's fiancé eased into view, Mary Elise couldn't help but welcome the distraction. She scrambled to gather thoughts scattered further than the expanse of ocean with tiny dolphin fins slicing lazy paths in the moonlit distance.

Silently Spike dropped a quick kiss on Darcy's mouth, the wren tattooed over his heart proclaiming his devotion as loud as any bullhorn. "You got the party for a while?"

"Yeah, hon, everything's winding up."

"Thanks. And no grilling the guests, okay?"

She slugged his tattooed arm, dead center on the diver-down symbol. "Love ya."

"You, too." He dropped another kiss on her lips before sprinting away.

So much devotion glowed in the woman's eyes, as she watched her spike-haired fiancé hop the fence to make his way toward the ocean, that Mary Elise felt like an intruder. "Why don't you go join him? I'm fine on my own."

Darcy shifted her attention back. "No way. We're having girl talk, and God knows I don't get much of that around these bozos." She shook her head. "Honestly, Max was pretty much an antisocial hermit when I met him. And while he's come out somewhat, he still needs his cave time on occasion. He has a cabin on one of the more remote spots of a barrier island for when the surfer dude within him needs to have a Poseidon moment," she explained with an understanding that boded well for the long term.

"I'm sure he appreciates your accepting him as he is."

"He does. And honest to God, it's a two-way street. He's given up so much for me, changing jobs, relocating from the West Coast to Charleston. He even wears a coat and tie to work when he's not out on assignment."

Darcy reached across to Austin to smooth baby-soft curls, a wistful look in her eyes. Her hand fell back to her lap. "Okay, I confess, I'm so ga-ga happy with Max I can't help but see romance everywhere. But folks really are dying to learn more about you two."

"Guess my calling him Danny gave things away." In spite of her decision to share, Mary Elise found the words tougher to spill than she'd thought. She seldom granted herself permission to look back on those times. Hadn't dared look, knowing the strong person Danny had challenged her to be then might not approve of the more cautious creature she'd become.

"We call him lots of things. But never Danny."

"Old habits are hard to break." In more ways than one. She forced herself not to let her eyes linger on the crinkle in the corner of Daniel's eyes as he smiled. "My family moved down south when I was eight. My mother's lung specialist was located in Savannah, so my father made the transfer there."

"Crusty's from Savannah? I thought he might be from the South with that hint of an accent, but I wasn't sure."

A twinge of surprise nipped her. Danny seemed close to these people, and yet they didn't even know the most basic facts about his background. "We were neighbors. Best friends since elementary school."

Laughter rode the wind, Bo flirting with Hannah as she cooed over his generosity with the bicycles.

Mary Elise smiled, pool memories merging with bike-riding jaunts. "Daniel even taught me to ride a bicycle. I was catching a lot of ribbing from the neighbors over being eight and still using training wheels. I'd fallen once before." She pointed to the scar on her knee. "One day he got a wrench and took off the training wheels, presenting me with my shiny, dangerous two-wheeler. No way did I want to climb back on that bike again. But somehow when Danny told me I could do it, that this time would be different, I believed him."

Again Daniel scooped a passing Trey into the air for a canonball splash, but without any repeat protests from Trey. Daniel inspired trust with his oozing confidence and invincibility. Only, the stakes were so much higher now than a dunking or scraped knee.

Darcy angled back on her elbows. "I can just see you sailing down that sidewalk, red pigtails streaming behind you while Danny whooped it up cheering you on."

Mary Elise smiled at the memory close to the one Darcy described. Those soaring two minutes of freedom were incredible. Until… "I broke my wrist."

Handful of sunflower seeds pausing midway to her mouth, Darcy flinched. "Ouch."

Mary Elise nodded. He'd gotten her right back on that bike again the minute her cast had been sawed off, albeit running alongside her to steady the handlebars. But unbending in his assertion that she could do it. She wasn't going to enter the fourth grade with training wheels.

"I was a real klutz in those days, arms and legs tangling. I did fine pedaling downhill on the straight and narrow, but once it came time to turn. Bam. Right into a hundred-year-old tree. Man, did his father ever chew him out."

"Kinda like Darth did today at the squadron."

"Darth?"

Darcy rolled her eyes. "Our private name for the new Squadron Commander. Daniel decided Evil Emperor was too long and opted for Darth, as in Darth Vader."

Mary Elise shivered, remembering well the stealthy man on the runway, dark, a little menacing—and conspicuously absent from a gathering where even the prior Squadron Commander had attended.

How bad had the reaming been? Yet Danny hadn't shown the slightest sign of tension all afternoon while shopping. Had he needed support or a confidant earlier, and she'd been too wrapped up in her own problems to notice? She would have never let that happen in the old days.

Of course they'd been more in tune with each other then. Still, she was surprised how much it ruffled her feathers to think of someone giving him a hard time. "Is he in trouble at work over the flight?"

"Sort of, but not really." Darcy waggled her hand. "Crusty has…connections. And he knows how to skirt the rules, push some boundaries, but he's careful not to risk his job by stepping over the line."

Apparently, Daniel hadn't changed much after all, merely upped the stakes of his boundary pushing.

Darcy laced her fingers over her stomach. "Sometimes Crusty reminds me of my Max, willing to bypass recognition for the higher good of the mission. Men like those two don't care about pinning on general. And from the shadows they make the world a better place."

A faraway smile played with her face before she turned to Mary Elise. "So? Will you be sticking around here? There's always a market for good teachers, and with your overseas experience—"

"I'm not staying." Enough confiding. She needed to

erect some barriers before she slipped into Daniel's world along with those stories. Mary Elise cuddled the warm weight of sleeping Austin closer, her arms already aching at the impending emptiness.

"Does Crusty know that?"

"He will."

Across the chlorine waters, Daniel's eyes met hers. Held. Mesmerizing. Unrelenting.

For all his easygoing ways, Mary Elise knew Danny possessed a steely will. Well, so did she now—at least when it came to keeping herself and those around her safe. She just hoped the battle took place with them both wearing a few more clothes.

Friendship could sure be a mixed blessing.

Walking beside Mary Elise in the late-night surf, Daniel wasn't certain whether to thank or curse his squadron buds. As if Darcy and Spike hadn't already done enough for him, now they insisted on watching Trey and Austin while the boys slept so Daniel and Mary Elise could take a breather. Stroll down the beach. In the moonlight. Alone but for the occasional passerby and dim lights of distant houses.

Thanks, pals. He jammed his fists into the pockets of his damp cutoffs. Clammy jean shorts didn't help cool the steam of frustration. The need to act.

Moored sailboats bobbed, wind snapping and pinging slack lines against the masts in an erratic tune. More than a walk, he wanted a solid twenty minutes with Max for feedback on the answering machine message from his father. Could be nothing. Could be something. He should be talking to Max. Or loading new games on his computer for the boys. Or plotting out flight plans to Timbuktu, just in case he got any ridiculous ideas about his new house-guest.

Anything except taking a cornball, romantic, seaside walk with Mary Elise, their shoulders brushing every other step.

He kept his eyes locked on a wooden dock fingering into the ocean. Yeah, he needed to make something happen, take action. Now would be the perfect time to lock in persuading Mary Elise to stay in the area. For the boys. Not for more moonlit walks and shared peanut butter Pop-Tarts, damn it.

Practical, right? He would still manage the boys on his own, but could check in with Mary Elise. Maybe they could find that friendship again. As adults. Wiser adults. Without the messy emotions. He opened his mouth—

"You are loved, Danny."

His jaw slammed shut. He risked a look at moonlit Mary Elise. "Uh, wanna run that by me again?"

She slung her hair over her shoulder, the gentle curves of her breasts straining against silk as creamy as her skin. "All these people jumping right in to help you. It's amazing to see how quickly they turned out with the perfect presents. More than just liking you, they know you and perceived your needs. That's a rare gift and you have it in abundance."

He might not be the most sensitive guy on the planet, but even he could see the woman had her brain wrapped around something heavy. Upsetting.

Please, Lord, no tears. Those made him long for the bottom of a pool more than discussions of "not swimming."

And then the memory hit him. An image of Darcy leaning over the porch rail to shout her announcement of a baby shower, tension promptly rippling up Mary Elise's spine. "Are you okay?"

"What do you mean?"

Hell, even he'd been knocked back a step by the notion of attending a baby shower with Mary Elise eleven years too late. "I gotta admit the whole baby-shower thing blindsided me."

She strolled without speaking, her arms swinging as she splashed through the low sipping surf. Suddenly he found something he feared more than her tears—knowing she might have tears locked inside. The girl who'd been a willing crusader for others had always been reluctant to share her own fears.

Words he hadn't known were within him churned. Wanted out. More of that old connection urged him to fill the silence rife with her hurt. Even if he was eleven years too late in addressing a subject that no amount of back-pedaling could fix.

For a man who thrived on logical solutions, that bit.

Once upon a time prior to their sexual marathon days, they'd been able to talk about anything. Surely he could recapture that ease for a short walk.

For Mary Elise, he pushed the churning words free. "I think about him or her sometimes. Wonder what our kid would have looked like. What we'd be doing now, if…" And the question he wondered about most, even if he suspected the answer. "Whether you and I would have made it."

She tipped her face up to his, red hair streaming across skin turned translucent in the moonlight. "Likely not."

Regret dulled her eyes, stirring protector instincts stronger than any he'd felt in a job that had taken him to some of the most twisted hellholes of the world. He wanted to fight a tangible battle to swipe away the stain in her eyes from memories past. Which of course meant taking on himself.

Way to go, bud.

He forged ahead. "You're probably right. My relationship history hasn't been any better than my father's."

"At least you were smart enough not to marry your mistakes."

He grabbed her arm and pulled her to a stop. "You can shut that talk down right now. We may have made mistakes, you and I, but knowing you was the best damned thing that ever happened to me."

A tender smile crept over her face. "You are so sweet, Danny."

"Sweet?" Crap. She obviously had him mixed up with someone else.

Her hand eased away as she trailed ahead. "But I wasn't talking about us. I meant my marrying Kent."

Her words carried so quietly on the night air, he let them kick around in his head for a few seconds to make sure he'd heard her right.

"So Kent McRae was a mistake?" He couldn't stop the question. He was human after all.

"Obviously, or I wouldn't have divorced him." She pulled ahead with long-legged strides that drew his eyes and his libido.

And then her words soaked into his brain. He stopped. "*You* left *him*." A fact that meant a lot more to him than it should. "I never knew for sure."

She continued ahead for five tide-swishing steps. He stood unmoving, seaweed twining around his ankles as tenaciously as thoughts of this woman. Thoughts and curiosity about the man she'd chosen to marry without the coercion of a shotgun wedding.

Finally she spun to face him, all traces of regret and

could-have-beens erased from her face. She was getting better at hiding her emotions. Much more practice and she'd be gone from him altogether, even if she never crossed the county line.

A bizarre thought for him, a man who kept life simple. Fact based. But he knew. She was easing her way out of his world. She'd thrown him out last time. This time she would stride away with a long-legged grace.

She smiled, signaled her end to deeper discussions, another freaking odd thought since that was usually his role.

"Anyhow, it's wonderful how everyone turned out for you with more than just gifts. They're here with support, for you and the boys. You're going to be fine." She held his gaze for one of those long, Mary Elise moments that carried peace and intensity all at once. "I'm so happy for you, Danny. You deserve to be loved."

"So do you." Where had that come from?

Well, hell. Of course he'd never been the right man for her, but that didn't mean he didn't want her to be happy. He'd always wanted that for her.

Her mask slipped, not much. But enough.

He pressed his advantage. "You don't have to go." Daniel closed the steps between them. "I know you'll need your own place and a job, so why not settle in Charleston? I'm not looking for you to take on my responsibilities, but it would be good for the boys to have you near. And I could help you relocate."

She backed up a step, tidewaters swirling between them. "I'm not staying here."

He'd expected that, realized he'd have to push her on this. He hadn't, however, expected the jab of disappointment. Eleven years had passed just fine without her.

Well, maybe more like the last nine of them.

Why the hell should a handful of days together change

that? ''Where are you going? Back to Savannah after all?''

She shook her head. ''I want to start over somewhere new, fresh.''

''Where?''

Since when was she the kind of woman who wanted to see the world? She'd been the girl who planned to settle in Savannah and fight battles with award-winning editorials that would shape the future of her hometown.

''Midwest or up north,'' she answered evasively.

Enough of this bull. He gripped her shoulders and drew her close, closer until the current made circles around their ankles. ''What's going on here, Mary 'Lise?''

He tightened his hold before she could slip away from him again like the sand under his feet; and tried like hell to ignore the sense that if she left, that would be the end. No more second or third chances to get her out of his head. He would be stuck with her haunting his mind with regrets, clinging to his thoughts like one of those whispery strands of red hair blowing over him for the rest of his freaking life.

They might not be able to recapture their friendship. The soft give of womanly flesh heating through his hands and sending blood straight south fast confirmed that. But damn it, he would not let this woman go until he knew she was settled, editorial pen in hand, crusades in place.

Smiling again.

He stepped closer and let the heat of his body filter through the air and his words. ''Why haven't you called your parents? Or anyone other than me? Don't get me wrong, I want to be here for you, whatever you need, you know you can count on me. Doesn't matter what the hell happened eleven years ago. One call, and I'm there.''

''The call was for the boys, Danny.''

Anger chafed like the broken shells under his feet. "I know there's not a chance you would have contacted me otherwise."

"Because I don't need anything." She softened her steely declaration with a gentle smile and hand on his forearm.

A hand that shook.

"You're a good liar. You say it with a straight face, no wince, looking me right in the eye. But the thing is, I know you learned that from me after the trouble I pulled us through as kids."

"Then how do you know I'm not telling the truth?"

"I'm a better liar now than I was before." Military training and covert ops had taught him well. He raised his hand, pressed two fingers to the side of her neck, her pulse throbbing against his skin. "I can feel your lie right here."

Her heart rate kicked up a notch under his touch, a wariness tinting her eyes that almost stirred guilt. Almost. He wouldn't be deterred from prying answers out of her this time.

Eleven years ago that cornered look in her eyes might have swayed him. But not now. He'd seen the worst the world had to offer. Fought it. Conquered it more than once, and damned if he would let this woman bring him down with a simple wince.

He was doing this for her.

Then the flash in her eyes shifted, she shifted, changing into a different woman, a steely, determined woman who may have visited some of those hells he'd seen. He saw a different Mary Elise, but one who still sent jolts of awareness rocking through him until his gut clenched with need, his pulse now echoing hers. Hard and fast.

Definitely hard.

Mary Elise gripped his wrist and pulled his hand down, trailing his fingers over her collarbone until his palm flattened over her heart. ''There are plenty of reasons a woman's heart rate speeds up, Danny.''

Chapter 9

Desperation chewed through her. Mary Elise wrapped her hand tighter around the warm strength of Danny's wrist, his fingers riding the beginning curve of her breast. Heat seared silk.

It had to be desperation and fear of her past being uncovered, of others taking on the risk and danger of her foolish mistakes. She wouldn't allow the emotions burning through her to be anything else.

Still, why hadn't she opted for a different distraction from Danny's persistence? Like a leg cramp? She'd walked off the real cramps and backache, but why hadn't she faked they were back again? Even a mad dash in the opposite direction would have made more sense than this.

Touching. Wanting. Needing. And there weren't nearly enough people on this patch of beach to offer chaperoning, a lone dog walker already disappearing around a dune.

At least she had the satisfaction of knowing she'd

shocked Daniel as much as herself because the man stared down at her with dark eyes, stunned silent—but not moving away. Desire curled smoky paths through her veins.

She wanted to believe the pulsing heat came from abstinence. Except she knew better. Never had she wanted a man's touch as much as she wanted Danny's. Now. Right now, with a surety that if it didn't happen soon, she would spontaneously combust.

Danny's brows lowered and his hand twitched back, away, callused fingers snagging on silk. Involuntary muscles held his hand firm with a strength she hadn't known she possessed.

And suddenly, more than ever, she wanted something to take with her when she left in four days. A memory. A kiss. The question answered about whether her imagination had exaggerated the impact of his mouth against hers.

She couldn't stay, so what the hell did it matter now if she blew any chance of friendship? Her peace of mind was already shot. Yes, even fleetingly, she definitely deserved something. This. Him.

"You should know what you do to my heart rate, Danny. And I think maybe I do the same to yours." Mary Elise arched up, into him, against him, not a far stretch as he topped her by no more than four inches.

Surprise nipped. This new man seemed so much larger than the young lover from her memories. But in her arms, he was her Danny. She took comfort in that as she leaned in to take his mouth.

And then he wasn't her Danny at all.

A hungry growl of possession rumbled low in his throat. His mouth took hers right back in the kiss of a man. Not a hungry youth who, yes, had style and exuberance. But a man of intensity, strength.

Experience.

All man. And he made her feel all woman. A sensation she hadn't experienced in so long she'd forgotten the heady rush of being wanted. Desired. Even while sex with Kent had been physically satisfying at the beginning, all too soon any mating had become just that. Mating. She'd been nothing more than a vessel to bear his child, and somewhere along the way had lost the wonder of being a woman.

Danny reminded, reassured her with the bold possession of his mouth, tongue, hands traveling down her back to urge her closer to the undeniable proof that he desired her. A precious gift she hadn't realized she needed, and now she couldn't face losing it.

Losing him?

She shunted that thought away, too much, too dangerous, and focused on his kiss, the warm play of muscles under her hands. The roar in her ears swelled like ocean echoes in a conch shell. Somehow she knew that in years to come she would listen to a shell whisper reminders of passion.

Mary Elise hooked her leg around Daniel's bare calf and gloried in the gentle rasp of his bristly hairs and sand against her sensitive skin. Reveled in the masculine growl the rub of her heel elicited low in his throat.

Drinking in the taste of him tinged with beer and memories, Mary Elise clung to his broad shoulders and the moment. A moment so much hotter than her memories, and her memories of wrapping herself around Daniel Baker had been mighty damned hot. Keeping her awake and hungry and longing on more than one night.

And now after just one kiss from the adult Daniel, she feared she might never sleep again.

* * *

Daniel gathered a fistful of Mary Elise's hair, anchoring her sweet mouth to his, and wondered how he was going to sleep through another night on that damned sofa. Then thought about how much he didn't want to sleep tonight, wanted to spend the night peeling those silk shorts down Mary Elise's long legs.

What the hell was wrong with him? He couldn't freaking control his shaking hands or the consuming drive to possess this woman. Now. Here. Who needed a wide inviting stretch of bed where a couple of nosy kids might spring in on them anyway?

Kids.

The boys. Responsibilities and life and a woman with problems she wasn't sharing and plenty of his own she didn't need to shoulder.

He tore his mouth from hers, a tougher proposition than slipping past enemy radar in a combat zone. Her foot glided down his leg back into the water, moonlight sparking fiery glints in her hair. His forehead fell to rest on hers and he inhaled the scent of her honeysuckle shampoo. Of her.

His arms draped over her shoulders, their hips still grazing a tantalizing dance against each other as his libido defied his reason. "Good God, Mary Elise. What was that about?"

"You didn't want to kiss me?"

Oh, he wanted to and a lot more, but that didn't make it any wiser. Not that he could lie to her. This was his doing as much as hers.

He pressed her fingers to his neck where his pulse double-timed. "What do you think?"

Femininity and more desire flared in her bottle-green eyes searing through half the slipping threads of his self-control. He cupped her shoulders to keep from sliding his arms around her back again. "But I don't understand why you initiated this when you say you're leaving."

She traced the line of his jaw, square, stubborn and the one thing he'd inherited from his father. He suspected he might need every ounce of that stubborn will to make it through this conversation.

"Chalk it up to a weak moment brought on by moonlight and old memories." She cupped his cheek, her finger tracking up to trace the chicken pox scar on his temple. "We did make some wonderful memories together, and right now I *so* don't want to think about the bad ones, if you don't mind. We can get to those another time."

He waited, searching for the tiniest chink in her defenses, but this woman was tougher to read than the open Mary Elise from before.

Finally her fingers fell to rest on his chest, branding his skin, except she was pushing him away.

"Danny, as wonderful as that was, I really can't stay."

He looked, studied. She wasn't lying.

"Damn it, why not? I don't expect you to move in with me or take on responsibility for the boys. They're mine now. But it would be nice for them to know you're close. There are schools and newspapers here where you could work, and it's not like you want to go back to Savannah. Heard and understood on that point. But you haven't come up with a place you do want to be since Rubistan is out."

"What happens when you're transferred? Am I supposed to follow you forever because the boys need my help? You're not making sense, Danny, and that's not like you."

Hell no, he wasn't making sense. Nothing tumbling around inside him made sense right now and that pissed him off. His whole freaking world was flipping, first his father dying, then the boys moving in. Now Mary Elise was back in his life. Once he'd depended on her to be his voice of reason and now he didn't want to grant her any more importance in his life, power over his thoughts.

But he couldn't let her walk away again with things so unresolved. He couldn't live the rest of his life chasing redheaded women who weren't her. "You're going to make me say it, aren't you? The real reason I don't want you to go."

Panic flared in her eyes. She backed away. "No. Forget it. I'm not trying to do anything except convince you to—"

He clapped a hand over her mouth. "*I* want you to stay."

Her eyes closed as if that would distance her from him.

Screw this evasive crap. He might not be Captain Happily Ever After, but he wasn't a coward. He would find some closure for both of them. Even if it meant—he shuddered—talking about feelings.

"The first year without you was the strangest damned year of my life. I kept looking for you. Picking up the phone to tell you something. Hell, sometimes I even started talking before I realized you weren't there. But the next year was a bit better. Then I hit a groove, moved on. Yeah, I thought about you sometimes, but I was living my life." A life full of redheaded women. "Now it's like those eleven years are gone, and the thought of telling you goodbye is tearing me up."

Her eyes drifted open, so full of pain it hit him like a load of shrapnel to the gut.

"But, Danny, those eleven years did happen. We're different people now."

Damn, he was in over his head here. But he had her talking, and he intended to press whatever advantage he could. "I'll be straight up with you, Mary Elise. You can

check my pulse if you want to prove it.'' He gripped her
wrist and flattened her palm to his chest again, over his
heart. ''I still suck at romance. Don't want it and usually
manage to screw it up if it comes my way. But I make a
damned good friend. Just ask that pool full of people.''

Her fingers flexed in an involuntary caress. ''I don't
have to ask them. I remember.''

''Let me help you.'' He gripped her shoulders to keep
her from running.

What the hell had gotten into him that she'd become
so important to him all over again? Maybe that call from
his dad had messed with his head—his control—more
than he'd realized. He wasn't the kind of guy who needed
more than superficial friendships, fun pals, often. But
damn it all, between inheriting two kids to take care of
and the cryptic message from his father that he couldn't
follow up on because of those two new responsibilities,
this was one of those times he could use a little backup.

Preferably from someone he knew without question he
could trust. ''Tell me what's wrong so you can stay and
be my friend again.''

The tide tugged sand from beneath their touching toes
for four ripping waves and he thought maybe, just maybe
he'd gotten through to her.

A sigh shuddered through her and into him. Her fingers
dug deeper in his skin, held. Each breath moved harder,
faster through her until… What the hell was tearing her
up so much?

Forget distance. He hauled her to his chest before she
could blow him off with an evasive remark. Folded his
arms around her and absorbed the tremors racking through
her. ''God, Mary Elise. What's going on here? Talk to
me.''

Her fingernails bit deeper into his skin, as if she

The Silhouette Reader Service™ — Here's how it works:

Accepting your 2 free books and mystery gift places you under no obligation to buy anything. You may keep the books and gift and return the shipping statement marked "cancel." If you do not cancel, about a month later we'll send you 6 additional books and bill you just $3.99 each in the U.S., or $4.74 each in Canada, plus 25¢ shipping & handling per book and applicable taxes if any.* That's the complete price and — compared to cover prices of $4.75 each in the U.S. and $5.75 each in Canada — it's quite a bargain! You may cancel at any time, but if you choose to continue, every month we'll send you 6 more books, which you may either purchase at the discount price or return to us and cancel your subscription.

*Terms and prices subject to change without notice. Sales tax applicable in N.Y. Canadian residents will be charged applicable provincial taxes and GST. Credit or debit balances in a customer's account(s) may be offset by any other outstanding balance owed by or to the customer.

Play the *Lucky Hearts* Game

and get...

2 FREE BOOKS
and a FREE MYSTERY GIFT...

yes! **YOURS to KEEP!**

I have scratched off the silver card. Please send me my *2 FREE BOOKS* and *FREE mystery GIFT*. I understand that I am under no obligation to purchase any books as explained on the back of this card.

Scratch Here!

then look below to see what your cards get you... 2 Free Books & a Free Mystery Gift!

345 SDL DU6U   245 SDL DU7C

FIRST NAME   LAST NAME

ADDRESS

APT.#   CITY

STATE/PROV.   ZIP/POSTAL CODE   (S-IM-08/03)

Twenty-one gets you
2 FREE BOOKS
and a **FREE MYSTERY GIFT!**

Twenty gets you
2 FREE BOOKS!

Nineteen gets you
1 FREE BOOK!

TRY AGAIN!

Offer limited to one per household and not valid to current Silhouette Intimate Moments® subscribers. All orders subject to approval.

couldn't get close enough. "I'm so damned scared, Danny."

Mary Elise's thready words barely whispered against his neck until he might have questioned his hearing. But he felt each word and all her fear soak into him along with the heat of her rapid breaths.

His hands roved her back, no bold lover's caress this time, instead resurrecting that friend within him. "Tell me," he coaxed. "Tell me what to do for you."

She inched back, her hand sliding up his face again. "Oh, Danny, can't you see that you and all this," she slipped her hand around his neck in a sensual glide, "this tension between us that we can't ignore is a big part of the problem? You need to believe me when I say I just can't risk staying here with you."

He sifted through her words, thought back to her sparse confidences about her divorce—marrying her "mistake." No question she closed off any time the man's name was mentioned. How badly had the ass hurt her?

Hell, who was he to talk when he'd hurt her himself years ago? And apparently she wanted to avoid an encore.

His arms around her twitched, muscles convulsively tensing to hold her closer, safer. As much as he wanted to reassure her, he couldn't. He knew himself too well. So he held her and stroked her back.

How long they stood there he didn't know. Yeah, the sex and friendship might be tangled in his head, but it felt damned good to have her back in his arms.

Finally, her breathing slowed to normal. She pulled away to let the wind slide an invisible wall between them.

Her mouth tipped in a half smile, a friend smile as if trying to jam more bricks on that wall between them. "Since I can't stay, do you want to have a quickie affair before I go?"

In spite of her kiss, she didn't mean it and they both knew it. And, hell yeah, while he wanted to sleep with her, stay awake with her, no way could he answer that one truthfully since it would send her running.

He might be confused about a boatload of things at the moment, but he knew one thing for certain. She could spit out excuses until sunrise, jam layer after layer of bricks between them, and it wouldn't change his course. More than ever they both needed closure so he didn't spend his life chasing redheads.

He would convince her to stay. He considered himself a master at tactics, his logical mind paying off big time in that arena. And a strategic retreat to regroup seemed the wisest battle plan.

Picking up her attempt at a lighthearted escape out of a land mine discussion, Daniel resurrected his best-bud smile and slung his arm around her shoulders. "Well, friend, if we do opt for that quickie, let's make sure at least one of us thinks to bring condoms this time."

Four days later, Daniel poured his third cup of coffee and scooped up a second peanut-butter-topped Pop-Tart. Only a week into his leave time and he'd made decent strides at settling the boys, thanks to Mary Elise, the master list maker.

Her lists picked up speed and length by the minute as if she had to get everything documented for him before she left. If they brushed chests passing in the kitchen, she logged the boys' favorite foods. An accidental walk in on her in her underwear—lime-green satin, heaven help him—and she'd spent an entire afternoon penning every childhood story she could remember the boys' parents ever sharing.

And he was running out of excuses for her to stay.

The boys were enrolled and ready to start school in another week, after Thanksgiving break. House hunting would come after Christmas. He'd interviewed a battalion of nannies and lucked into a woman he could swear was a clone of Alice from the Brady Bunch, no less. Hell, if things went much better, Mary Elise would hit the road by sundown.

Which should be cause for rejoicing since he was losing his freaking mind locked in the condo with her. The bunk beds might be offering the boys a better night's sleep, but visions of Mary Elise alone in his queen-size bed had him twisted into trigonometric knots.

Their attraction multiplied exponentially by the minute, thanks to one kiss on the beach. Ending up horizontal together was a given before much longer.

But she would be gone soon. He could see it in her eyes even as she smiled and went through the motions of helping the boys start a new life. He knew her too well, and what parts he didn't remember from before or had changed over the years, he'd relearned with alarming speed.

That same crusader spirit of hers also made for a damned stubborn woman. It could well be his smart, crusader buddy knew what a rotten risk he was and thus had opted to stay staunchly vertical.

Of course he could see definite possibilities in vertical as well.

Sagging onto his sofa, Daniel sifted through the junk mail he'd ignored earlier in the week, tearing and pitching now that he finally had a free moment.

Free minutes sucked. Busy was better. He'd already run, worked out, showered and changed into his flight suit for a quick stop by the squadron.

But still the rest of the house snoozed on, so he would

keep quiet. He felt guilty enough over how much he was demanding of Mary Elise. Her pale exhaustion tugged at him. Sure he wanted her to stay, but not because he and the boys had made her sick, for God's sake.

Shuffling the pile, he saved pizza coupons. Tore a vacation giveaway sweepstakes. Flipped over a flyer on a local women's clinic, complete with stats on infertility and other birth control factoids. He ripped that sucker in half. "Where was this when I could have used it eleven years ago?"

Daniel pitched the rest of the stack back onto the coffee table, brochures and flyers skidding into a fan across the glass top. A quick glance at the clock told him Spike wouldn't be up yet. Of course, the guy would have come by the night before if there had been any more on the answering machine message, since he'd turned the tape over to the CIA for analysis.

He had to hope his father had simply called about Mary Elise and not anything related to his death the next day. Otherwise, the international implications in an already rocky region boggled his mind. As if the military wasn't already maxed from the recent conflicts. Just what they freaking needed, another Afghanistan on their hands.

Feet shuffled down the hall, easing Daniel back to the present, home life overriding big world. He glanced up and found…a buck-naked Austin.

He sighed. Crap. Another load of laundry. Who'd have thought two kids could quadruple the wash load? The math defied logic.

Austin danced from bare foot to foot. "I gotta go."

Uh-oh. The potty dance. No arguing with that.

Sprinting across the carpet, Daniel scooped his brother up under his armpits. No direct pressure to the bladder. And face the kid forward. He'd learned that one the hard way. Nope, he didn't plan to add his own clothes to the packed hamper before he'd even finished breakfast. "Why'd you take off your pull-ups, pal?"

"Gotta go."

Ah, hell. He didn't even want to check out that bed. His revamped budget would have to stretch to cleaning help as well as a nanny.

Daniel sidestepped discarded pj's and performed a military pivot round the corner into the bathroom. He plopped Austin on the tile floor.

In front of the neon-green plastic attachment to the john.

God. His bachelor digs now sported a freaking training seat. He liked the kid and all. Even Trey wasn't a major pain in the ass anymore, his snotty attitude having downgraded to *minor* pain in the ass, with the occasional quip that actually had Daniel laughing the minute the kid left the room.

He was managing. Doing okay. But that training seat pushed it.

Austin climbed up the step and took aim. Daniel leaned against the doorjamb and waited. And waited. Man, the kid was going like a racehorse. Daniel snagged the footed pj's off the hall carpet along with the pull-up.

Huh?

Well, hell. The thing was dry.

He spun back to Austin. "Way to go, bud."

"Oo-rah." With a big-toothed grin, Austin reached over the sink and pumped purple soap from a dinosaur dispenser.

The spare room door cracked open, Trey stepping out, his yawn closing into a frown. Big surprise. Not. "Wanna hold the party down? Some of us are trying to sleep."

Austin's smile faltered, and Daniel vowed he'd slip

peanut butter and marshmallow sandwiches in the kid's lunch for a week if Trey didn't ditch the attitude at light speed.

"We're celebrating Austin staying dry through the night. And so should you, pal, since Austin sleeps on the top bunk."

A grin tugged Trey's somber face. He held up a high-five palm.

Austin launched off the footstool and smacked his brother's hand, shouting, "Oo-rah!"

"Hoo-ya," Trey parried with the Navy grunt, anything other than a nod to the Air Force.

Yesterday Trey had chanted an Army cadence as he circled the pool. The day before that he'd taped a computer printout of the "Marine Hymn" to Daniel's bag of licorice—a bag that was suspiciously light.

Trey let loose another hoo-ya. Daniel snorted on a chuckle. Trey turned, a wicked glint sparking his brown eyes. The way would never be easy with this kid, but at least Trey had found his sense of humor.

Daniel burrowed a hand into a laundry basket—of clean stuff, he hoped—and yanked free a pair of Austin's shorts and a T-shirt. Once they passed a quick sniff test, he tossed them to the little guy. "What do ya say we head out to IHOP for breakfast before I swing by base so Mary Elise can sleep in?"

Guilt bit over how he'd kept her up late more than once grilling her about where she'd go. What she'd do. Of course, now he wondered if maybe she did have a plan and just didn't care to share it with him.

"Pancakes?" Austin cheered, pushing his head through his wrong-side-out T-shirt.

"IHOP?" Trey echoed with a shrug and an almost disguised grin. "Yeah, I guess that's okay, even if it is a regular hangout for you Chair Force dudes."

"Don't push your luck, kid." He thumped Trey in the stomach with his shoes.

Eyes well off the master bedroom door, Daniel charged down the hall. Leave a note and let her sleep. He wasn't up for resisting a sleep-mussed Mary Elise, anyway.

She might be stubborn, but so was he, and he had reinforcements. Each day that passed, it was obvious she loved Trey and Austin. The boys were his trump card for convincing her to stay.

He locked the front door while his brothers sprinted toward Darcy Renshaw's Firebird easing into her parking spot after her night flight. The boys launched at her as she stepped out. She had to be dead on her feet but didn't wince. He owed Wren and Max more than he could repay.

Daniel finished bolting the door and turned to thumb the remote on the truck lock. "Come on, fellas," he called, striding down the walkway past the mailboxes. "Leave Wren alone so she can go to sleep. Let's get a move on, or I'm ordering Trey chocolate chip pancakes."

"Eww!" Trey's exaggerated gag drifted across the lot.

"You're talking to a man who ate rabbit eyeballs in survival training. I'm not impressed with your bellyaching about the menu, kid."

When Trey didn't snap a ready comeback, Daniel glanced over his shoulder. Wren was long gone, Trey and Austin now standing with some businessman, tie flapping in the breeze over his shoulder.

Alarms jangled in his head. Not the work instincts he'd come to expect and trust, but a strange new protectiveness. Didn't schools teach kids not to talk to strangers?

Daniel charged forward. "Come on, boys. Now."

Trey jogged toward him, dragging Austin by one hand.

"That man was just asking about the condos, said he's thinking about moving here."

"Yeah, well, the guy's outta luck, then." He knew damned well there weren't any condos available since he'd already called to check that out for himself in the midst of a stupid whim thinking maybe he could coerce Mary Elise into staying a few doors down.

Just to be close to the boys, of course. And because he wanted to help her as much as she'd helped him. Not because he damn well couldn't stomach the thought of her long-legged stride walking out of his life.

Daniel scooped Austin up under one arm and "flew" him to the truck. "We'll talk about staying away from strangers some more over your milk, kid."

Austin stretched his arms out, airplane-style. "Man's got funny birds on his tie."

"Yeah, yeah." Daniel swung Austin upright and snapped him into the car seat with a newfound skill.

Tucking behind the wheel, Daniel watched the man cross the parking lot to the main office. Okay, that seemed to support his claim of condo hunting. Instincts were there for a reason, however.

He popped open the glove compartment and snagged a pad and pencil, jotting the license plate number on the guy's Mercedes. He'd get Spike to run the number when he checked in about the answering machine tape.

Daniel shifted the truck into reverse and glanced over his shoulder. Two pairs of brown eyes stared back at him.

Those eyes filled with trust, albeit begrudging on Trey's part, until something twisted inside Daniel. He'd been so damned busy thinking about how he would do his duty and take care of them, he'd never even seen it coming.

These weren't trump cards.

They were his brothers, his blood, not just some burdensome responsibility. They needed more from him than a set of bunk beds and a ride to school. God, if he felt this much for the two runts after only a week…

As much as he wanted to break through whatever walls Mary Elise had erected between them, if he screwed up again—a likely scenario—two sets of trusting brown eyes would pay as well. A prospect a helluva lot more daunting than the addition of a neon-green training seat to his bachelor condo.

Chapter 10

Mary Elise tugged the T-shirt over her knees, chin resting on her folded arms, and listened to the door slam as Daniel and the boys headed out for breakfast. The scent of bay rum—of Danny—drifted up from the rumpled sheets where she'd lain awake, too aware of him with every breath.

As if sleeping in the soft warmth of his shirt wasn't tempting enough. Almost as tempting as the fading echo of his laughter mingled with Austin's giggles and a repeat hoo-ya from Trey.

She was so damned proud of Danny.

He'd pulled it together with his brothers. Sure, they'd only been together about a week, and no doubt more bumps would jostle them in the future. Trey was still prickly, but Daniel had his number. Austin would adjust faster because of his youth. The rest would sort out, now that they'd begun to forge a family unit.

They didn't need her anymore. Her suitcase waited in a corner, calling to be packed.

She'd known he could manage—smart, determined, with a heart bigger and softer than he realized. She worried more about him submerging his own needs. The boys would be fine. But what about Daniel? The friend inside her wanted to be the one to take care of him in what would still be an ungodly stressful time.

The woman within her just flat-out wanted to take him.

Her gaze gravitated toward the half-open closet to Daniel's uniforms dangling across two-thirds of the space. How such neatly hung clothes could end up wrinkled within seconds of hitting his body defied logic.

But then, Daniel was as complex a puzzle as the artwork and toys he favored.

From the closet rod, the deep blue of a formal uniform gave way to the lighter blue shirts, shifted to splotchy green military camouflage, desert-tan cammo, then flight suits in both green and beige. All shapes of hats. Vests with canteens dangling and a scary-looking knife attached but sheathed in black leather. The Daniel who'd streaked grease paint on his face to jump a fence had turned his hobby into a profession.

Or perhaps it hadn't been a hobby, just a sense of direction from the cradle.

Pride hummed through her anew over the man he'd become. And, oh, my, was he ever a man. The heat of his kiss from the beach still tingled along her nerves. Tough not to think about it while she sat in his bed. Wanting him.

Mary Elise thunked her forehead against her hands folded over her knees. She could laze around feeling sorry for herself. Ick! Or she could shake off the blahs and get her butt in gear. Be satisfied that she had helped Danny build a strong foundation for a future with the boys in a few short days.

Get up, get a move on. And pretend her heart wasn't breaking in two.

Snick. The click of the front door opening echoed through the condo. Daniel must have forgotten something. Facing him now when sleep still mussed her defenses seemed a reckless move. Time to hit the shower.

She swung her feet over the edge of the bed and arched up to stretch out sore muscles, vowing to visit a clinic first thing in the morning. But after her mother's endless doctor appointments, live-in nurses, medicine bottles lining the kitchen windowsill, Mary Elise hated admitting to a physical weakness.

Prideful. Silly. Reckless. She could almost hear Danny ticking through her illogical reasoning.

Whipping the well-worn T-shirt over her head, she padded to his master bathroom. For the last time. Once Daniel and the boys returned, she would have to say her goodbyes.

The shower spray hit her with stinging needles of heat. *Stay.*

Danny's words from the beach rolled over her in a tidal wave. Give their friendship another chance.

Friendship? Thoughts of him walking around the condo looking for Austin's favorite blanket while she stood naked in the shower led her mind to thoughts far from friendlike.

Honestly, she wanted to stay. And, yes, she even wanted to try again. The friendship. Maybe even more. The past days with Danny and the boys had been… everything.

Mary Elise snagged her bottle of shampoo from beside Daniel's. How could she escape the fact that she had to leave? To stay another day would be selfish and not worth the risk. Life seemed to be telling her in a hundred different ways that Kent was still out there.

Returning to the States had brought old memories forward. Stronger. Which likely heightened her emotions to supersensitivity. Or perhaps her subconscious was tormenting her so she wouldn't be tempted to stay.

And that pissed her off.

Her hands slowed in working the shampoo through her hair. Where was the fear? The ache over Kent's betrayal? All she could feel was a stinging anger like soap in her eyes over all Kent had taken from her.

Well damn. She'd gained something from the past days too.

Seeing herself through Danny's eyes reminded her how far she'd strayed from her essential self. First, losing pieces of her will through Kent's subtle control, then later by hiding while she licked her wounds.

Strength seeped into her with each waft of steam carrying the lingering scent of Daniel's aftershave. Yes, she had to leave. She accepted that. But she didn't have to cower.

She would fight back, scavenge for a plan to reclaim her life. Plans were in short supply at the moment, beyond saving to finance a private detective, but already the renewed strength fueled determination. How odd that until a few days ago she hadn't realized just how much had been stolen from her.

And once she had her life back?

Simply because she'd reclaimed her inner self didn't make her any more right for Danny than she'd been eleven years before. Not that he was even the same person. Parts of Danny remained, mingled with the newer, darker Daniel. Even if he stayed single after however long it took her to reclaim her life…

She didn't know. But for the first time in years, she knew she wanted to dare. To dream.

And the steamy whispers of possibility made packing somehow easier and tougher at the same time.

"Hey, Mary Elise, where ya going?" Austin piped from four steps ahead as he sprinted into the condo, his blankie dragging.

Going? Daniel's brain went numb.

He stood in the open doorway staring at Mary Elise's suitcase, and freaking couldn't process what he was seeing.

Didn't want to.

Hell, his mind never stopped working. Never. His thoughts always operated three paces ahead of his feet, and his feet were mighty damned fast even on a bad day.

And thanks to Austin's question, this promised to be a sucky day. Once again Mary Elise flipped his world.

Daniel double-timed into the condo, his boots traveling ahead of his reason. He charged past the boys, stopping toe-to-toe with Mary Elise and her small suitcase.

Austin shuffled to a stop in front of her, his bottom lip trembling.

Mary Elise knelt eye level with Austin's blueberry-syrup-stained face. She licked her thumb and swiped it over his cheek until the smudge disappeared. "Well, sweetie, it's time for me to get a place of my own."

"Why ya gotta go? I want you to stay."

"I'd like to stay, too. But this isn't my home."

He hitched his blanket under his nose and sniffed. "Are you gonna be close? Are we gonna see you again?"

She smoothed back sweaty brown curls off his forehead. ''You bet you will.'' She answered the latter question while avoiding the first. ''It may take a while for me to get everything…settled, but I'll be back here to see you sometime. And when I come back, I want you to show me all your new dives into the pool, and I'll bet you won't even need water wings anymore.''

Damn it, he could see the tears in her eyes. Why was she doing this to herself? To the boys.

To him. ''Mary Elise, let's talk without the boys here.''

''Daniel, I'll be sending you the money I owe you for all the clothes and such. And I made a list of things Austin and Trey have mentioned wanting for Christmas.'' She avoided his eyes by rifling through her suitcase with jerky agitation. ''Where did I put them?''

Trey leaned forward to tug the side zipper pouch. ''Are they in here?''

''No. I don't think so. I haven't used that pocket yet.''

''But it's half-zipped.''

Hell, did the kid have to flipping help her out the door with a hoo-ya just to piss him off?

''Hmm.'' She yanked open the zipper and jammed her hand inside. ''Maybe I put it in here without think—''

She shrieked. Her hand whipped back out of the bag. Blood dripped from her fingertip. ''Ouch.''

Daniel knelt beside her, pressing his thumb to the pinprick. ''Trey, run back to the bathroom and get one of those Winnie the Pooh Band-Aids.''

Maybe he could stretch this into a trip to the hospital for a tetanus shot to buy him time to talk her around. Or he could stand here and hold her hand for another hour and stare into the damned prettiest eyes he'd ever seen.

Mary Elise tugged her hand free and stuck her finger in her mouth. She looked away, taking all that endless green with her.

Prying open the side pouch, she peered inside. Color drained from her already-pale face. Swaying, she withdrew a small medicine bottle for a shot.

Daniel supported her shoulders with one arm and grabbed the bag from her. A syringe lay in the side pouch, and from the stunned glaze in Mary Elise's eyes, it didn't belong there.

Instincts went on full alert. Something wasn't right.

Trey charged back down the hall, Band-Aids waving from his hand like banners. "Got it. Two of them. One Tigger and one Ee-yore."

"Thanks, pal." Daniel snagged the bandages and wrapped an orange Tigger Band-Aid around the tip of Mary Elise's finger. "How about you fellas take your Game Boys to your room for a minute."

Austin's bottom lip trembled. "But I wanna say goodbye to Mary Elise."

"I promise you'll get to." He scruffed a hand through the tousled curls. "Meanwhile, let me see if I can talk her into staying a little longer."

Mary Elise exhaled, shaking free whatever had gripped her. "Please, Trey? Could you keep Austin busy for a bit? I promise not to go anywhere without talking to you first."

Trey shuffled from foot to foot, then shrugged. "Yeah, okay, but I want eggplant parmesan for supper."

Daniel faked a smile. "Sure kid, whatever."

Trey yanked his little brother by the arm, promises of Pokémon Nintendo fading with the close of their bedroom door.

Anger on a tight rein, Daniel jabbed a finger toward her. "Cut the crap. I'm not letting you walk out until you tell me exactly what's going on."

Mary Elise sunk back on her bottom. "Oh, God, Danny. I've screwed up so bad."

Mary Elise forced her hand to stay steady around the empty bottle, willed her teeth not to chatter. Still, the shaking swelled inside her.

She'd tried so damned hard to weigh the options and make the right choices to keep the boys from being traumatized. Yet, once the cargo plane had become airborne, her life had spiraled out of control until every option absolutely stunk.

Even if little Austin hadn't been frightened to the point of being immobilized and she could have run right away, Daniel would have been curious. Which would have led him—and therefore the boys—directly to Kent.

Except Kent had found her anyway.

She'd expected fear, and hell yes, fear stirred a storm within her. But she hadn't anticipated the blind explosion of fury.

How dare he do this to her? To the family she'd grown to care about so much? Rhetorical questions that served no purpose. Kent dared anything. And now she had to tell Daniel. Surely he would understand he needed to stay near the boys, protect them. Once he heard the truth, he would realize the farther all three were from her now, the better.

A horrific notion took root. She knew Kent had planted the bottle, but when? Her mind echoed with the rustlings when she'd showered. "Danny, once you and the boys left for IHOP, did you come back to pick up anything?"

"No." Impatience stamped his face. "The boys stopped to talk with Wren for a minute and then we left. What the hell's going on here?"

She flattened a hand to the carpet, slumping back against the couch. Nausea roiled. Bile burned. She dropped the bottle like a snake onto the glass-topped coffee table. "This isn't mine. Someone broke into the condo and put it here."

Kent, the man who dared anything and respected no boundaries, had placed it there. While she was naked in the shower.

Incredulity furrowed Daniel's brow, feeding her worries that he wouldn't believe her, either.

"What the hell for? Ah hell, whatever the reason," he reached for the phone on the chrome end table, "we need to call the cops, now."

"Wait!" She lurched to the side, flinging her hands over the telephone, the pinprick forgotten in a new panic.

He paused midreach. "The longer we wait, the farther away whoever it was will get."

"I know who it was, and no way is he anywhere near here now. He's left his message and will undoubtedly leave another, but not today."

His hand fell back to his knee as he sank down beside her. "Run that by me again?"

"I know who planted it there. Or at least I know who was responsible." And damn it, she prayed she hadn't made a huge mistake in lingering at Danny's this long.

"Want to share that nugget? Because I'm getting pretty torqued off thinking about someone slipping in here when the boys may have been around."

"The boys are fine." She would have never stayed at Danny's for so much as one night if she'd thought for a second Kent would come near the boys. He'd always been precise in his sanctimonious anger. "It's me he wants to rattle."

"He?"

"My ex-husband."

"Your ex did this? How can you be sure? You haven't

even let him know you're here.'' His eyes narrowed with a glint of…jealousy? ''Have you?''

''No! Of course not. But somehow he must have found out.'' She nudged the bottle beside a stack of junk mail on the table. ''Only he would think to leave behind a medicine bottle with my name on it, used back when we were married.''

Medicines to increase fertility.

A bottle from one of her daily shots.

As much as she hated giving Daniel details, she had to convince him, for his own safety and the boys'. ''Kent didn't take our breakup well. He pulled stunts like this all the time right after I left him.''

''You still haven't explained why you know this is from him.''

''I had difficulty conceiving. We tried…everything. I wanted to adopt. Kent wanted to keep trying for a biological child.'' She couldn't make herself tell him about the miscarriages. Her precious son born too early. But Daniel needed to know her suspicions, no matter how paranoid they sounded. ''I think maybe this wasn't the first time he's attempted to rattle me since I returned to the States. There was a plant mixed in with your neighbor's potted garden, a plant that's supposed to promote fertility. I thought it was a coincidence, and now I'm not so sure. I'm so very sorry for not telling you then.''

Daniel's hand fell to rest beside the bottle, inching over to straighten the stack of junk mail beside it with an odd precision. ''Why not just contact you?''

Long-buried resentment clawed its way to the surface, having been denied light too long, due to her more basic survival needs of the past year.

''Because he's a sick bastard who enjoys tormenting me. God, I could go on forever. Regardless, he's a nut

case, Danny. And I'm so, so sorry for bringing him anywhere near the boys. I didn't think there was any way he
could know where I was. Even if he'd tracked me to Rubistan, it's not like my leaving the country was exactly out
in the open.''

''You went to Rubistan to get away from him?''

''I'd have gone to the moon to get away from Kent
McRae.'' She pushed out the words she'd told her parents,
only to be patted on the hand and ignored by them.
''Danny, my ex-husband was more than just a mistake.
He's dangerous.''

''The bastard hit you?'' Daniel's eyes flamed.

He canted forward, already on the offensive just as
she'd predicted. As much as her heart cheered his ready
acceptance, she also feared his reaction.

With her own anger building by the microsecond, how
would she stay calm enough through the rest of her explanation to keep him from going ballistic? She forced
herself to sit still when her feet wanted nothing more than
to pace out the edgy bite of emotions.

She shook her head. ''No. He never raised a hand to
me. He's much more subtle than that, like with leaving
this old medication bottle. You can call the police, but
what are they going to do? Unless we can prove he broke
in here, they'll just issue another restraining order, all the
while looking at me like I'm a hysterical woman because
I don't have bruises to show for proof.''

Sometimes she wondered if things might not have spiraled down so if only she'd left sooner, once Kent started
changing from the charming man she'd married into a
manipulative control freak. Easy to second-guess now
with hindsight, but at the time she'd let guilt blind her to
the signs. Deep in her heart she'd been certain the fault

was hers because, God help her, she didn't love Kent as much as she'd once loved Daniel.

The guilt had torn her. She'd chosen to marry Kent, after all. She owed him better than she'd given him, half of herself. Now from the clearer perspective of distance, she wondered if he'd somehow sensed her feelings and manipulated them all the more to persuade her to give him whatever he wanted.

Daniel shoved to his feet, pacing enough to wear tread marks in the carpet with his boots. "We'll get another restraining order. I'm here to help keep space between you and the jerk before things turn violent. Mary Elise, you can't just keep running."

"It's too late for that. I know this may be difficult to take in. There are certainly plenty of people out there who think I'm only out to tarnish his reputation. But Kent went off the deep end when I left him." She closed her eyes and sucked in air to keep her voice steady. What would she do if Danny didn't accept her story?

Mary Elise rose to her feet. She didn't have a choice but to make him believe her. He stood with his back to her, which seemed the perfect time to tell him. She wouldn't have to see his skepticism. Not right away.

"Danny, I moved to Rubistan because Kent hired a hit man to kill me." Even the words chilled her. She tamped down the images and concentrated on reading Daniel.

Tension rippled the muscles along his shoulders in visible waves under his flight suit, but still he didn't turn. Thank God, because she wasn't sure she could keep talking if she found disbelief on his face. But she would talk, had to. Damn Kent straight to hell, she wasn't the wounded woman who ran to Rubistan anymore.

"Shortly after I left him, I suspected I was being followed, but I thought it was just Kent and more of his hurtful *messages,* like the bottle or the plant. Then a man with a gun caught me getting out of my car in front of my apartment. He planned to fake my suicide.'' The remembered cold press of the gun to her temple pushed through her concentration. ''He told me Kent had sent him. Even gave me a message from Kent no one else could have known.''

Her secret name for their last child, a name she hadn't dared share with anyone except Kent because she couldn't take the hesitant looks from people if she dared be hopeful.

''I realize it sounds crazy. God knows the cops and even my parents were skeptics.'' She winced. Great. Way to go giving him the idea if he hadn't already thought of it himself. ''I never dreamed something like that could happen to me. It seems the sort of story you only hear about from celebrities or in tabloids. But it happens. It happened to me.''

She waited.

And waited, reassuring herself that no matter what his reaction, she would hang tough. She would be strong and walk out the door today despite Danny's offer to help. The time had come for her to deal with the shambles Kent had made of her life, but she couldn't do it here. She'd leave to protect the boys. To protect Danny.

Slowly he pivoted on his boot heel with military precision. Fury vibrated through him, so tightly reined the low hum of rage reached to her from across the room. Not at her, but for her.

He believed her.

She reached back for the arm of the sofa and let herself sit. Relief rattled her teeth for three blessed seconds. Until she realized that yes he believed her, and planned to right the wrong done to her.

Any veneer of civilized niceties peeled away from him in strips, leaving behind raw man. Man at his most elemental protector self, a primal essence that centuries ago enabled him to charge into battle with only a sword in his hand or a knife between his teeth.

To protect.

What should have brought her breath-stealing relief instead chilled her. Daniel—she couldn't think of him as Danny right now—yes, Daniel would throw away his life to keep her safe. Looking deep into his eyes, she knew without question.

Kent was a dead man.

Chapter 11

Daniel deadened his emotions.

His brain assumed control, assimilated information. Video chirps and blasts reverberated from behind the boys' closed bedroom door. Two little boys he was almost certain had come inches away from Kent McRae in the parking lot earlier. A sick son of a bitch who'd dared to walk into Daniel's apartment. Who'd dared breathe the same air as Mary Elise.

A tic twitched the corner of Daniel's eye. Yeah, deadened inside was better. Otherwise the molten rage bubbling deep within him would melt his logic with a burning need to take out the bastard.

Damn straight Kent McRae had tried his scare tactics before with that junk-mail brochure. Coincidental that it landed in the mail this week? Not a chance. And he would pay.

But first, get the facts straight. Make a plan. And don't

fall victim to the distraction of vulnerable green eyes. "How long?"

"How long what?" She lifted the telephone from the end table and placed it on her knees, as if that could keep him from dialing the cops if he chose.

He let her have her phone victory for the moment. He needed every ounce of information he could wring out of her before he spoke to them, anyway. "When did you leave for Rubistan?"

"I started the teaching job at the embassy school a year ago."

A job his father had arranged for her.

More anger piled on top of a towering load. She hadn't even considered coming to him with this.

Later he would deal with the fact that he would have to reassess his father's call from Rubistan shortly before his death. His dad hadn't been informing him about Mary Elise's arrival. In fact, had known about her slimeball ex and hadn't bothered to share with Daniel, another betrayal from a man he already resented like hell. A man he would never have the chance to chew out.

But Franklin Baker had kept her safe.

As much as Daniel wished he could have been the one she'd run to, he owed his father a debt for keeping her alive so she could sit there on his sofa and frustrate him with every defensive twitch of her head. Sunlight through the window glinted along the wet sheen of her hair.

She'd been in the shower.

Mary Elise had been vulnerable in the shower while McRae had rifled her bags. Walked through Daniel's place. Touched everything that was his.

Whoa. Full speed emergency stop on a short runway. Mary Elise was *not* his.

Wrong.

She was under his roof. Under his protection. And hell yes, she'd once been his. If he hadn't allowed the ties to be severed between them, she would have come to him. This might well have never happened at all.

Anger and guilt tangoed big-time. "You should have told me everything when we landed. Hell, before that."

"This isn't your problem. It's mine. I didn't mean to bring you in at all. You were right that crawling into the crate was a mistake." She speared her fingers through her tangled mass of wet hair. "But I still don't know how I could have sent those boys off with Austin crying. The guard would have been on them in a minute. And once I was in that crate, everything rolled out of control so fast."

He backed up a step to keep from yanking her close again. Thoughts of her risking her life a few days ago hammered too hard and fast on the out-of-control mess at their feet right now. "That's a crock, Mary Elise. You know I would have been there for you. Why didn't you tell me?"

"Maybe there's a better answer somewhere, but I did the best I could." She freed a lock of damp hair twisted around a gold hoop earring, no doubt to avoid looking at him. "God knows Kent told me what a screw-up I was often enough. I know better, damn it. I do. But sometimes it's just hard as hell to trust your instincts. Not everyone can be so all-fired certain their choices are perfect, like you are, Danny."

Daniel's slowing steps drew him to her with the seeping realization from her words. He may not agree with her choice to stay silent, yet there was no question but that this woman selflessly had his brothers' best interest at heart. Always.

She was scared and he was grilling her. Way to go, bud.

He brushed her hand aside and finished untwisting the hair from her earring. ''Damn it, Mary Elise, don't clam up now. This is too important for you to deal me half parcels of truth.''

''Yes, Danny, I do know you, and I knew you'd be just like this. That you'd throw yourself in the middle of my mess, which is the last thing I want for you. Or for those boys.''

His fingers gripped tighter around the silky lock. ''You would have left today, without telling me.''

''Of course,'' she answered without even a blink.

More of that anger and something else he damned well didn't want to define scratched through the numbed state. Letting her go eleven years ago had been the toughest thing he'd ever done. And yet she could just write him off. She'd put the boys first and once they didn't need her anymore, she was gone. Over and done without a wince about losing him.

That bit. Too much.

''Yes, I would have left. Would that have been the right decision? Have any of my choices been the best option? God, I don't know.'' Her steady gaze pinned him. ''Where is it written that every choice is clear cut? Even in your logical brain, there's got to be room for shades of gray. And who says that we're perfect and had better damn well make the perfect, right decision or we're too stupid to live?''

She fisted her hands by her sides. ''Kent told me for years I was defective. Incompetent. Incomplete, if I didn't live my life his way. I almost bought into it. Almost. But I got away. And I'll be damned if I'll let you take away something harder to rebuild than you'll ever understand.''

Her voice didn't so much as quaver. But pain laced her words.

Psychological warfare on the home front.

He'd studied and experienced the power of mental mind games in the POW phase of military survival training. And for her, the propaganda crap had come from someone she had every right to trust, someone who'd vowed to love and cherish her.

When had anyone cherished this woman?

Damn straight he didn't agree with her decisions, but he understood how she'd arrived there. She'd been betrayed by her husband and her parents. Why should she trust him, someone who'd already let her down before?.

Yet even as he saw the wounded pieces of her, he couldn't mistake the grit. Hell, yeah, she may not have made his kind of choices,. but she'd kept right on moving.

He'd seen bravery and cowardice in a hundred different forms. And, God, was he ever in awe of this woman right now.

She inched her hair from between his fingers. "Are we clear? I'm leaving, and I'll be careful. I'm going to find a private investigator and try to put an end to this. But I can't let it touch you and the boys anymore. I only told you this much so you're aware and can be careful for their sakes. I did *not* tell you so you could launch into a commando protector and solve my problems for me. I *am* leaving."

Like hell.

She wasn't taking one step out that door without him five steps in front of her, between her and whatever waited. Daniel shook off the sentimental fog, emotional crap that would distract him, get her hurt. She could make this easy. Or she could make it tough.

Mary Elise picked up her suitcase.

Okay, so it would be tough.

Ducking a shoulder into her stomach, Danny hefted her up. She gasped, deep. Damn. She was gonna get vocal.

Planting a hand on her bottom—ah, hell—he forestalled her with, "Shout and you'll upset the boys."

"Danny," she threatened through gritted teeth. "Put me down." Her suitcase thumped his leg.

Deliberate? Or accidental.

Ow, damn it. Deliberate.

Daniel flung her on the sofa. On her back. Already she arched up.

Something snapped in her eyes. All that Mary Elise calm and restraint unraveled into a tangle as convoluted as her hair twisting through her hoop earrings. Any minute she would lose it, and he couldn't let that happen, for her or his brothers.

Daniel dropped, flattened her fast. His body pinned hers in a full-length press to the sofa. "You're not going anywhere."

She bucked under him. "I'm damned tired of people controlling my life."

No way could he let her fly out of the apartment like this. He struggled to make sense of her words, a hard-as-hell proposition with her writhing under him. The glide of her body against his numbed his brain while heating other parts of him.

She clipped him on the chin.

All right, then. Passion tempered. He grabbed her flailing fists, manacled them with his hands over her head. "You need to rein it in, Mary Elise."

"Get off me, you son of a bitch, and I'll be just fine."

She glared up at him, her green eyes sparking with a mix of fury and a desperation that knocked him harder than her punch. She wasn't fighting him but some demon he couldn't combat until she let him in.

God, he never, never wanted to frighten her. As much as he knew of the old Mary Elise, he was beginning to realize he would need new instincts in dealing with this wary woman.

He gentled his grip. ''Southern boys get particularly pissed when you talk bad about their mamas. Now hush up and listen for a minute.'' He trailed a finger down to loosen a strand of hair clinging to her full bottom lip. ''You know I would never hurt you.''

She stilled under his touch, breasts pressed to his chest, legs twined. Back and forth, he traced the pad of his thumb over the giving softness of her mouth, felt the steamy rushes of breath gust over his skin.

Into him.

Her eyes darkened to that deep green of late summer grass. Oh, yeah, he remembered the shade well, felt the hitch in her breath that had nothing to do with fear and everything to do with wanting.

Adrenaline-fueled desire. Logical explanation. Not that logic would stop him from—

Her face rose to meet him as he angled down. Mouth to mouth, open, ready, hungry. More adrenaline and heat and too long not touching sent his hands into the pooling mass of her hair.

He needed to hold her again and kiss her senseless and find out if being inside her was as un-freaking-believable as he remembered before she hauled ass out of his life. Not that she seemed pointed toward that door at the moment.

She was damned near tearing his flight suit off. Her fingers yanked at his zipper, crawled inside to stroke his shoulders. Sweeping the warm recesses of her mouth with his tongue, he tasted Mary Elise, wondered if the honeysuckle sensation was taste or scent but couldn't tell with her jumbling all his senses.

Daniel struggled for reason. He couldn't let this spin out of control, as much as he might want to roll her to the floor and lose himself inside her with a deep rightness he hadn't felt since…her. He needed to get his head on straight. Two boys waited down the hall, and regardless of what she said, the cops would have to be called. They would have to face her past.

Together, damn it.

He let her soft touch seep into his anger, even feed the protective urges. Whatever it took to keep her safe, he embraced it.

Daniel pulled away, let his gaze land on her, immobilizing her with only his will. "You're not going anywhere without me."

The cloudy passion in her eyes dissipated. "Danny—"

"How closely did you look at that bottle?"

Her head angled to the side, toward the coffee table where the bottle rested. Her hand inched closer to graze the numbers handwritten across the label.

He forced himself to say the words, even knowing they would scare the hell out of her.

Whatever it took to keep her safe.

"You can talk about walking away to protect me all day long, but McRae has already made the choice for you." Daniel pointed to the penciled scrawl across the label on the medicine bottle. "My social security number. He's not just after you anymore."

Time passed in a haze.

Standing by the queen-size bed, Mary Elise sorted through the laundry basket, folding the boys' clothes into a suitcase, her body on autopilot. Beside her, Daniel jammed gear into a big green bag—a webbed vest, canteens, knife.

A gun.

His stark announcement about his social security number on the bottle still thundered through her head. She'd brought Kent's wrath to Daniel.

She would never be able to forgive herself.

Danny had insisted on calling the cops and filing the official complaint. Prints had been lifted. A restraining order requested. She'd been this route before.

At least the boys would be protected, safely hidden away with Darcy and Max until the threat passed. The engaged couple had already planned to spend Thanksgiving with Darcy's sister stationed at Seymour Johnson Air Force Base in Goldsboro, North Carolina. The boys would be ensconced in a family full of service members and an OSI special agent. She would stay alone with Daniel in a secluded fishing cabin Max kept for his "cave time" as Darcy called it.

Totally alone. Gulp.

Daniel had calmly explained this would give him and Max time to track information through CIA and OSI internet files. The remote locale would also keep the threat away from others if Kent found them.

Mary Elise willed her hands to keep folding little boy boxers and pairing up socks. Darcy and Max would finish their own accelerated packing soon. It still boggled her mind that Daniel could ask this of them and that they wouldn't even hesitate to help. The level of friendship went beyond anything she could fathom.

Made her question the depth of her friendship with Danny.

She tunneled a hand into the basket and came up with…one of Daniel's shirts. Hard Rock Café: Bangkok.

Once they'd shared so much, and now there were countless unshared memories and experiences between them. She smoothed a hand over the logo, then tugged the shirt inside out for Danny before folding it.

They *had* been close, damn it. She'd only turned to his father because she'd known Franklin wouldn't ask too many questions.

Or had she secretly been hoping Franklin would notify Danny? A disturbing notion that left her swaying on her feet.

"Would you quit before you fall over?" Daniel palmed her waist, stirring embers barely banked after their kiss earlier.

The two of them would be alone together soon. No more secrets. Well, not many. Already she could feel the inevitable draw they hadn't been able to resist eleven years ago.

She didn't want this. Especially not now.

Mary Elise ducked from under the temptation of his broad palm. "It's only a little laundry. Do you really want to subject Darcy and Max to the sonic shriek that will come if you forget Austin's blanket?"

Daniel jammed a pen and paper in her hands. "Make a list. You're great at details. There's plenty of crap Darcy and Max don't know about the kids that you didn't need to include on my lists."

What? He didn't think she could even handle climbing Mount Washmore? Being relegated to nonactive roles stung on a day where she'd taken a few too many hits. "I've already written everything out."

His hands landed on her shoulders, urging her to sit on the bed. "Do you have any freaking idea how pale you are?"

Yes, she did. The mirror didn't lie as well as she could.

"It's been a helluva day. Maybe I'm a little shaky, but then, who wouldn't be?"

Slowly he shook his head. "What the hell else aren't you telling me? Why would your ex leave a medicine bottle in your bag? And you'd better come clean now because I don't want any more surprises knocking me on my ass for at least another twenty-four hours, if you don't mind."

Two fingers slid from her shoulders up to the bare skin of her neck. "No lies."

Mary Elise swallowed her anger. The last thing they needed was more sparks. She stared into his smoky-brown eyes and found plenty of anger...and concern. The guy genuinely thought there might be something wrong with her.

She'd pushed him far enough.

"I mean it when I say I'm fine, Daniel. I told you already that the bottle was linked to fertility drugs. I just have a...condition...called endometriosis. A chick thing, and you really don't need to hear all the details. I hadn't planned on this trip back to the States, and my meds are still in Rubistan. But it's not like I'm terminal. Women lived with this for centuries without any more medical help than herbs and a warmed brick."

"Well you look like hell."

Just what a girl wanted to hear from an old lover who was even hotter eleven years later. "I get a little achy." Understatement of the year, but hopefully she'd kept her pulse steady enough. "I'm a tad anemic, too, which is why I seem run-down to you. And thank you very much for letting me know I'm a hag. That makes me feel much better."

"Nice try with the diversion. Not working. Although later I'm going to want to hear what the hell the brick was for.'' He tapped her nose. ''You know you're beautiful, so don't fish for compliments. Do you need a specialist or can any doctor take care of this?''

Beautiful?

''Mary Elise? I want an answer.''

Oh. Yeah. She shook off silly vanity.

She had a specialist, but… ''This can wait until we have everything settled.''

His stubborn chin jutted. ''A specialist or a regular doctor.''

''A regular doctor can handle this, but Danny—''

''Fine.'' He wrenched the zipper on the green military-issue bag closed, then slid a laptop computer off the dresser to rest beside the suitcases. ''We have to swing through base, anyway, to mask our tracks and make sure no one sees us trading the boys off to Wren and Spike. We'll check in with Kathleen while we're there. Now that I think about it, Bronco's TDY—temporary duty—to McChord for two weeks. We can swap out my truck for his SUV when we leave base. I can clear a tail even if McRae's got help, but changing cars wouldn't hurt.''

Damn it, she understood he had more expertise in these things, but she wouldn't be relegated to a sick bed with her pen and paper. She could pitch in with something besides lists.

She respected that Danny was loading his gun and packing for the worst, but he didn't realize Kent would never fight the kind of head-to-head battle that Danny must excel at. ''Do I get *any* say here?''

''No.''

Frustration swelled. Built. She owed him, but why did he have to be so damned stubborn with the whole his-way-no-matter-what attitude?

The doorbell pealed once, twice.

Daniel backed one step at a time. "You won't be any help to me if you pass out."

He spun away on his boot heel.

Great. He got to be bossy *and* right. As if the hag comment wasn't bad enough, damn his cute departing ass in a wrinkled flight suit, he had to go Cro-Magnon on her.

She should be thanking him for fixing her mess of a life, not cursing him. Except rogue thoughts of the future kept teasing her with how much these boys would need a mother's softening influence long-term so their knuckles wouldn't drag the ground on occasion, as well.

Compressing the stack of clothes, Mary Elise tucked Trey's nebulizer, an extra inhaler and the rest of his asthma meds on top, and zipped the suitcase closed.

"Boys?" She crossed the hall and opened the door to find both children perched on the bottom bunk with Game Boys in hand. They'd been told about the change in plans, but with so much to assimilate in the past week, she wasn't sure they fully understood.

Hell, she still didn't understand everything.

She held out her arms. Flinging aside the video game, Austin launched toward her and hopped up. He clung to her, spindly arms and chubby cheek pressed against her neck while Trey's thumbs flew over the handheld video.

Voices drifted from the living room, Darcy and Max with Daniel. Austin's hold tightened. Tears burned her eyes. Oh, God, she couldn't lose it in front of the kids.

"Don't wanna go wif' Wren and Spike." Austin's muffled voice rang with the steely resolve of a temper tantrum on the rise.

Guilt jabbed her like the unrelenting stab of endless needles.

She pushed back her tears and straightened his Winnie the Pooh shirt. "I'm sorry, sweetie, but it's just for a little while. You'll have fun playing with all of Darcy's family.''

He shook his head against her neck. ''Don't know them.''

''But you do know Darcy and Spike.'' She sank to the edge of the bottom bunk amid rumpled sailboat sheets, ducking her head to accommodate the upper bed. And you'll get to play with Darcy's big sister and brother and her dad. I'll bet they even take you to McDonald's, and Danny's going to give them money to buy two new cartridges for your Game Boy Advance.''

Chiming bells from the video signified a leap to the next level. Trey's fingers flew. ''You might as well give it up,'' he confided without pausing. ''He doesn't want to leave you and go with them.''

''Trey,'' Mary Elise warned low.

''He's just a big baby.''

Mary Elise gasped, reached to clap her hand over Trey's mouth. Just what they needed. An all out battle on their hands.

Austin's head popped up from Mary Elise's neck. ''Am not a baby.''

''Are so.''

''Am not.''

''Then why are you hanging on her like one?''

Realization clicked. The kid was maneuvering his brother with tactics reminiscent of his big brother scamming an extra helping of ice cream out of a neighbor. She stifled the urge to give Trey a tight hug and blow the whole gig.

Trey flipped the off switch on his game. ''Danny and Mary Elise need some time by themselves, you big bozo. Like Mom and Dad did.''

''So they don't get a di-borce.''

Divorce? Franklin Baker had been heading to divorce

court again? She'd known they were having trouble, but apparently not how much.

Trey nodded. "Yeah, dweeb. Come on, I want that new Zelda: Ruler of the Universe game really bad." He rolled his eyes. "But it would probably scare you, anyway."

Mary Elise held her breath. Had Trey overplayed his hand with that one?

Austin squirmed, working his way down and out of Mary Elise's arms. Apparently sibling rivalry was a mighty strong motivator. She mouthed over Austin's head to Trey, "Thank you."

A grin creased his face.

Well, hell. He did look a little like his big brother after all.

Austin tugged her shirttail until she leaned forward.

"Love you. Have fun with Danny." He planted a wet kiss on her cheek along with a final hug.

Footsteps sounded down the hall just before Darcy poked her head into the room, looking rested from her power nap after her night flight. "Hey, kids, let's go raid your brother's junk-food cabinet and find some snacks for the road."

"Treats? Oo-rah!" Austin launched into Darcy's arms.

Mary Elise forced her feet to stay still while Darcy led the boys away. Austin was settled and she would only make it worse by following Darcy and pointing out what Austin and Trey preferred.

Relief and jealousy duked it out inside her. Thank God Austin would be okay for now. But damn it, she wanted to stop making lists and start living life. She wanted to be the one packing snacks for those two boys who'd first tugged her heart because of Daniel and then stolen her heart by being themselves.

No way would she let Trey and Austin lose their big brother. Captain Commando would have to learn to accept her help whether he wanted it or not.

Chapter 12

In the home stretch.

Tucked in a corner of the living room, Daniel memorized security codes from Max, for the fishing cabin, for joint computer access. Only a few more minutes and he could hit the road, hide Mary Elise safely away, then forge ahead with his plans to neutralize Kent McRae. Ensuring that ex of hers stayed locked up for life offered the only guarantee of safety.

With a little luck, he and Spike could dig deep enough into intelligence files for some kind of connection between Kent and a too-damned-cold trail for a hired gun. And pray the police landed a lead, as well. If the dusting for prints turned up anything.

According to the cops, Daniel's positive ID of Kent McRae outside the condo wasn't enough to place him inside. Meanwhile a restraining order was in the works. Apparently, it was the third Mary Elise had taken out on the bastard.

For all the good the others had done her.

Max clapped a hand on Daniel's shoulder. "Anything else you need?"

Answers? "Nah, we're set. I can't thank you enough for this. I already owed you for helping me get the boys out of Rubistan, and now this, too."

"You don't owe me a thing. Just keep your eyes peeled whenever you're flying wingman for Darcy."

"Don't let Wren hear you say that or she'll deck you."

Darcy poked her head through the kitchen bar opening and waggled a fruit roll-up at them. "I heard, anyhow. Wrestling match later, Max. Me and you, *mano a mano.*"

"Looking forward to it." Max winked, then thumped Daniel's back. "We'll take good care of them. You just take care of the two of you, and we'll be ready to throw another party by the end of next week."

"I hope so."

"I'll be in touch with you via the secure line 24/7 with updates about the boys and…anything else that comes through."

Daniel nodded.

"Hey, Darce," Max called, hitching his Technicolor swim trunks higher on his hips as he strode toward the kitchenette, "don't forget to pack some of those juice box things, grape-blaster flavor. Baker here has gotten me hooked on them."

Max rounded the corner, dodging Trey ducking back into the living room. Trey clutched a fistful of red licorice in his hands, eyes broadcasting more questions with each step toward the sofa. Damn, but he owed Trey a boatload of eggplant for keeping his little brother occupied today.

Daniel scrubbed a hand over his face, prepping himself for Trey's next round of questions. He wanted to be up-front with him. But as much as Trey put on that hoo-ya brave face, he was still just a kid.

A persistent kid. Interrogations in the Air Force training mock POW camp were a cakewalk compared to the inquisition of two little boys.

Plunking down on the leather couch, Trey waited, his eyes demanding answers with the same imperious right-to-know their old man had mastered well.

Daniel dropped to sit beside him. ''Trey, I'm sorry about all of this.''

''It's okay.''

''No, big guy. It's not. But I'm going to do my best to make it okay again.''

Trey peeled a strand of licorice off. ''Is Mary Elise in trouble?''

''She didn't do anything wrong, if that's what you're asking.'' Other than not come to him in the first place, but then that was as much his fault for closing the door between them years ago. ''But yes, things are a mess for her right now, and she needs a friend.''

Trey unraveled another strand, slowly, then another. ''My dad was trying to help her, wasn't he?''

My dad? Daniel wondered why the kid had the power to rile him with one little freaking pronoun. ''Yeah, Trey,'' Franklin Baker the third, ''your dad was trying to help her.''

''Help her with what?''

His brother couldn't be bought off with a video-game promise. Honesty worked for a reason. He just hoped the kid could understand something that damn well bemused him. ''Her ex-husband isn't a nice guy. He wants to hurt her, and I can't let that happen.''

''Kind of like how you kept me and Austin away from Uncle Ammar back in Rubistan.''

And to think he'd worried about the boy understanding. Life had given Trey a crash course in life's injustices. "Exactly like that."

One day, when he'd ensured the boys' safety, he looked forward to making sure they saw the beauty of their mother's heritage, as well. Man this parenting gig was a complex bag. But he didn't want his brothers' view of a part of themselves to be tainted by experiences with their uncle.

Trey nibbled the end off a strand of licorice. "Well then, I think it's probably a good idea for me and Austin to go to North Carolina."

Daniel let the pride build inside him. Yeah, the kid had to make it seem like his own decision, but no problem. He could live with that. He clapped Trey on the shoulder. "Thank you. I'm trusting you to take care of Austin. It'll hurt Mary Elise to think he's popping out those tears."

Trey rolled his eyes. "Yeah, two of those big fat leaky ones and Mary Elise was crawling inside the crate with us."

The enormity of her sacrifice nailed him dead center like an on-target missile, no warning. He'd respected her bravery before, but he'd been clueless on how difficult it must have been for her to risk a return to the States, to expose her sanctuary with the call for help in the first place. Anonymous or no, the trail was there.

Her call. His father's call. His father's death.

Pieces of information jostled in Daniel's head, searching for edges to make a clean fit. Except connector pieces were missing.

"Danny?"

He startled back out of his pensive trance. "Yeah, kid?"

"Who were you named for?" A simple question with a weight of importance reflected in the boy's eyes.

"For Great-grandpa Baker."

"Our father's grandfather?"

Our. "Yes."

"Cool."

Silence descended. Trey peeled the last strands of licorice apart, sorting them into two piles on the leather sofa. He clutched one stack, leaving the other beside Daniel.

And then his little brother was hugging him. So quick Daniel almost missed the chance to hug those bony shoulders back.

Trey stepped away, stubborn chin jutting just like their father. Like his older brother. "I still hate peanut butter."

"Oo-rah."

"Hoo-ya."

Daniel scooped up the pile of licorice Trey had left behind. *Love you, too, bro.*

Who knew red licorice had such a distinctive scent?

Of course, after an hour alone in the car with Danny, Mary Elise feared she would soon keel over from sensory overload from the different facets of him bombarding her.

Daniel's aftershave drifting with each gust of the vent.

Danny's licorice disappearing strand by strand.

The captain's military paraphernalia wafting an odd hydraulic fluid scent she'd come to realize permeated Air Force gear. Even a well-washed flight suit carried the air.

She lowered the window on the SUV, Daniel's truck having been traded for Bronco's vehicle on base after her doctor visit. After a quick trip to the BX, where Daniel bought the most bizarre assortment of supplies, they'd hit the road. Two dozen plastic buckets rattled around in the back with a bag of twenty-penny nails and heaven only knew what else.

Moss-draped oaks arched over the narrow road, the marshy coastline peeking through on her right out the open window. Reeds bowed a welcome in the breeze.

Mary Elise wriggled in the seat to get comfortable. At least her medicines would be kicking in soon, throwing her body chemistry back in sync, hopefully lightening her mood. This was worse than that day by the pool years ago. At least then Danny had been her friend. She vowed if he offered her boatloads of chocolate, she'd deck him.

Or hug him.

It was a close contest.

She adjusted the angle of the seat.

Daniel tore off another bite of licorice. "Why the hell didn't you let me know you're in pain this week?"

"What did Kathleen Bennett tell you?"

"Nothing." And he didn't look too happy about it.

"But you asked her."

"Hell, yeah, I asked her. And she got her flight suit all in a twist over rules."

Three cheers for patient confidentiality. "Danny, I'm fine, and feeling better by the minute thanks to Kathleen. By tomorrow I'll be a hundred percent, and your chocolate will be safe from me."

"Funny. Not. Why the hell are you so sensitive over a flipping trip to the doctor?"

Boggy wind whipped between them while she searched for a simple answer that would bring the fewest questions. "I didn't want to draw any undue attention to myself that might tip off Kent."

For all the good that had done her. If that False Unicorn plant had been intentionally placed, which she firmly believed, Kent had known about her return within hours of her landing. She shuddered.

"There are a thousand ways around that and you know it. Not to mention we've been to the doctor, and you're still so flipping prickly on the subject you have cactus written all over you. Why?"

Because her mother's calendar carried nothing but doctor's appointments. Because she didn't want to be a burden to anyone. Because Kent had parked her in more doctor offices during three years than most people saw in a lifetime.

She pitched those thoughts out the window with the salty breeze. Hadn't she resolved only a few hours ago to reclaim her strength? She'd had enough morbidity for one day. Real worries would close in soon enough, and for now she just wanted to enjoy her time with Danny. "Like I said before, women have lived with this since the beginning of time, and the last thing we want is to discuss it with men who wince."

The big brave warrior threw back his shoulders. "I did not wince."

"Oh, really?" She jabbed him in the side with a teasing poke. "You wouldn't turn green over the mere mention of a shopping expedition for feminine hygiene products?"

She had to give him credit. He didn't turn green. However, he *was* giving pale a run for its money.

"Okay, maybe you have a point. But I think I could have handled buying you a bottle of Motrin or a request for Kathleen to give you a checkup after she finished with Trey. I'm a modern guy. What's the big deal?"

She snorted and snitched a piece of licorice from his hand. "Liar."

"Aw, now cut it out. Be fair. Like you wouldn't wince

over shopping for...for—'' he paused, then snapped his fingers ''—for a jock strap.''

A laugh bubbled. God she missed laughing with him.

''And just think of the poor sales clerk at the sporting store if you had to quiz him on what size you should buy.''

''I remember your size just fine, Danny.''

Had she said that?

His eyes widened, focused on crossing a low rail bridge with exaggerated care.

Oh, yeah. She sure had said it.

''Uh, thank you?''

''No problem.'' Well, actually it was starting to be a problem as need snapped along the air between them.

And they would be spending an indeterminate amount of time alone. No tiny chaperones. No secrets. And a teenage need that had matured into an adult hunger. Now all those memories swirled through the car, the medicine buzz not unlike the champagne buzz all those years ago that had led her to pitch her clothes off.

She sagged back against the headrest. With the lulling pass of each mossy oak, she fought the sensory overload draw of Daniel's smile and bay-rum-tinged hydraulic fluid riding the ocean breeze....

She didn't want to be pregnant. Mary Elise touched a bare foot to the ground and launched her old tire swing into motion under the ancient oak while watching Danny's back door. He'd just pulled into the driveway, home for the summer, and she knew he wouldn't wait long to see her.

To find out if their night together—long, hot hours— had left her pregnant.

Who wanted to be pregnant and unmarried at nineteen with three years of college left to finish? And it wasn't like she even loved the baby's father. Well, she loved him. *She just wasn't in* love *with him. Like, geez, it was Danny. Her best friend.*

Her best friend who really knew how to do it.

Well, as best she could tell then, from her limited— okay, nonexistent—experience. Now she had a weekend of experience under her tightening belt, along with a growing baby. No Air Force Academy graduation for Danny. No journalism degree and crime-beat-reporter job for her.

And the part that sucked most was she hurt more over Danny losing his dreams than she did over losing her own.

She knew without a doubt he would offer to marry her. Would insist on marrying her. She wanted to tell him no, but the thing was, as much as she didn't want to be pregnant, she was. And it was Danny's baby, which made the kid already cute and special and deserving of the best she could manage.

So yeah, if he pushed, she'd marry him. Maybe they could work out one of those married-for-a-year deals so the baby would have his name.

But he'd still be booted out of the Air Force Academy. Would still lose his dream. And an ache started low in the pit of her belly at even the thought of pushing him out of her life in something so harsh sounding as a divorce.

Geez. They should be making plans to go to the beach, not wedding plans.

Then there he was. Danny, striding across the glass-enclosed back porch, through the screen door.

The military precision slipped into his walk a little more with each year at the Air Force Academy. He could wear wrinkled clothes all he wanted. The walk gave him away.

Pushing up from the swing, she made her way past a blooming dogwood tree, through the ivy-covered gate. He looked older, too. His parents' split hit him hard. He kept saying it didn't matter, since he was grown. She knew better. Senator Baker's trophy marriage shrieked cliché to a son who personified uniqueness.

That had to be the reason worry lines creased Danny's face. Not because they both knew they'd been stupid, stupid, stupid not to use birth control.

"Hey, Mary 'Lise." His smile pulled tight as he drew her in for a hug. Are you?

She could feel his unspoken question reach to her. His arms wrapped around her with the familiarity of a hundred other hugs. The awareness tinged with fear, however, was all new.

Are you pregnant? *Again, the silent question pulsed from him.*

Mary Elise swallowed and forced the words out. "I am."

She didn't have to say anything else. He would know what she meant. That damned unspoken connection between them was working just fine. She'd prepped herself for his proposal, knew Danny well enough to understand his sense of honor wouldn't let him do anything else.

But please, please, please, with her hormones in an ungodly tangle she wasn't sure she could handle seeing disappointment in his eyes, even though he had every right.

He held so still, unmoving for four deep breaths of her own. With their connection in total working order, she felt it all rock through his motionless body—the shock, frustration, anger…the resolution.

Finally he stepped back. She opened her eyes, slowly, in no great hurry to face him just yet, and found… Danny's smile at its most kick-ass vibrant.

"Well, Mary Elise, then I guess there's no reason we can't go lock ourselves in the pool house, tear off all our

clothes and have out-of-control screaming sex.'' Scooping *her up into his arms, Danny planted a deep kiss on her lips and made fast tracks past the diving board.*

Mary Elise laughed, tension easing at least a bit. Her hand snuck up to play with the close-cropped hair at the nape of his neck. Yeah, she knew the proposal would come once their clothes lay in a pile by their sweaty, sated bodies. But he understood her enough to realize she couldn't hear those words yet.

And in that moment she fell a little in love with Danny after all.

Daniel scooped up sleeping Mary Elise and kicked the car door closed. Softly. Keeping his motions quiet, steady, although Mary Elise slept like the dead.

Dead.

Not his favorite word today. Pine straw muffled the thud of his boots toward the rectangular cabin—a shotgun-style house, one room deep, long and thin. Nowhere for anyone to hide inside.

He hitched his hold on her, his survival vest and belt dangling from the crook of his arm. He'd unload the rest of the gear once he had her inside, but not a chance would he let his gun out of his reach.

His eyes scanned, assessing for vulnerability with each step closer to the clapboard fishing retreat on stilts. He would have to put trip wires around the open underway to stop anyone from lurking beneath.

Shallow tides bordered the house on three sides, rotting marsh grass emitting a methane scent into the air. At least they would have prior warning of ''visitors'' on those three fronts from the water.

A single road in. Two minor paths. Manageable to defend with traps positioned to disable intruders.

Daniel ducked to avoid the drape of Spanish moss trailing from the limbs of an ancient oak, sidestepped a hammock blowing in the salty breeze.

What a haven this would be any other time, with its uninterrupted view of the water, dock stretching into the reedy surf rippling out into the main ocean way. Max had chosen his retreat well for peace…and safety.

Thudding up the wooden steps, Daniel shifted Mary Elise in his arms, the late-afternoon sun casting pasty shadows across the hollows in her cheeks. He cursed Kent McRae for at least the fiftieth time. Bending at the knees, Daniel flipped open the metal box by the door and punched in the security code he'd memorized from Max, before opening the dead bolt.

She could talk all damned day about how she would be fine, and that didn't change the fact that she should be putting her feet up until her medicines took effect.

Daniel toed open the door and stepped inside the rustic one-room cabin with nothing more than a few pieces of sparse furniture and a walk-in closet bathroom/shower stall. A man's dream retreat. And the least romantic getaway he could think of to offer a woman in need of pampering and R&R.

If he even knew what to do for her in the first place.

Kathleen Bennett and her damn rule book. Screw patient confidentiality. The best she'd given him was directions to check out the Internet, since he already knew Mary Elise had endometriosis and fertility problems. The most freaking unfair thing he could imagine, this woman not having her arms and heart full of babies.

Daniel shut down the image he'd carried for years, a mental picture of what Mary Elise might have looked like holding their kid. Focus on the here and now. He made tracks through the efficiency kitchen with a small counter and two bar stools, past the single sofa in front of a stone fireplace to the quilt-covered bed tucked against the back wall.

Not that Mary Elise would voice a complaint about their accommodations. Of course he appreciated her grit, but only to a point. And if he tried to discuss her medical needs with her again, who knew where she'd flip the conversation this time. The jock-strap-size discussion still had him swallowing his damned tongue.

He grinned.

Yeah, he liked her grit, all wrapped up in a subtle package and gentle smile, which gave the surprise wallop all the more punch. He hated like hell what had brought them here, but couldn't stop the surge of excitement over having her all to himself.

He was one messed-up dude. No doubt.

Daniel lowered her to the bed, surprised at the give under his hands. A water bed. He fixed his eyes on her face for the least sign of stirring. The gentle roll of enclosed waves welcomed her in a lulling embrace.

Unable to resist, a given around Mary Elise lately, he slid his survival vest and belt to the floor and pressed a kiss to her forehead. Lingered. He inhaled the honeysuckle scent of her shampoo like some infatuated adolescent. Except, the powerful tangle of frustration, anger, protectiveness pounding through him had little to do with tender teen emotions.

"I swear I won't let that bastard ever hurt you again," he whispered against her skin.

Her hand glided up to his chest. "Danny?"

She lay so still he missed the motion until he felt the warm weight of her palm seep through his uniform. He stared down into eyes the green of deep summer. And damned if it wasn't just the two of them. Completely alone for the first time in eleven years.

Chapter 13

Water bed rolling lightly beneath her, Mary Elise struggled to shake off the fuzzy dream remnants of long ago riding in Danny's warm embrace. A tough proposition when she could still feel the imprint of his strong arms banded around her after he carried her from the car.

The roar of the ocean outside lulled her, but she fought sleep's call. She brushed the pads of her fingers against the raspy texture of Daniel's flight suit. The whole dark-wood cabin decor and dim light through thick panes offered an ends-of-the-earth solitude her sleep-mussed brain couldn't seem to recall why she should resist. "Were you going to tell me we're here?"

She flicked his zipper tab with one finger.

Daniel jumped back as if burned. "Were you going to tell me you're awake? I damn near threw my back out carrying you."

Angling up on her elbow, she started to bristle, the thrown-out-back comment coming mighty damn close on the heels of his pale-hag remark. She looked deeper, found an edgy tension in him that she might have attributed to their dangerous position, except with her own eyes opening and her defenses lowering, she recognized the glint well.

Desire. He wanted her. Bad. Or rather, oh-so-good.

A trill of feminine power sounded through her. It had been so long since she'd felt attractive. She and Danny may have kissed, but only when either she'd come on to him or when they'd been in a full-body press with her leg nestled between his. Against *him.*

Oh yeah, she remembered *him* very well.

"Put your back out? Liar." She sat the rest of the way up and tucked her legs to the side, the gentle glide of the enclosed waves of the water bed undulating against her suddenly sensitive skin. "I think you got a he-man kick out of carrying me in here."

He snagged his survival vest from the floor beside the bed. "Why don't you try to sleep? I should be through before you wake up."

Through? Encroaching panic edged out desire. "Where are you going?"

"To scope the area. Set some warning devices in place."

Warning devices. Her throat closed. She'd just assumed the distant locale and Danny's weaponry would be enough protection, and that she and Danny could use this rustic-haven time to sort through past feelings.

Present feelings.

She wasn't sure whether to be reassured or scared spit-less that he saw the need for more security.

Mary Elise swung her legs off the side of the bed. "Tell me what to do."

"Sleep."

"Get real."

"I mean it." He jerked on the green mesh vest, the knife sheathed in black leather attached to his shoulder a harsh reminder of real-world worries. "Rest. You're no good to me dead on your feet."

"Sleep can come later. I may be a little groggy." Understatement. She wished Kathleen had been less pushy with the muscle relaxants. "But I'm far from passing out. The sooner we have this place secured, the sooner I can get that rest you keep insisting I need. Do you really think I could just kick back now?"

"You did in the car."

"That was different. There was nothing I could do."

He buckled a gear belt around his waist with canteens—a gun holster. He pulled free the 9 mm, tugged out the magazine, checked, clicked it in place again before returning the weapon to the holster with clean efficiency. "How about whip up something to eat."

No way was she playing Betty Crocker to his John Wayne. "Oh, yeah, that's really a pressing survival issue right now after the two Big Macs and order of supersize fries you banged back in the car."

The first signs of a grin creased the corners of his eyes. "Well, I'm still hungry. You know me. Never full, jaws just get tired of chewing."

"Great. If Kent finds us, I'll toss up a smoke screen by burning some fried Spam."

Mary Elise shadowed him around the tiny cabin, staying smack dab in his peripheral line of sight. Danny swung his foot up onto the arm of the brown plaid sofa and tucked a second knife inside his boot.

Suppressing a shiver over just the thought of him having to use it, she stepped closer. "Give me something constructive to do or I'm going to follow you around and be a real pain in the butt. You should know from our growing-up years, I can do it.''

"You're already doing it right now," he mumbled without glancing her way.

"Good. Now give me a job that doesn't involve a spatula." Her hand fell to his forearm. Gripped. Held with a determination she infused in her voice as well. "Danny, I won't be relegated to a passive role ever again."

He dropped his foot to hardwood floor, a sigh riding a long trip out his lungs. "Do you know how to shoot?"

"I took lessons after I arrived in Rubistan." Never again would she be caught unprepared. And as much as she wanted to find a peaceful middle ground with Danny, she would battle him to the end for her right to defend herself.

Daniel recognized well the dogged glint in Mary Elise's steady gaze. The woman was in full fighting form.

At least she wasn't gliding those soft hands up his body with a distraction he couldn't afford. Security came first.

And after?

He'd face that later. And pray that by then he could remember all the reasons why he shouldn't lay her back on that water bed and rediscover every inch of her.

First priority, arm Mary Elise with a weapon.

Hooking his hands under the end of the sofa, Daniel hefted the far edge a couple feet to the right. He flipped back the edge of the brown braid rug and knelt, working his fingers down the ridges in the boarded floor.

"Danny?"

"Shhh." He waved her silent as he concentrated on finding…bull's eye.

He pried three loose boards up, revealing, just as Max promised, a small gun safe. Spinning up the combination, Daniel opened the door. A gasp sounded from behind him.

He glanced over his shoulder. "What?"

"I just didn't expect to see that."

He tracked her wide-eyed gaze down to the two hand-guns—a Browning M9 and a .45 automatic—surrounded by stacks of ammunition. "What do you think we do for a living?"

"You fly planes. Spike investigates. I mean, well, I figured you took a gun with you on missions or assignments, like the one in your closet. I just didn't expect to see all of this here, too."

"Maybe Spike packs a little more firepower than some of us. But like a cop, a military serviceman is never off duty." He dug out ammo and tossed it on the sofa. Sitting on the couch, he checked and began loading both weapons.

She eased down beside him. "Never off duty?"

"Back when you were working for the paper," he answered without taking his eyes off his task, "if you got a three-day weekend, you could hop a plane and go anywhere you wanted as long as you were back at work on time."

"Yeah. So?"

"If I travel outside the area, I have to apply for official leave and let admin know where I'll be at all times. Even on a weekend."

"Why?"

"We may not sit alert anymore, but we're always on call, 24/7." He pressed bullets into the magazine. Click. Click. Click against the spring action. "If the world goes to hell, we have to be ready to roll."

She sank down beside him. "How can you live that way?"

"How can I not?" With the heel of his palm, he jammed the magazine home on the 9 mm.

That she even had to ask the question offered a great big reason why he should reconsider a mattress dance with this woman.

"Darcy said you have...connections."

"She did?" His fingers paused in loading the .45, a damned big gun with even bigger stopping power.

"What kind of connections?"

He didn't answer. Couldn't. More reasons to avoid sleeping with anyone he genuinely cared about.

Whoa. Back up. Echoes of *emotionally unavailable* ricocheted like an out-of-control bullet in his skull.

"Danny?"

"I fly airplanes."

She waited.

He rolled a bullet between two fingers. "There's a lot more to being in the military than fighting wars, and that includes things we can't talk about. At times we walk out the door with no indication of where we're going or when we'll be home. Some of those missions bring connections."

End of discussion. He had more current concerns, anyway. Like keeping her alive.

And deciphering why he felt anything but emotionally unavailable at the moment.

He placed the 9 mm in her hands before she could press him to talk anymore. "Don't aim unless you're willing to follow through." Daniel tucked the .45 into his survival vest and strode toward the door.

She followed. "If you have problems with me pitching in once we step through the door, you're just going to have to get over yourself."

The pounding of her determined steps echoed behind him.

An all-out smile pulled free, so damned incongruous at

the moment that he smiled even more. For better or worse, emotionally unavailable was never an option around Mary Elise. A low chuckle rode up and out. "That's my girl."

"What?"

He stopped her in the open doorway, palming the metal frame over her head. And it hit him, full force like the power of the so-damned-pretty green eyes staring back at him. He knew just what had him smiling in the middle of the worst day of his life. "You're back."

"Pardon me?"

Grazing his knuckles along her cheek, over skin still a shade too pale but the woman beneath humming with renewed vitality that had nothing to do with medications. "Before, you were half here, holding pieces away from me."

"I thought we already covered why I felt I couldn't tell you—"

With one finger to her lips, he silenced her. "That's not what I meant. You were holding pieces of *yourself* back, but not anymore. You're here and in my face, and, yeah, it can be annoying as hell, but I'm so damned glad to see *you* again, I can't bring myself to do anything more than…"

Screw wise decisions. He'd have to deal with enough of those after he finished securing the perimeter and locked himself inside alone with Mary Elise who deserved a helluva lot more than what he had to offer.

He kissed her, hard, fast and on the mouth before pulling back. His hand still cupped her head, fingers in tangled red curls that would cling to his memory.

"Welcome home, Mary Elise. I missed you."

Eyes fixed on the purples and mauves of the darkening skyline as she jogged down the cabin steps, Mary Elise wondered how the world could look so level when surely the ground under her feet tipped decidedly to the left. Right when she had her feet steady under her, purpose set... Bam! Danny shook things up again.

Welcome home, Mary Elise.

She followed Daniel, hand on the wooden rail just to be safe from the rocking-world problem, and tried to reconcile the conflicting images. The man who'd stroked such a gentle caress down her face was the same man who'd dug out an arsenal from under the floorboards. And both fascinated her.

I missed you.

Shadowed by the graceful arch of an oak, Daniel popped the hatch on the SUV and reached inside, providing too tempting a view. Sheesh. She might as well be nineteen again given the way her hormones were acting.

From deep inside, he pulled a stack of buckets. ''Before you get your knickers in knot, I'm not asking you to mop a floor.'' He glanced back over his shoulder.

Busted. Scavenger birds squawked a mocking call from the shoreline. A grin teased her lips as she gave him a wide-eyed look of innocence so overplayed she knew she hadn't fooled him for a second.

How bizarre to feel lighthearted with the worst of threats looming. Not unlike that moment years ago when Daniel had scooped her up in his arms, and while she knew they were both in a mess, somehow his smile made it okay.

A tickle of unease fluttered in her stomach.

She didn't want to depend on anyone for her happiness. And most of all, she did *not* want to be a little in love with Daniel Baker again.

He hefted out another bag, a jingling sounding inside. She peered inside to find...

"Twenty-penny nails."

Large. Spike-size. Well there was a hefty dose of reality for a girl. "What am I supposed to do with these?"

"Hang tough and watch. You'll need to do this with twenty-three more buckets."

Daniel sat on the back bumper, a handful of the metal spikes beside him. One by one he shoved three through the plastic on one side, then three more on the other. An industrial-size roll of duct tape in his hand, he encircled the outside to secure the nail heads so the points angled slightly down on the inside.

He passed her the bag of nails. "Do this with the other buckets while I fan out and work on the first line of protection. This will be our second ring of defense."

"I'm still not understanding."

"We'll dig holes around the cabin at the most logical places where someone might approach. Drop these inside, cover each hole with a layer of pine needles and leaves over thin twigs. When a foot goes in, it's not coming back out—at least not without a lengthy process and a lot of pain. Even if he works free before we get there, he'll be slowed from the injury."

We. Funny how one word could speed that tickle in her stomach. "Amazing."

"Untwisted bed springs work as spikes, too." He tore the duct tape with his teeth. A hank of hair fell over his brow, and he could have been the boy building a rocket out of his mama's Corning Ware.

She started to reach to brush aside his stray lock of hair.

He jammed the completed bucket trap in her hand as if he wanted space between them. "Here. You try now."

Why was he being so brusque? Hadn't he spent the past

days trying to convince her to stay? Of course that was before he found out what she'd been hiding.

She would have known how to break the tension eleven years ago. Now she wasn't so certain.

Mary Elise hopped up to sit in the back of the SUV. She set to work on a second bucket while Daniel hefted out rope, fishing wire and a bag of electronics that looked as if they should have been gifts for the boys.

Wind rustled through the trees, shaking loose a shower of pine needles in the widening silence between them. Where had the guy gone who'd kissed her on the porch? She should be relieved. This Daniel offered fewer complications.

"Where did you learn all of this?"

"Survival training. Study. It's…wise to stay up-to-date." He kept his eyes off her and on the unloading. "There are countless options. Chinese Chopper, Cuban Water Trap, Sheepeaters' Rockfall. But we have to adapt to the situation and means available. The traditional pit takes forever to dig and then you've wasted time on one line of defense."

The reality of it all washed over her again. He was arming for battle when he should be swimming or breaking in the new Zelda game with the boys, prepping for Thanksgiving.

"We're going to use the Malaysian Hawk on the main path in. A log strung high, attached to a trip wire. On the two minor trails in, I'll string Jivaro Catapults using this."

He slid a canoe paddle out of the back. One swift move brought it down on his knee to snap off the handle. "The paddle will be fixed inside a twisted-tight rope tied to a tree limb. Foliage and moss is thick enough here to cover. A stick trigger sets this sucker to spin fast and hard enough to crack ribs. If he finds us before we can nail him with traditional evidence, we'll be ready.''

That *we* word again. Strange how it stirred the same strange mix of hope and trepidation as the traps.

No more passive roles, she reminded herself. Except, thinking about all those maybes with Danny scared her hair straight.

Danny's determined strides down the main road took him farther away from her. No surprise, her eyes devoured the look of him. She accepted the attraction, yet in a day full of revelations a final realization settled.

She might not know about tomorrow. And while she felt safer, she knew better than ever to underestimate Kent again.

All she could control were her decisions in the here and now. She was through running from experiencing life, and she damn well intended to make full use of that water bed at the first opportunity.

Sunrise fingering through the bulletproof panes, Danny hooked a foot on the rung of the bar stool. He clicked through computer keys, logging on to the green screen that signified secured communications with Max.

Reaching for his coffee mug, Daniel kept his back to Mary Elise. A power nap, cold shower and two PBJs had recharged him, not enough to face Mary Elise just yet, however. Watching her sleep was a torturous hell, and he wasn't interested in incineration.

Well, maybe he was interested.

But he couldn't afford the distraction, and no question, the woman was one endless distraction. At least the security preparations had worked her into an exhausted sleep through the night. Guilt nicked, but Mary Elise at her pit bull most persistent hadn't been budging. Of course she'd been right in asserting they would work faster together.

He glanced at the second laptop sitting alongside, this one set up with security monitors. He'd rigged two video cameras on opposite corners of the cabin, as well as setting alarms on his three major traps, alarms sending radio pulses back to his computer.

His credit card bill would be hell next month, but when it came to Mary Elise, his peace of mind was priceless.

"Come on, come on, come on, Max." Daniel watched for incoming mail. He'd passed along seven possibilities for underworld types who worked the Savannah area. All fit the profile and description in Mary Elise's initial police report.

The fact that no one followed the too-damned-easy trail a year ago turned his vision red. And why the hell had no one questioned the number of McRaes in the Savannah PD signing off on Mary Elise's reports?

Red turned scarlet.

Daniel channeled his anger into productivity, best line of defense for Mary Elise. Any second now he hoped Max would fill in the next block with his feedback on McRae's overseas bank accounts.

The mail icon flashed. Anticipation chugged. "Thanks, Spike."

Daniel opened the file and scrolled through Max's notations, lists of suspicious bank transfers from an overseas account, crossing multiple state and country lines. McRae would burn for this once Max turned the findings over to the FBI.

Scanning, his eye snagging on a line item. A transfer that routed through three accounts before finally ending…in the Middle East four weeks ago.

McRae had tracked her to Rubistan. She'd been that

close to death. Could that have been why his father had called? Because of a heightened threat level to Mary Elise?

Unable to resist looking at her, hungry for reassurance that she still breathed, lived, Daniel kicked his heel to spin the revolving bar stool to face her.

Protectiveness fired into afterburners. Thank God she slept deeply and he didn't have to hide anything for once. While waiting for Max's response earlier, Daniel had cruised the Internet for information on endometriosis—a painful, chronic disease he now knew affected at least ten percent of all women.

Had he invaded her privacy? Maybe. No doubt Mary Elise would be pissed. But he needed to reassure himself the stubborn woman wasn't pushing herself.

And yeah, being locked up with Mary Elise made him think of sex and he wanted to be certain he didn't make a lame-ass mistake that would hurt her. Heaven knew the woman went out of her way to downplay her medical needs.

So now he knew. Discomfort during sex could be a side effect for some. Talk about a splash of cold water. And how exactly would he bring that up if the situation arose where they happened to find themselves naked together?

An image he did not need but wanted, so much his teeth hurt.

Mary Elise stirred under the patchwork quilt. He turned away from too much temptation arching awake before his eyes. His ears, however, filled in the blanks. The rustle of covers shoved aside to reveal a sleep-mussed Mary Elise. Soft, bare feet hitting the floor. A gentle sigh accompanying a stretch.

He swallowed hard.

Her feet shuffled a groggy path across the floor. The

bathroom door snicked open, then closed. Daniel exhaled long and loud. Then straightened. His ears really didn't need to hear the…

Shower.

The whooshing of water tormented him when his reserves already spiraled in a nosedive. The tenor of the water hitting altered with the intrusion of a body.

He had earplugs in his flight suit.

Fliers carried them to combat flight-line noise and he seriously considered using them now for combating insanity. Except he couldn't afford to miss the warning alarms set on the traps. Not that he expected McRae to track them for at least another twelve hours, if at all.

Just the same, Daniel steeled his ears against the shoosh of the shower beading against Mary Elise's naked body and concentrated on typing a response with feedback for Max.

Ten torturous years—or maybe ten minutes—later she padded into the room, barefoot and smelling so good his mouth watered.

He pulled away from the chair, made tracks for the kitchen. Not near enough space in the cabin.

"I cooked." He unwrapped the paper towel from around the sandwich he'd made for her earlier when he'd slapped together two for himself. "Well, if you call a PBJ cooking."

Silk clung to her damp skin, her shorts and shirt already baring a tempting stretch of arms and legs. "Thank you. Definitely a good sign you've moved out of Cro-Magnon mode."

"Cro-Magnon? Who me?" he asked, although feeling very primal. "Lady, I'm more than willing to let you pull your fair share around here."

"Right after you drag me to your cave by my hair."

He had other ideas of what he'd like to do with all that wet hair. Instead, he nudged the open jar of strawberry preserves toward her on the counter. "Fresh open, canned preserves. I figure we'd better use the bread now and save the military MREs—meals ready to eat—for later."

How long would they be here? He wanted this over and done fast for Mary Elise, but also for his brothers. Trey and Austin didn't need any more disruption in their lives.

Mary Elise tore off a corner of her sandwich and popped it in her mouth. Her eyes widened with surprise before she rushed the sandwich up to her face for another bite. He watched, couldn't take his eyes off her as she savored the simplicity of strawberry preserves with a sensualist's delight.

Damn, but she was a woman after his own heart.

"Happy Thanksgiving, 'Lise. Not exactly a turkey dinner. But actually much better than the chicken à la king MRE." Shuddering, he passed her a bottle of water. "Even I can't stomach that one unless I'm starving."

"Have you ever been…starving, I mean?" Her elegant throat moved with swallows of water, her mouth fitting perfectly around the bottle.

Answer the question, bud. "Survival training was rough for a guy like me who needs a few thousand extra calories a day to burn up all the energy pinging around."

She placed the bottle on the counter and stepped closer. "All the flyers go through this survival training?"

"Yep." He took a step back. "By the end of the course, rabbit eyeballs actually tasted good."

"Eww!" Laughing, she popped the last corner of her sandwich into her mouth, her tongue swiping a hint of strawberry from her lips.

Words fell out but he lost track of them. "Rabbit eyeballs are a great source of iodine."

Remnants of laughter painting her eyes jewel tones, she sucked jelly off the tip of one of her fingers. ''You can't throw me off the track with gross-out stories, Danny Baker. Although I gotta confess, now it's tough to think about kissing your mouth.''

''Did you want to before?''

Crap. Shut the yap, Baker. The woman might have a backbone of steel, but she needed time to get over the hell McRae had put her through. Having to fend off someone who should damn well be protecting her wasn't honorable.

Mary Elise's eyes deepened, darkened with two slow blinks.

Uh-oh.

She dipped two fingers into the strawberry preserves. If she put those fingers in her mouth to taste again, he'd die. Right here. Right now. His obituary would read, ''Toxic case of deadly testosterone overload.''

He had to remember about keeping his distance. For her. And, yeah, for his own freaking sanity.

She placed her fingers…against *his* lips. ''How about a palate cleanser?''

No mistaking her intent. And no way did he intend to die just yet.

Don't do it, Baker.

Too late.

His open mouth closed around her fingers. Mary Elise and sugar. Uh-huh. He was a dead man.

In no hurry, she withdrew her fingers while stepping closer. Maybe he wouldn't be taking advantage of her after all. She obviously knew her own mind.

Yes! His libido shouted while his mind cautioned with logical reasoning—as if logic stood a chance against his need for this woman. He would just control himself while enjoying this torturous-as-hell moment.

Daniel dipped two fingers in the jelly jar still held in her hand. Without once breaking eye contact, he brought his fingers to her mouth.

Oh, yeah.

Her lips closed over him, the subtle suction drawing him inside, deeper. Her tongue circled his fingers.

His vision clouded.

Okay, maybe he didn't need to stay completely away from her. He would just be gentle. Careful. After all, the woman knew her mind and understood her body.

Hell, she'd about decked him over a "pale" comment. If he pushed her away... Giving in would be good.

He could almost hear Mary Elise laughing at his reasoning. *Oh, Danny, you are such a man.*

And she would be right. He was feeling very much a man.

Gentle, big guy, he reminded himself. He withdrew his fingers from her mouth, his body throbbing at the moist friction against his skin. He reassured himself that his logic wasn't so far gone that he lost sight of what she'd been through with that bastard.

Take it easy. Take it slow. He hooked his arms low on her waist, eased her to him. Brushed her lips once, twice, found more strawberry preserves on the corner of her lips.

Yeah, slow and tender definitely had its merits.

With a wealth of security surrounding the cabin and at least a few hours' window from detection, Daniel intended to peel every piece of clothing off Mary Elise's body. Worshiping this woman with an attention to detail she deserved.

He would be sensitive, damn it, even if it killed him.

Mary Elise slid her arm from around his neck and

hauled her purse across the counter, just as he reached in his back pocket. Simultaneously they both pulled free... condoms.

Her smile met his. "You know, Danny, since we both remembered contraception this time, there's no reason we can't tear off all our clothes and have out-of-control screaming sex."

Chapter 14

She wanted him. Intense, fast, now, until she forgot everything but him.

Mary Elise arched on her toes to taste fully of Daniel and strawberries and a passion just as vibrantly red. Hers or his? Deepening the kiss, she wasn't sure because that old connection of theirs flowed back and forth and back again until she couldn't ascertain where the need began.

Couldn't imagine its end.

Daniel breezed his fingers down a shivery path over her neck, along her breasts, leaving her aching for more when his hand fell away. Nipping her bottom lip, tracing her ear with growled words about how damned hot he found her, he shucked his vest, hooked it over a chair.

Placed his gun by the bed.

She mentally shoved away that stark image and listened, savored. So what if he was being practical and safe? He was also filling her mind with incredible promises of what he planned to do to her. He dropped the condoms beside the gun, her Daniel never losing sight of his protector role.

She tugged his zipper, yanked his flight suit over his shoulders and down.

"Take it easy, 'Lise. Slow."

Featherlight strokes traveled up and down her back in tantalizing whispers at odds with the bold hands delivering them. She wanted this and more and everything, after so long of nothing. So long wanting just this man.

And if he shoved her away?

"Not a chance," he answered her unspoken thoughts with an ease recaptured from the past.

Relief weakened her knees. Having Danny now meant so damned much to her, almost too much. Something she hadn't realized until she faced his possible rejection.

For a moment she faltered. This was supposed to be about uncomplicated sex, taking charge of what she wanted from life.

Sex with Danny had never been uncomplicated.

Of its own volition and without her permission, the moment became about more, much more. It became about broad hands shaking from restraint. A familiar lock of hair falling over a brow furrowed deep with concentration. On her. The past and the present blended into a combustible need that surpassed just sex.

Her silk shirt glided down her arms, hooked on her elbows before slithering to pool at her feet. A quick snap of the front clasp on her bra bared her.

Would he find her thirty-year-old body less enticing than her nineteen-year-old self?

She didn't have to wonder long. His appreciative eyes burned a slow ride, lingering, moving on to linger and heat again. With an almost worshipful reverence, he reached. Touched. The line of her collarbone. Who'd have expected that to be an erogenous zone?

Mary Elise shivered.

"You're even more beautiful than I remembered."

Such a silly thing, to be pleased over a compliment, yet it wasn't the compliment so much as the desire that accompanied it. For too long, her body had been nothing more than…

She refused to think about any of that now. Not with a rock-solid man in nothing but his boxers and dog tags wanting her every bit as much as she wanted him.

He rested his forehead on hers, his hands hooked low on her waist. "Are you okay with this? I mean physically."

Oh, Danny.

She should have remembered this man had a decidedly earthy, practical side. "Do you think I would come on to you like this if I didn't intend to follow through? And, while I appreciate that you're being careful, I'm finding it rather unromantic to talk about medical conditions right now."

He angled back, pensive Danny in a full-out think mode in direct contrast to an abandon-thought need she could feel hot and hard against her.

"Do you want romantic, 'Lise? Because I'm not much good at that. Never have been. I'm an inside-out-shirt kind of guy. Beer and chips on the beach. Blunt. And, yeah, once I've decided on a course I forget to ask if anyone else has input." He grimaced. "I believe some might even call it intellectual arrogance."

Guilt pinched over having tossed much those same sorts of words at him years ago to push him away. "You're also funny and have a tender heart under all those muscles."

She gave her hands free rein to rove his shoulders, trail forward to skim his dog tags, the light bristle of skin and man. Hard planes and tendons jumped under her fingers.

He rewarded her with a smile. "You've been checking out my muscles, have you?"

She slugged his shoulder. "And you're also a jerk sometimes."

"But you want me?"

Her fist unfurled on his bicep. "Yes, Danny, I do. Very much."

Looping her arms around his neck, she fell backward to drag him down with her on the bed. Waves rocked beneath them as the rest of their clothes found their way down, off, into the air.

Daniel eased over her, holding himself away with his elbows, air sliding between them. She wanted more. Forget his slow dictates.

She hooked her leg around his and knocked him off balance with the help of a rogue wave. He bolted from her, rolling to his side. She would have thought he didn't want this if it weren't for the trembling in his arms, muscles bunched from undeniable restraint.

"Danny? What's going on here?"

A broad hand grazed down her damp hair. "Hon, if you don't know that, then apparently I really didn't have a clue what the hell I was doing back then."

"You knew just fine." Although she had a feeling he knew a lot more now. A tingle of anticipation tripped up her spine, then back down again, sparking lower. Hotter. "And you're just arrogant enough to realize it. You never held back then, but you're holding back now."

"It's called self-control." With more of that agonizing precision, he untwisted a strand of hair from her hoop earring. "Something a guy that young doesn't always understand."

A giggle teased her throat, making her laugh all the more because she was *so* not a giggler. She'd forgotten how fun Danny could be in bed. She wanted that lightness, the ease of being with him.

Still, something wasn't quite right here. "You made me be honest with you. I expect the same."

His hand trekked into her hair, gathered up a fistful and cradled her against his chest. "I don't want to hurt you."

Her breath hitched in her chest. She'd thought her heart too worn to be hurt again. Could she have been wrong?

The ache of his leaving before crashed back, even when she knew she'd sent him on his way by accusing him of being all his father ever said. Not that she believed any of it. But she'd been so wounded by his obvious relief at freedom. And no matter how much she told herself otherwise, he had that power to hurt her again.

His fingers rubbed a sensuous massage into her scalp. "You can tell me all day long that you're fine. Kathleen could give me a freaking printout of your records, and that still wouldn't stop me from worrying about you."

Clarity dawned. He meant physically hurt, minor in comparison to what she'd been imagining. The body—so transient in comparison to the heart. The soul. Her emotions started to scramble her resolve, a mighty inconvenient occurrence with her naked body plastered to his.

She wanted this, damn it. He wanted this. After all they'd been through together, they deserved at least this much. And they deserved to enjoy it to the fullest.

"Do you remember what I said earlier?"

He stroked her hair back with a hand so tender she almost crumbled. "You said a lot of things, 'Lise."

Maybe too much. "I won't be relegated to passive roles."

Taking advantage of his surprise, she flipped him to his back.

Heat flamed his eyes to smoky black. She draped herself down and over Daniel, blanketing him with her body and hair just before she took his mouth. Searched deep and long, with all the pent-up need she yearned to pour all over him.

Groaning, he gripped her hips. "You want to be in control?"

She walked her fingers down his chest, lower, counting the ridged flexing of his stomach. "Do you have a problem with that?"

His heart slammed in his chest against her. "No, ma'am."

"I'm not going to break, Danny." Her hand dipped lower still until she encircled him, sheathed him in a condom with languorous strokes. "But I'm thinking it might be incredible to break your restraint."

His fingers flexed on her hips. "And I'm thinking you won't have to try very much."

She lowered herself onto him, took him into her body as once she'd taken him into her heart. Fully, the pressure of his presence within her maybe a bit too much at first until she adjusted to him being there again.

And then so very right she couldn't remember a time he hadn't been a part of her.

His head pressed back into the pillow, eyes closed, jaw clenched tight. She was damned tired of his restraint. She was tired of being half-alive.

She stopped. Waited.

Knees bracketing his hips, she stared down at him, suddenly realizing how much all that restraint cost him, because doing the same was killing her now.

His eyes opened and he stared back up at her. She brought her hands down to his chest, touched him with the same light caresses he'd given her, strokes that at first enticed, then grew progressively more frustrating.

With one teasing finger, she outlined his flat nipple, watching his eyes until… She pulled her hand away, circled her hips once. Stopped again.

His eyes widened then narrowed. Oh, yeah, he was on to her. And who would win? Hopefully both of them.

She could even see him smolder at the challenge. Their battle of wills continued with traded caresses that tempted without satisfying until…

With a growl of surrender that conversely brought his aggressive advance, he sat up. Mary Elise shifted her legs to wrap around his waist, welcome him in further, closer, wrenching another growl from low in his throat. He palmed her back, holding them chest to chest, heart to pounding heart as she glided down while he thrust up.

Restraints fell away. His. Hers. Until everything became *theirs* as they moved together in a frenzied pace of gasping breaths and demands.

His mouth closed over her breast, pulled, drew. The rock of waves beneath them increased the hot friction of skin against skin until she wasn't in control anymore. But then, neither was he.

His dog tags pressed, almost cut into her slick skin. Not that she could think or care, her mind focused totally on Daniel and completion.

Yet also not wanting that end and the afterward that would accompany it when they would have to face each other. Deal with the line they'd crossed that couldn't be retraced. Had she won or lost in demanding his surrender?

And then she couldn't think anymore, just felt the quickening of his pace, his heart, his heated breath against her flesh.

Her memory must have been faulty because no way could she have forgotten this. Knew she never would forget.

"Danny."

His name rode her scream of release. Her name swelled from his hoarse shout against her neck as he buried his face in her shoulder.

And echoing in her head with a resonation that soothed and excited and scared the hell out of her all at once, she heard…

Welcome home.

Daniel sprawled in the hammock, scanning the expanse of ocean in the fading light, his booted foot on the dirt nudging a lulling sway. Mary Elise lounged with her head at the opposite end, keeping watch over the other stretch of ocean. He drew lazy circles along her ankles and wondered when he'd developed a foot fetish. Of course, the woman did have pretty toes in those sandals.

Toes? He was in big trouble here.

As much as he'd enjoyed the hell out of Mary Elise when they'd been younger, this woman flattened him. There was an intensity about her now that demanded more from him than before.

And he didn't just mean in bed.

"I asked you a question, Daniel."

Man she had that schoolteacher tone down pat, and damned if he could remember the question because he'd been busy drooling over her feet.

"Danny?" She scooped up a pinecone and pelted him on the chest, dead center on his survival vest. "I'm tired of talking about me. What have you been doing with your life since finishing the Academy?''

Talk would be good, keep his mind on task rather than on thoughts of taking her back into the cabin.

But once the sun set… He cleared his throat and mind. Talk. ''I started out in a regular flying squadron—then became a test pilot with C-17s out at Edwards Air Force Base in California for a few years. Flew with all the newest cutting-edge gizmos on the planes. Figured out which ones worked, which ones didn't and why.''

''You enjoyed that.'' Her soft affirmation blended with the rustling branches and gushing waves.

''Oh, yeah.'' Almost as much as he would enjoy peeling those copper-colored shorts from her body in another hour.

''Sounds dangerous.''

''Sometimes.'' His thoughts skidded over to less tempting terrain. Would she run screaming from stories of his more-than-one emergency landing? Even a crash landing in the middle of the California desert?

''So you have connections.''

Her question yanked him back to the present. ''So you're a dog with a bone you're not letting go of.''

She toed him in the side. ''You're calling me a dog? First washed-out hag and now dog?''

He grabbed her foot in a firm hold before she could damage a kidney. ''You have the prettiest feet.''

She snorted.

Still, he couldn't unwrap his brain from the notion that his job bothered her, a problem he should have considered before. The stresses of military life had broken up plenty of marriages in the squadron.

Whoa. Marriage?

Wasn't he thinking about trying the dating thing as

grown-ups? Not that they'd ever really dated in the first place, just shot straight from pals to nonstop sex. The next logical step included taking things slow, spending time together, healing old wounds and progressing from there.

But he couldn't stop thinking about her old engagement ring in his flight suit pocket, his permanent reminder not to repeat past mistakes. Couldn't stop remembering what it had once looked like planted on Mary Elise's finger.

She scrunched her toes, drawing him from his haze. "Ouch," she squawked.

His hand jerked away from her foot. "Damn, 'Lise, I'm sorry."

"Gotcha!" She toed him in the side again, her gaze unrelenting. "I told you already. I'm not going to break."

He smiled. God, he loved her spunk, her steely will. This woman was far from breakable.

Memories bombarded him of their hours together, rediscovering each other on the water bed. The floor. The sofa. "I figured that out."

"I'm stronger out of bed, too. I realize there are things about your job you can't tell me. But don't hold back on what you *can* share because you're worried I'll turn all Victorian on you and you'll need smelling salts. Got it?"

He forestalled her lethal toe. "Yes, ma'am."

The ring in his pocket seemed to scorch a brand through the fabric and into his skin. If he even intended to consider those thoughts, then she needed to know more about him before they both landed in way over their heads. "About connections, let's just say once you get a high-security clearance for one mission they tend to tap you for other missions since you're already in the loop."

"And you enjoy that," she answered with understanding and no censure.

"Oh, yeah."

Her fingers trekked inside the leg of his flight suit, scratched along his calf. "And you enjoy that?"

"Oh, yeah," he repeated. "I think I could really get into this shared control gig."

Next thing he knew, he had the ring out of his pocket and wasn't sure who was more shocked, him or Mary Elise.

Her hand flew out of his pants leg. "You kept it."

He worked the solitaire between two fingers until the diamond caught the fading sunlight, casting multifaceted sparks. "So I wouldn't forget what a relationship screwup I am like my father."

"Danny," her fingers slid to his knee, "you made a single mistake at twenty-one. For God's sake, that doesn't make you like your father."

"I don't do relationships well, never have. There are plenty of women besides you who can attest to that. And just look at the mess with my father."

"He was proud of you."

Daniel jammed the ring back in his pocket where it could brand a reminder he needed before he ended up doing something totally illogical like asking this woman to marry him. "So damned much he didn't trust me enough to tell me when you came to Rubistan."

"I told him not to."

"So?" If that sounded arrogant, big freaking deal. His father should have called him, anyway.

"I wasn't in a good place right then." She plucked a leaf from a low-hanging branch, crumpled it in her hand.

"I can understand having someone try to kill you must have been rattling as hell. All the more reason extra support and protection should have been a good thing."

"Not just that." She studied him for four lazy swishes of the Pawley's hammock, her fist further mangling the leaf. "How much did you learn about endometriosis on the Internet while I was sleeping?"

"What makes you think—" He swung his foot back up on the hammock. "Ah hell, you used to do that when we were kids, too, read my mind and then follow me right into my messes. Yeah, I did some reading, wanted to understand how to help you. Where's the crime in that?"

"You can back off the defensive, Baker. I just wanted to confirm you have a core knowledge here."

He gave her a simple nod. This was obviously tough enough for her. He didn't want to make it worse by shoving his boot in his mouth.

"Then you know the more scar tissue that builds up, the more difficult it is to conceive, which explains how it was easier for me to become pregnant when I younger. But then in some cases with endometriosis, even if pregnancy occurs, the body—" she unfurled her fist and let the wind carry away the shredded leaf "—my body can be a hostile environment. Miscarriage rates are higher."

Hostile environment? He could hear too well the repeat of McRae's propaganda crap.

"After three more miscarriages, I told Kent I'd had enough. Enough of the doctors and hormone injections and surgeries. I just wanted a baby. I really thought he was okay with adoption." Her head fell back against the webbed ropes. "God, he had me fooled."

Her eyes slid away from him for the first time, which should have been a warning to prepare himself. But thinking about himself was the least of his concerns right now. He lifted her cold hand from her side and linked their fingers. A damned paltry offering, but all he could think of at the moment.

"Kent swapped my birth control pills for placebos. I got pregnant." Her flat tones carried on the wind, the hollow tones of a person with no tears left. "After all those treatments, for some damned reason I finally conceived on my own again. And then I made it past my first trimester. That had never happened before. The hope was…worse than anything else."

His gut twisted. Tight. Already he could see where this was going. It hurt like hell to breathe just thinking of what she'd been through. Images of their one lost baby had haunted him for a year. How much more had she suffered?

Alone.

"At twenty-four weeks, I gave birth to a stillborn son."

Her words gut punched him. Even expecting it hadn't prepped him for the silent ache radiating from her. Nothing could have.

Here he'd been arrogant in wondering if she could handle hearing about his freaking job, and he was the one who damn well couldn't breathe. At least he had his head together enough to know she wasn't ready for him to talk or ask questions. She needed him to listen. He could do that much.

He should have been in her life to do so much more, but he'd been too busy staying out of Savannah because he didn't want to run into Mrs. Kent McRae.

"I overheard him with my damn traitorous doctor. Heard what they'd done to me with swapping the birth control pills." Her voice faltered for the first time. "What they intended to try again." One shaky breath and she continued, "I put on my clothes, walked out of the hospital and left Kent. Once the divorce was final, he tried to kill me."

Rage, barely banked from the day before, exploded within him, riding a silent curse and vow to send Kent McRae straight to hell.

Her fingers tightened around his. "No, I really wasn't

in very good shape when I arrived in Rubistan. And your father just put his hand on my shoulder and told me it would be okay.''

Waves echoed in the background for five gushes, six, seven and with each one, Daniel thanked his father for giving her that calm acceptance, that quiet strength that he never would have been able to manage. Nothing else mattered.

''He seemed to know the right balance to strike between helping me and urging me to do for myself. Giving me room to heal, room to grow.'' Her thumb brushed his wrist. ''No offense my dear friend, but, Danny, you would have taken over, and I wouldn't have been strong enough to stand up to you then. And maybe I was prideful in not wanting you to see me like that. Weak.''

His fingers tightened around hers. Damn staying quiet. He wouldn't let her buy into any more of McRae's garbage. ''Weak is the last word I would ever apply to you.''

''Thank you.'' She squeezed his hand back. ''I asked your father once why he never told you where I was. He said he'd learned the hard way about letting a person find their own path in the world.''

And in a flash of intuition Daniel had only just begun to acquire from his own brief stint at parenting the boys, he understood. His father had been making amends. Making peace through Mary Elise.

Daniel stopped fighting with his father's shadow long enough to identify his own. ''I'm glad he was there for you.''

And he meant it.

She nodded. Spent.

''Come here.'' He opened his arms.

She smiled one of those gentle Mary Elise smiles he'd

once thought whimsical. Now he knew they held more strength than most combat veterans.

"I'm not about to fall apart, Danny."

"I know. Come here, anyway."

She crawled up the hammock until she tucked in beside him. Her head fell to rest on his shoulder, over his heart that wasn't as numb as he'd thought.

Well, hell. He wasn't emotionally unavailable at all. His emotions were in total and complete working order. They'd just been in deep freeze from the moment he made the mistake of walking away from this woman.

Now he felt it all churn to life inside him. Her pain was his. His heart was hers.

He wouldn't have a second chance with his father, but his father had given him a second chance with Mary Elise. He only had to figure out how to win her back, how to be the man she deserved. Because no way in hell could he lose her again.

Chapter 15

Mary Elise flung her arm over her eyes, even though little light filtered from the moon into the cabin, and tugged the sheet higher. It inched down again.

God, Danny was a covers hog. Except she couldn't remember him going to sleep after they'd made love again.

Hmm. She snuggled deeper under the sheet. Now there was a beautiful thought to savor, the way they'd come together after their discussion on the hammock.

At first she'd been worried he would stomp around, angry at Kent, or push her to talk. Instead he'd just let them both find escape from the roar of emotions through great sex. Awesome sex. Can't-imagine-it-ever-being-that-incredible-again sex.

Wrapped in her memories—if not that darned slippery sheet—Mary Elise mentally listed ways to torment Danny in turn later.

A warm tickle teased along her stomach, whisper thin and…smelling of strawberries?

Her eyes snapped open. Daniel stood over her. Gloriously naked and obviously very happy to see her. Sheet in one hand, jar of preserves in the other, he poured a thin stream of the warmed syrup onto her. Warm?

Danny grinned. "Wonders of the microwave."

Oh, my. Anticipation curled within her. Curious as to how far he would take this, she sank back, even arched into the flow.

He drizzled higher up her body, closer, until with perfect aim, he tipped one breast, then the other. Her nipples tightened under the teasing torment of the heated liquid and Daniel's unrelenting gaze. Her hand drifted up, her body languid.

She swiped a finger through the sugary red thread, traced the hot length of him, tasted.

A growl tore from his throat. Daniel dropped the sheet and straddled her in a clean move. "Good morning."

And it was—for the first time in too long. She tore open a condom with lightning speed and sheathed him. "I sure do like the spin you put on breakfast in bed."

Daniel dipped a finger into the soupy preserves pooled in the hollow of her belly and drew a circle. Then again. Until she tuned in to the pattern of him swirling her initials against her oversensitized skin.

"I may not do romance well, 'Lise, but I do know about thorough, mathematical attention to detail."

"Details. I like your details."

"What else do you like? Maybe I could make a list of all the things I plan to do to you." He continued to write a veritable epistle on her body with bold fingers inking red strokes over her, all of her. "Or maybe you could make a list for me of everything you want, everything you need."

Playfulness lit his eyes, tinged with a deeper intensity,

even an agenda of some kind. Just a byproduct of maturity? The old Danny blending with the new? Visions of him pulling the ring out of his pocket earlier edged into her mind with thoughts of the past and future.

The flicker of nerves tickling her stomach had nothing to do with syrup. While she might be finding her footing in regaining her sense of self, there was only so much a person could handle in a few short days.

And at the moment Danny was giving her all she could handle…and more. She'd faced so many life-changing decisions in the past month, she wanted, needed a brief respite of light, simple.

This.

The rest would have to be faced eventually. If nothing else, she'd learned from the past months a person couldn't run forever. Right now she wanted to embrace Danny's playfulness and ignore the niggling questions in his eyes and her nervous belly.

Daniel watched Mary Elise's eyes slide closed, pleasure flushing her skin almost as rosy as the thin sheen of syrup. Victory chugged through him. He wanted her so hot for him she couldn't remember anything or anyone else. He wanted to drive them both into forgetfulness until he evaded the impending sense of doom dogging his steps. Not so much over McRae. That battle he could fight with strategy and logic and tangible defenses.

But he couldn't shake the fear that had gripped him once he acknowledged his feelings for Mary Elise. The risk of losing her multiplied tenfold without any formula or equation for what he could do to keep her.

This freaking intuitive crap was driving him nuts. And the best he could come up with was a damned heated jar of jelly to mark her.

"Well, 'Lise, my list would include everything I find

totally hot about you.'' With dabs of jelly on his fingertip, he stroked, claimed her as his to touch, taste. Love. ''But I need you to let me know what you want.''

The million-dollar question.

''All of that. I adore it when—'' her words jumbled over themselves in nonsensical affirmations ''—I really like it when you…''

He filled her.

''Yes.'' A purr vibrated her chest against his. ''When you do that.''

He moved again. And again, all the while grappling for self-control, a damned elusive commodity around Mary Elise.

Love wasn't easy and warm like friendship. This gripped him and held him as firmly as her body gliding against his, faster, leaving him no choice but to just move with it, with her, because he'd tried running, only to find she would always be a part of him, anyway.

He gritted his teeth against release, waiting, watching her, touching until he saw, heard her unravel in his arms. Her purr swelled into a cry of pleasure so sweet he waited until the last echoes faded from his head before he cut the bands of control, surrendered to a flat spin fall, ending in an explosion of emotion and raw need.

Each slug of his heart taunted him. No, he wouldn't walk away, but this new Mary Elise had a will of steel he couldn't bend, and this time he could be the one left behind.

Mary Elise perched on a bar stool, monitoring the two laptop computers while Danny took a power nap on the sofa. He'd vowed no way would he be able to drift off in the water bed scented with strawberries and sex.

She smiled. She was officially a strawberry addict.

The computers hummed reassurance beside her with video views of sunrise filtering over the trees, the marshy beach clear except for the occasional pelican or egret scrounging for breakfast. Alarms stayed silent.

Quiet settled, deep and odd after so long on the run with fear roaring in her ears. For the first time since she'd found that hypodermic needle in her bag, she allowed herself to contemplate a future beyond the cabin. She thought…and came up blank. She knew all the logical answers, but taking the last step toward them seemed a bigger stretch than everything that had come before.

Because of everything that had come before with Danny.

Start small. Think about basics. She picked up an ink pen and pad, paused, exchanged the blue ballpoint for a red pen, strawberry red. Surely that was a good omen to use for making a list of the things she would need to do to reestablish her life. Where?

Charleston?

Logically, yes. She loved Danny. Now admitted she always had. How could she not? She loved the boys too. So why the can't-breathe feeling constricting her chest?

The last step stretched further in front of her.

With Kent out of the way, she wouldn't have any more excuses. She would have to face Danny. Face herself. Face risking forever with someone. She should be rejoicing.

Instead she was scared to death.

It was one thing to dream of a future, another to actually live it. Risk it.

And therein lay her core fear—how much it would hurt to fail with him again. Taking Danny's diamond solitaire off her finger had been hell before. This time her emotions went well beyond the teenage swells of first love that had characterized her feelings for him a decade ago.

Her hand slowed on the paper. She glanced down at her list of things to accomplish, things she wanted to tell the boys. Her hand stopped altogether. How strange. Her list had taken on a more conversational tone than a note written in bullet statements.

Slowly she began adding connector phrases, and a letter to Trey and Austin took shape. She let the words flow into a second letter, this time to her parents. Another to Kent that left her hand shaking.

She was writing, certainly not anything like the editorials she'd once written in hope of shaping readers' thoughts and politics. But words poured from her fingers in a healing balm she'd denied herself as if denying the need for a cure negated the ailment.

Time melded into a stack of papers scattering the counter, even the floor around her feet as she wrote to everyone.

Except Daniel.

Words failed her there. She let the half-spent pad of paper fall to her lap and studied him instead. Arms folded tightly over his chest, he didn't seem to be in the least relaxed. She would have thought him awake if it weren't for the soft snore and the quirky twitch of his booted foot propped on the end of the sofa.

That hint of movement spoke of restless dreams. Her fault, no doubt. She considered nudging him, but he needed the sleep, restless though it was, to prep for possible waking nightmares later outside.

Setting the notebook aside, she walked around the edge of the sofa to sit cross-legged on the rug beside him. Her hand lifted, carefully. She smoothed his hair back, and when he didn't stir, stroked again and again until his foot slowed.

Would he have let her soothe him if he'd been awake?

Part of her shouted to quit with the psychobabble self-analysis and grab at this chance for happiness. Once upon a time she would have, except this newer Daniel had reminded her she should expect more from life, herself. Even him.

And if the pushing for more shoved him away again? Her foot twitched this time at even the thought of losing him. If only he would tell her what rumbled around in that thick, dear head of his, maybe then she wouldn't be so afraid of that last step.

Leaning forward on her knees, she brushed her lips to his brow and let the bottled words flow free, an easy enough risk while he slept. "I love you, Danny Baker."

"I love you, Danny Baker."

Daniel forgot to tread, almost choked on a gulp of chlorinated water, before he made his feet move again. "Uh, me, too."

Correct response, right? He was going to be her husband in four days. So, sure, he loved her, too.

Damn. Except he didn't know what the hell he was feeling these days, mostly just putting one foot in front of the other. Marching, focused on the steps like in PT training or cadence calls in formation.

Daniel slid his hands down Mary Elise's slick sides, bared by her bikini, leaned to kiss her so they wouldn't have to talk anymore. Laughing, she ducked away at the last second, diving beneath him. He took chase, both knowing she wouldn't get far, but still enjoying the ritual of their water games. Why did things have to change?

He had his application to the University of Georgia

ready to hand-carry to the dean, with his father's help—a fact that chewed his pride almost as much as leaving the Academy when he'd reached his senior year. Another administrative mess his father would have to smooth over.

Only four more days and it would all be real, marriage, different college...baby on the way.

For now he just wanted to pretend he was home for the summer. Of course his newly invented reality would still include sex with Mary Elise. He sure didn't want to backtrack that far.

But marriage. Kid. Love. That had him cricking his tense neck to the side.

Four days. He kicked through the clear waters, deeper, until there was nowhere left to go, and still he could hear her declaration of love echo in his ears. Same words he'd heard his parents say to each other.

Damned if he'd seen any example of love lasting.

He preferred what he and Mary Elise had and he didn't want to screw it up. Crap. He was acting like a whiny kid rather than an adult. Get it together, Baker.

Daniel kicked upward, snagging Mary Elise and drawing them both to the surface. "Gotcha."

"What do you plan to do with me, Danny?"

"This." He drew her closer, brushed her bikini-clad breasts against his bare chest, eliciting a rewarding purr. He cupped a breast—fuller, more sensitive. The pregnancy thing had definite side benefits, like the visit from the oh-so-generous Breast Fairy.

"Danny," Mary Elise panted against his mouth.

"Pool house, or take a drive and park. Your choice, but make the decision fast." He prayed for the pool house. Closer. Sooner.

She stiffened against him. "Danny, I'm not feeling too good. Something's wrong..."

Daniel struggled to pull himself awake. Awake? But he was in the pool with Mary Elise.

Reality and dreams mussed. He wanted out of the pool or the dream or wherever the hell he was before the rest of the events unfolded: Mary Elise wrapping an arm around her stomach, a drive in the car that hadn't led to parking but instead to the emergency room.

He forced his feet to keep treading water as if that could stave off the end, keep them both from moving to the end of everything. Their baby. Them.

Water churned around them, someone else in the pool, beneath, drawing near Mary Elise to take her, blasting to the surface...

Kent McRae.

Daniel bolted upright on the sofa.

Dragging a hand over his face, he shook off the nightmare fog.

Mary Elise sat cross-legged on the floor beside him, hands in her lap, emerald eyes wide with worry. ''Are you okay?''

He nodded, throat still too tight for talk. Swinging his boots to the floor with a thud, he braced his elbows on his knees and sucked in air, steadied his heartbeat. He kept his hands clasped between his knees rather than gathering Mary Elise hard against his chest to feel her warm and alive against him. ''I'm fine.''

''Bad dreams suck.''

Leave it to Mary Elise not to let him dodge the issue by pretending. ''Yep.''

''You've had a lot on your plate lately, too, not just the boys, but losing your father, not even being able to make the memorial service for closure.''

Death wasn't high on his list of topics for discussion, the word riding too hard on the heels of a time he'd thought Mary Elise might die. The doctor may have called it a routine, first trimester miscarriage. But the doctor hadn't been the one carrying her across the yard to the car while she cried in pain.

Daniel stared at his clenched hands and remembered the weight of Mary Elise in his arms. His father had met him at the emergency room, silent but there. Odd how he'd forgotten that part over the years. "I'll always regret that he and I didn't have a chance to talk."

"Life can change so fast. And when I think of how close I came to being in the car with him that day…"

Daniel's mind raced back to the present. "What?"

"I was supposed to be with your father the day he died. I had a doctor visit in town, but had to cancel it at the last minute because of an emergency teacher's meeting. Your father decided to take his wife along instead, make a day of it and see if they could start working though their problems."

Her words nailed him like relentless mortar rounds. How she should have been in the car. McRae's money transfer to Rubistan shortly before. Daniel blanked his face and prayed she wouldn't draw inferences. He should have known better.

All too soon, dawning horror stained her face. "You don't think? Kent couldn't have been responsible. Could he? Oh, God, Danny, please don't let me have caused your father's death."

Think before opening the yap, Baker.

He forced his mind to work, remember that she needed to be a part of whatever happened. A tough-as-hell thing to do when his instincts blared for him to lock her in the bathroom and barricade her there while he stood between her and the rest of the world.

"Stop looking for trouble, Mary Elise. Ammar makes

the more likely suspect if my father's death wasn't an accident. Killing my father would give Ammar control over the widow, the boys and all their inherited money.'' His conscience kicked him, reminded him of Mary Elise's insistence on no more passive roles. Damn it, he just wanted to keep her safe. His conscience gave him another hefty punt. ''But it's possible he could have been working with McRae.''

''How so?''

''McRae has been funneling money into the Middle East underworld. The FBI has already been alerted.''

''Terrorism?''

''That. And Rubistan is one of the largest suppliers of opium. There are any number of likelihoods. But yes, I think McRae tracked you. And I think it's possible he and Ammar hooked up.'' Daniel paused, ready to pull her close if she fell apart, wondered if he was a sick bastard for wanting the excuse to hold her.

Mary Elise blinked once, tears glinting but not falling, then nodded for him to continue.

''Regardless, I think Ammar was gunning for my father.''

''And Kent would have found help even without Ammar.''

''Exactly.''

The glaze of tears disappeared, replaced by a different glint altogether. Suspicion. ''When did you find out about the overseas transactions?''

Damn. ''Yesterday.''

''Last night?''

Baker, you are so busted. ''Yesterday morning.''

Silently she stood, walked away from him, made a freaking production out of straightening a stack of papers by the computers.

"Go ahead and say it, 'Lise."

"Obviously, I don't need to." The papers slid from her hands in a scattered mess, making lie of her seeming calm.

Not unlike the mess he was making of this conversation. "You'll feel better if you chew me out."

A dry smile twitched as she collected the pages. "I doubt it."

Talk, damn it. Shout. Care enough to fight back so he would have a clue what she was thinking. Then he could plan a counter-defense. Strategize so they wouldn't self-destruct their relationship this time.

He shot to his feet. His boots traced a restless path on the hardwood floor, across the brown braid rug, back and forth in front of the stone fireplace. He needed action. Decisions. All the waiting and inaction left him with too much time to think about the past.

Flashes of his nightmare had him ready to snap like one of those trip wires strung under the cabin. Watching her distance herself from him didn't help. He needed reassurance she wouldn't bolt, not a helluva lot to ask.

Damn it, he wanted to lock her up tight beside him so he wouldn't have to worry about her day and night. "We should probably try to find something in the same school district so the boys aren't uprooted again."

"What?" She tucked the papers in her suitcase.

He paced over to the computers, checked again, found the same uninhabited security picture of sunrise filtering over the deserted beach. Nothing but a pelican and some egrets hunting for breakfast. Alarms stayed silent.

Action. Even a simple e-mail from Max would give him something to do. He would settle for anything that would make him shut up before his rambling mouth pushed her away for good. "A house on the water is out of my price range, but then with Austin around, it wouldn't really be safe or practical long-term, anyway. Buying an older home, we can get more space, but then I don't want you to be stuck dealing with the extra repairs when I'm TDY."

"Daniel."

"Yeah, 'Lise?"

"Slow down." Her hand fell to his arm.

"Oh, yeah, right." He dropped onto a bar stool, his booted foot twitched on the lowest rung. Tap. Tap.

"I didn't mean your pacing."

"Oh." He frowned. What the hell had he been saying anyway? Something about house hunting, an attempt at making something happen to relieve the stretched-taut in-action when what he really wanted was to nail McRae to the wall.

And to make Mary Elise stay. Houses. Duh. His subconscious was having a field day with him. Way to steamroll the woman. "Hang on a second. I think I know what I'm supposed to say here. Uh, what kind of house do *you* want?"

She perched on the other stool beside him, her hands gliding up his thighs in an obvious attempt to distract him. "Danny, this isn't the time to take such a big step with life decisions."

"Why the hell not?" His frustrations swelled to the surface, inconvenient as hell when he knew calm would work better. But his feelings for Mary Elise were anything but placid. "Is it my job? I know the gun safe and the traps freaked you out. Damn, Mary Elise, I realize I'm not offering you much of a deal here, but I'll do my best to make it work for you. I can even back off the secret stuff, stick with more straightforward missions."

He trailed his fingers down a strand of her auburn hair as if he could bind her to him, pull her slim body to him and give her something to do with their mouths so she would quit worrying her rings in circles around her fingers.

"It's not your job. God, I know it's a part of you." She stroked up to his chest, tracing his collar, dipping inside to hook in his dog tags, tug him forward. "And if this past year has taught me anything, I know that life is dangerous no matter what you do. We should live to the fullest."

"Exactly." He manacled her wrist in his grip. "I understand that logic and facts indicate I'm not the best bet for the long haul, but determination can't be gauged, and damn it, I'm hell-bent set on making this work. So why are you holding back from me again?"

Her hand fell to her lap. "Why is it that if someone doesn't go along with your way, then they're holding back?"

Echoes of other arguments pummeled him, nose-to-nose battles with his father, defensive confrontations with the squadron commander. But, damn it, those had been different situations. "Do you love me?"

Where the hell had that come from? His dream.

"Yes."

Say it back, dumb ass. "Then what exactly did I offer up that was so hell-fire terrible? A house?" He fished in his sleeve pocket and pulled out the solitaire. "Or God forbid I should give you a ring."

He held it with two fingers, a silent question between them. Say it back, Baker. His mouth stayed closed.

She folded her hands over his, held his hands in hers without taking the ring. At least she wasn't shoving it in his face. Yet.

"Danny, think. I told you I love you. And I know you love me, too, even if you can't push the words out. I hear you, anyway. I only asked for space.'' She knocked on his forehead. ''Hello? Why does it have to be all or nothing, black or white with you?''

''Seems pretty clear cut to me. Yeah, you're right.'' He said the damn words, ridiculous to hide from them, anyway. ''I love you, too. So either you want to marry me or you don't.''

The words burned his throat, but they were out there like a big purple polka-dot elephant between them they'd been trying to ignore all morning.

''It's not as simple as a ring and love, or everything would have worked out eleven years ago. Why are you just assuming that if my timetable doesn't fit yours I must not want you at all? Maybe I want to take the next two months and go ice fishing.''

''Do you?''

''No. Maybe. I don't know. And that's my whole point. You're pushing too hard, too fast for me right now. I'm not like you, feetfirst jumping in. All I'm asking is that we table this discussion, and then take it slow once we get back to it again. Okay?''

The computer dinged behind him with incoming mail.

Damn. He'd wanted answers from Max, but why couldn't the guy have hit send on the e-mail five minutes prior and saved him from landing in this hellacious conversation? How many times did this woman have to shove the ring back in his face before he got the message?

Daniel jammed the solitaire in his pocket and opened the post from Max.

''Ammar has entered the U.S. Wren and I have the boys locked down and safe.''

Trey and Austin's uncle in the States? Warning bells clanged in his mind, louder, until he realized they were merely an echo of the alarm from the security computer.

Someone had breached the first line of defense.

Chapter 16

Mary Elise stared at the security computer, monitor images of the yard still uninhabited except for gulls. Alarm silent now. Except for in her head where the alarm still blared and the memory of Daniel slipping off into the band of oaks and pines stayed imprinted.

Of course it made sense that she shouldn't go with him. She didn't have the training to move silently enough to stay undetected. She would be a liability to him out in the open.

According to logical Danny, she should stay here, locked down tight behind a dead bolt with her loaded gun. Still, the situation chafed.

Nerves tangled into a snarl that rivaled her hair after a shower. Fear gummed the tangle to near unmanageable levels. Why had she wasted time arguing with Danny? Why couldn't she have waited to make her damned stand for independence—all because she was scared of taking a final step?

Stay calm. The alarm could be nothing worse than a rowdy raccoon setting off a trip wire. Right?

One really heavy raccoon.

If only she could do something besides stare at the freaking computer screen. She hated the inaction.

Well, hell. She was starting to sound like Danny. Part of her wanted to be just like him, able to dive into a situation, completely confident in her judgment. Sure, Danny was a little arrogant. But, doggone him, he was usually right.

And to give him credit, he was trying to include her. Once confronted, he shared more about tracking Kent's finances, working through Ammar's possible connection together when he could have bluffed his way through.

So why the knee-jerk need to pull back from Daniel?

Intellectually she knew he wasn't a threat to her independence. He might get angry and stomp around, but the man eventually listened. He cared.

Danny's words in the car tripped through her mind, his confusion about her reluctance to go for even a simple doctor visit. The answer sidled past her defenses with blinding clarity.

Those doctor visits symbolized weakness to her, and above all she couldn't bear to be weak, dependant. Just as it didn't help denying herself the healing balm of words to negate there was even a problem, staying away from Danny couldn't protect her from the risk of loving him.

The rest of the answer followed in a rush, now that her defenses had been breached. Sharing burdens didn't equate loss of control or weakness, with the right person by her side.

With Danny by her side.

His innate honor, his ever-logical sense of fairness

would make him a man to trust. He might not always agree with her, but he would listen to her. Respect her.

Love her.

How strange that Danny with his black-and-white reasoning helped her see the shades of gray to find the formula for making it all work. She sank back on the stool, exhausted and exhilarated all at once.

A flicker of movement on the screen snagged her attention. Danny?

Nerves drew taut, near to breaking. The figure cleared the trees. Not Danny.

Kent.

Icy pinpricks tingled over her scalp.

Her ex-husband stepped deeper into the clearing. Closer to her hiding place in the cabin. Sunlight played dappled shadows over his blond perfection. She'd once found the dimple in his chin endearing, his classic looks and clean-cut appearance safe.

She'd been so horribly wrong.

Bile roiled up her throat. Swaying, she gripped the edge of the counter. He stared at the cabin, eyes intense, as if he knew.

Of course he knew she was inside.

Oh, God, where was Danny? He couldn't be dead. She refused to believe that. What the hell should she do?

Kent pulled his hand out of his pants pocket, his fingers clenched around a rock-size object. Her methodical, understated ex couldn't have a grenade. Something so overt—so messy—wouldn't be Kent's style.

Still, she winced. Zoomed in with the camera and saw...a piece of paper banded around some kind of weight.

With a gentle underhand toss, Kent lobbed it onto the

porch. Mary Elise heard the thud echo in stereo from outside and through the computer's speaker.

He raised his hand, waved once in a mocking salute and waited.

She shifted on the bar stool, trying like crazy to adopt Daniel's logic and blend it with her own intuition about the madman she'd married. Stepping outside would be reckless, and undoubtedly Danny would be furious with her.

Unless Kent had already—

She sliced that thought away. Damn it, she couldn't even consider that, because then she couldn't think at all.

But what if Daniel had been hurt? Time became crucial. Or worse, what if he hadn't even discovered Kent as of yet and stumbled on him unaware? She knew with a certainty born of both intuition and logic that Kent was well armed in some fashion. Perhaps he had backup lurking in the cover of trees waiting to take her out while he watched.

Certainly a possibility. In which case Daniel would stumble on two people unaware. Which left her with only one choice. She would have to alert Daniel. All she needed was a single warning shout. Or shot.

The past year had taught her she could survive almost anything. But she knew without question, she wouldn't survive seeing Daniel die.

Daniel stared down at the dead body at his feet.

The Javaro paddle dangled from the rope, deactivated. The dead man's unblinking stare made checking for a pulse unnecessary. Problem was, the paddle hadn't killed him. A bullet through the temple from someone else's gun had, someone with a silencer, since he hadn't heard a shot.

All of which meant another armed party lurked out

there. Searching for Mary Elise. And the dead man couldn't help with any information, most likely the reason he'd been silenced once injured.

Daniel shifted the weight of the .45 in his hand. He didn't need to check the man for identification, either. The frozen face below was a direct mirror of one of the mug shots he'd pulled up from intelligence files.

The assassin who'd been hired to kill Mary Elise a year ago.

The dead bastard lying on the ground had been used the way sacrificial troops were run through land mines to clear the field for the next line to march through. Scanning the trees, the path, Daniel found disturbed pine straw continuing down the path. Toward the cabin.

Mary Elise.

A shot split the air.

He flattened to the ground, rolled to the side and steadied his gun in a fluid move. Nothing. Nobody in sight. Crouching, he darted through the trees, dried leaves crunching beneath his feet.

His heart pounded in time with his feet. Damn it, how could things have gone to hell so fast. What could he have done differently? He searched his mind—and came up with zip. Other than the fact he'd been lured out, separated from Mary Elise.

He'd expected McRae to be devious. He hadn't expected tactical savvy.

Of course he should have, if he'd listened to Mary Elise. The commander's warning from only days prior thundered through his head. Every flyer faced the possibility of meeting a missile some day.

His death he could face. Mary Elise's was unacceptable.

Daniel drew closer to the cabin. Voices carried on the

wind. Mary Elise's. Relief hammered him until he almost forgot to make his feet keep moving.

Another voice drifted. Male. The cabin showed through the cover of trees.

Mary Elise eased down the porch steps, gun drawn and steady on the man standing with his back to Daniel.

Good girl. She had McRae cornered, withstanding whatever garbage the bastard was pouring her way in his relentless talking, and holding her own.

Daniel strode closer, sight line clearing. A tie flapped over the man's shoulder, jacket long gone but white shirt a crisp beacon—with the harsh slash of a gun tucked in the waistband out of sight to Mary Elise.

Daniel stopped cold.

He couldn't let her see him now. If Mary Elise called a greeting, thinking she had McRae safely pinned, the bastard would have time to draw.

To shoot. Her.

Daniel blinked as if he could change the hell in front of him. He'd been so damned sure he could protect her. Of course he'd been concerned about injuries, but never, never had he allowed himself to consider that she could die.

Mary Elise dead.

The past and present merged in a blaze of reds—her hair, strawberries, blood. In the middle of the roaring fury, it hit him, why he'd run so hard from her eleven years ago. He hadn't run from commitment, or even from admitting how much she meant to him. Hell, he'd already realized now how damned much he loved her then. How much he loved her now.

He'd run because he was afraid of losing her.

And damned if he hadn't fallen right back into old patterns by picking a fight with her in the cabin. They'd

almost replayed the past all over again—the mistakes for-
givable in their youth but totally asinine now, given they
should know better. Be stronger. Wiser.

Ah, hell. Love wasn't wise, either.

But love did make a person stronger. He just prayed it
would make Mary Elise strong enough to stand down a
madman until he could come forward with reinforcements.

Training overrode emotions. Crouching low, Daniel
made his way around the perimeter of trees, dodging
through whatever cover he could to work his way closer.
He would have to take out McRae, but it would have to
be fast.

Daniel assessed the terrain. Counted steps. Organized
the plan of attack in his head.

He inched forward, eyes trained so firmly on McRae
he almost missed the flash of movement to his left.

Pivoting, he brought his arm up to defend his face just
as a knife came slashing down. Burned. Knocked the gun
from his hand. "What the—"

"Where are they?" Ammar asked in heavily accented
English, eyes wild with fanaticism. "Where are the
boys?"

Mary Elise stepped deeper into the yard, prayed, inched
another step, Kent subtly moving toward her every time
she did. Closer to the buried bucket trap.

If only she could keep him talking. Good Lord, why
had she never realized how much this man liked the sound
of his own voice?

"You still haven't unwrapped my gift, Mary Elise.
How rude."

Her fingers convulsed around the crystal paperweight

clenched in her fist, the paper crackling around it. No, she hadn't dared do anything after scooping it from the porch.

Was he trying to distract her so he could launch forward?

She locked her gaze with Kent's when she desperately wanted to look down for affirmation on the placement of the submerged spike trap.

God, she hoped her peripheral vision and memory were on target. She needed him disabled, couldn't risk him overpowering her, because heaven help her, she wasn't sure she could actually shoot him. "How about I check it out after you're in jail?"

"That's no fun." He tugged his tie back over his shoulder, tiny pelicans traipsing their pattern across blue silk. "Remember how much you enjoyed seeing me open this for my birthday? The bearer of gifts enjoys watching the receiver unwrap the present almost as much as selecting it." A slow smile crept across his face. "I enjoyed watching you find my other gift, the plant. You knew it was from me, didn't you?"

"You really are a twisted bastard." She willed her feet to adjust closer to the nearest bucket.

"And you're illogical. Old territory. Move on. Did you like the other gifts? The syringe? The fertility clinic flyer in Baker's mail?"

Flyer? Her mind winged back to the stack of junk mail in Daniel's condo on the coffee table, how he'd fidgeted with it after she'd told him about Kent.

Oh, Daniel. Always trying to flipping protect her.

Damn it, she absolutely refused to let Kent anywhere near him. Hatred spiked sarcasm. "As always, Kent, you're too generous."

His smile widened without reaching his eyes. "I do

miss your wit. Now, open your present and I'll tell you whether your lover is alive or dead.''

A frigid fist closed around her heart. She knew Kent was playing with her like a cat tormenting a mouse. And she wouldn't be a mouse. She would play his game and win.

Keeping one hand steady on the gun, and her eyes glued to him, she worked the paper free of the band around the weight. Thicker paper than she'd originally thought. She raised it and glanced at the last thing she would have expected. *Oh, God.*

Her fingers clenched around the funeral mass card for her stillborn child.

Cold hatred iced through her, although she wouldn't give Kent the satisfaction of seeing he'd stabbed her clean through. She thought perhaps she could shoot Kent after all. Fighting back for herself wasn't near as easy as fighting for her child.

Maternal instincts swelled further, encompassing Trey and Austin, demanding retribution for the fear this man had brought down upon *her* boys by working with their uncle. How dare he force Trey and Austin into hiding? Fury clogged her throat.

''It seems only right that you have one, too, since you left everything behind when you ran from me.''

She cleared the haze of emotions and adjusted another inch to the left. *Move, Kent. Move.* ''I didn't run from you. I ran *to* life. Something you could never understand.''

Her finger itched on the trigger until logic teased, reminding her if she gunned him down in cold blood she would be no better than him.

That argument almost swayed her. Almost.

Then logic pushed further that she owed it to Trey,

Austin, Danny to be a stronger person. As much as she wanted vengeance, her life was inexplicably woven with theirs. And that surrender made her all the stronger.

She took a bold step forward toward the trap, placing her within touching distance of pure evil.

Kent lunged.

An explosion of motion from the trees behind him yanked her vision up.

Danny?

Kent grabbed her wrist, twisted, squeezed. Her gun went flying.

She screamed. Jerked, yet was unable to take her eyes off Danny locked in hand-to-hand battle with a knife-wielding foreigner. Blood stained both of them. From which one?

Bodies shifted, revealing a face she'd hoped never again to see outside of Rubistan.

Ammar.

Daniel gripped both of the man's arms, brought his knee up, Ammar twisting to dodge. The man's heavily accented curse floated on the air. "That McRae bitch should have died in the car, not my sister."

Mary Elise shuddered. "Danny," she whispered.

Daniel appeared to have the upper hand, but—

Kent's hot breath grazed her face. Adrenaline gave her the strength to break free, powered her back away from Kent and in the direction she'd been trying to lead him earlier. She struggled to orient herself, keep from placing her own foot in a spiked trap. She stumbled, fell to the ground, pine straw offering little cushion.

Panting, she crawled, a gnarled root jamming her knee, her ears filled with harsh curses from Ammar and Danny. Thuds, grunts as fists met flesh.

She grappled for her gun. Kent advanced, foot landing

hard. Slamming through the earth and into the bucket. His scream of agony halted her. He fell to his knees, one leg trapped.

No time to waste.

Mary Elise searched the ground when more than anything she wanted to look at Daniel and reassure herself he was all right. Rustling through the pine needles, her hand grasped, found, closed around her gun.

She rolled to her back just as Kent whipped his hand from behind him. Gun drawn.

"You bitch."

Death winked in the steady steel barrel.

Heels pushing against dirt, she backed away, her arms outstretched in front of her, 9 mm aimed. "You might as well give up, Kent."

"Already have you running again, don't I? Never could stick with anything. Not even a marriage. Now you've ruined my plans. Bet you don't even have the guts to shoot me."

She wouldn't let him rile her. She kept her eyes trained on him, peripheral vision assuring her Daniel was still on his feet. She couldn't risk shots distracting him.

Let Kent talk. Ignore his words. Daniel would finish Ammar off in seconds. Kent would not win.

Dirt streaked his face, his perfectly groomed facade shot to hell and revealing the monster she knew him to be. "You believe I don't know what you're thinking, Mary Elise, but I do. I know I'm not going to make it. Ammar is no match for your lover there. And if I shoot you, no doubt Baker will kill me. Oddly enough, you inspire that kind of fanaticism in a man. I should know."

His twisted logic for love crawled over her like a lethal rash when she wanted more than ever to live. For Daniel. For the boys. For herself. She wanted life with a ferocity she hadn't expected after so long of simply existing. Daniel had brought her back to life.

Kent adjusted his knee, winced at the shift of his foot against the spikes. "Your leaving hurt me. Did you know that? I loved you and you threw our life together away. If only you'd been more patient, I wouldn't have had to hurt you, too."

The will to live flamed hotter. "Kent, you don't have to do this."

"Oh, but I do." Resolution froze his eyes to an icy blue full of certainty. "And I know the best way to hurt you back." Foot anchored in the bucket, he pivoted.

Toward Daniel.

"No!" The scream echoed in her heart, powering resolve.

She fired.

Kent bucked. Blood bloomed across his chest. Eyes widening with surprise, he fell over backward. His gun skittered from his lifeless hand as he lay, unmoving.

Mary Elise rushed to her feet, ran, toward Daniel, his hands twisted in Ammar's shirt. Daniel hauled back his fist and landed a final, knockout punch.

The boys' uncle crumpled to the ground.

Panting, Daniel barked, "Rope, from the porch."

Blood poured from the jagged tear on his flight suit sleeve, but she couldn't waste time thinking about that now. Mary Elise snagged the coil and pitched it to Daniel, her feet suddenly unsteady.

By the time she worked her way back, he'd finished tying Ammar.

Swaying, Daniel flattened a palm to the ground. Extended the other arm to her. Without hesitation or question, she fell forward, into his embrace.

Home.

* * *

Five hours later Daniel hefted his green duffle bag into the back of the SUV. His arm hurt like a son of a bitch from thirty-six freaking stitches, but he'd turned down painkillers.

He wanted a clear head to savor every minute of knowing Mary Elise lived. She had her life back, and damned if he wasn't alive, too.

The cops had already cleared the area, taken statements, hauled Ammar to a holding cell. International laws and extradition would make for a lengthy legal process. If Ammar ever saw the light of day again, at least Daniel would have time to formulate a plan for keeping the boys safe—with Mary Elise's help.

Yeah, he needed a clear head so he didn't screw up this second-chance gift with her. Whatever pace she wanted to set, he could handle, because at least they would be together. He was through running.

After all, she'd given him a gift he'd never received, not even from his father. Total acceptance. Mary Elise didn't want to change him or fix him. Damn, the woman was even okay with his job, a rare-as-hell find. All she asked was that he give her the same consideration in return.

However she wanted to take this, he'd follow and hang in for the long haul. She'd said she loved him. He could hold on to that—especially if she let him keep slathering strawberry preserves and anything else he could scavenge out of the cabinets all over her delicious body.

And he was a mighty damned good scavenger.

Daniel closed the hatch, his gaze skating over the top of the SUV out to the shoreline where Mary Elise stood. God, she was a trooper. McRae's parting "gift" to Mary Elise in the form of that funeral mass card would have leveled just about anyone. No question, if anyone deserved to die, McRae fit the bill, but still, taking a life left an irreparable bruise on a person's soul.

But Mary Elise was stronger than she'd known. His pigtailed buddy who'd needed a defender against playground bullies could bloody noses all on her own now.

She would make a helluva life partner.

Partner. A word he was only just beginning to understand, and he looked forward to a lifetime of learning more with Mary Elise's help.

He skirted the bumper, walking toward the shore. Mary Elise knelt, releasing the card into the tide before standing. He wrapped his arms around her waist and watched with her until it disappeared in the surf. Her head fell back against his chest. With that unspoken connection between them in full working order, he could feel her pain easing into a swelling acceptance.

She tipped her head, looked up at him. "I can't have children, Danny."

"I know."

"You're okay with that?"

He could only think of one reason she would ask him that question. Relief nearly drove him to his knees. Exactly where he wanted to be, on his knees proposing, begging this woman to make their love official. Instead he stayed on his feet and let her find her own pace.

After all, he was a smart guy, and more than his own happiness, he wanted hers. "Yes, I'm okay with that."

Her wise eyes held him. "That's all you have to say? Danny, I've had years to think about this, to accept it. It's more complex than just a single sentence."

Maybe to her. Not to him. But if she needed more words, more—he gulped—emotional analysis, he would dig inside himself for the words and feelings to reassure her. He turned her in his arms to face him.

"Straight-up honest, yeah, it hits me right here—" he thumped the area over his heart "—to think we'll never make a baby together, and I imagine you feel the same." He cupped her face with both hands. "But I also know in that exact same place that I'll love any child we adopt as much as any child we might have made."

Her jaw trembled.

Without a wince she'd risked the retaliation of Rubistanian guards to climb in a box with two frightened boys. No crying, she'd stood down Kent McRae, her worst nightmare, for him.

But now, two big fat tears to rival any from Austin pooled, fell over her eyelids and down her cheeks.

He brushed away the tears with his thumbs. "A child shouldn't be just an extension of me or you, or only my chromosomes and yours mixed up together. A child, our child, is a person."

A watery laugh bubbled free. "I do so love your logical mind."

"You do?" He knew but sure wouldn't mind hearing it again.

Her tears evaporated in the warmth of her smile. "Yes. Of course. I've loved you since you slugged Buddy Davis for me in the third grade."

She traced her hand gingerly over his bandage.

"Buddy's punch back then hurt a helluva lot worse than this." He captured her fingers tracing featherlight paths over his arm as if to heal it. He brought her hand to his lips. "I love you, too."

Whimsy lightened somber emerald eyes to spring grass. "More than Hostess Ho-Hos?"

"Oh, damn, that's a tough one."

She slugged his uninjured arm.

Laughing, he pulled her close, inhaled the scent of honeysuckle shampoo and the promise of forever. He held her while the wind encircled them and could have sworn there was something symbolic in the moment. A damned strange thought for a man more comfortable in the mathematical realm.

He held her closer. "You know I'm not a flowery-words kind of guy. I wish I could tell you how much I love you with the poetry that you deserve. All I can say is that I love you. No measurements. No limits."

Her hands hooked around his neck, she stood in his arms, unmoving while they both watched the fading sunlight stain the sky deeper hues of purple.

One hand slid from his neck to his shoulder, unzipping his sleeve pocket. He smiled, already planning his one-knee proposal once she passed him the ring.

Mary Elise inched away, the solitaire between two fingers. He reached to take it.

She pulled her hand back farther. "Wanna marry me, Danny Baker?"

Surprise nipped and he wasn't complaining at all. He was starting to like the way she assumed the aggressive role. "Yes, I do. Very much."

She placed the ring in his palm and extended her fingers. He slid the engagement diamond in place again. Forever.

He sealed its placement with a kiss on her finger, followed by one on her lips, and knew without question he would be challenged, entranced, in love with this woman for the rest of his life. A strong woman who would, hell yes, demand the best of him.

And would give her best in return.

Pulling back, he stared into eyes a shade of green he'd only ever found on one woman. "Are you ready to go?"

"Yeah, Danny," she answered, her voice echoing with surety along the salty breeze. "I'm all set."

He hooked his arm around her shoulders as he'd done a thousand times before with Mary Elise, his best friend, his love. "Then let's go get the boys and start putting our family together."

Epilogue

Mary Elise paced around the oval table, spinning each empty chair she passed. Waiting sucked. But the reward for patience would be worth every lap on the industrial carpet in the private hospital waiting room.

"Settle down, boys." Daniel hooked an arm around each brother, immobilizing the hyper kids with a pseudo-wrestling match that landed them on the blue-plaid sofa.

Thank goodness the hospital had provided a small conference room for gathering to meet the newest member of their family. The baby had been born nearly an hour ago, but Daniel had requested they not hear the gender until the infant was brought to them after the doctor finished the exam.

Even though the boys had only arrived a half hour prior, she had been waiting at the hospital with Danny from the minute the call came that the birth mother had gone into labor. Darcy and Max had brought the boys over later, and even now were down in the cafeteria picking up food. Maybe the boys should have gone with them, but she'd been so afraid they would miss "the moment."

Of course Trey and Austin had been more impatient in waiting for their new sibling than she would have expected. The aide from the adoption agency had suggested she and Danny might want to leave the boys home and bring them later.

The boys' crestfallen faces at the mere mention of delay had swayed her.

Danny gave both brothers noogies on the head before releasing them. "Hang tough and we'll go to IHOP soon."

"No chocolate chips," ten-year-old Trey insisted.

"Roger that, bro."

Mary Elise extended her arms for Austin and hitched him on her hip. "How about we check out all the pictures again?"

"Nuh-uh." The wriggling four-year-old slid from her grip back to the floor, seeming more in need of a run to the snack bar than another perusal of a doctor's diplomas.

Snick. The door opened.

Last-minute nerves tangled in her tummy. They knew without question the birth mother was firmly committed to giving up her child. Still, what if the nurse entered empty-handed....

A nurse wearing surgical scrubs backed in, tugging a rolling basinet, the clear sides revealing the wrapped and squirming infant inside.

A newborn with a pink cap.

Mary Elise clutched Danny's arm, endlessly grateful she could share this moment with him. "A girl."

A tide of tender emotion wiped all the traces of nervous butterflies away. At long last, they had their baby.

Smiling, Danny looped an arm around her and drew

her against him for a quick kiss full of joy and even tears. "Yeah, 'Lise, we have a daughter."

The past year as Danny's wife had been a gift worth waiting for, like this child. Sure, the path hadn't always been easy with long TDYs, the boys adjusting to their new life, her finding her way as an education columnist. But with Danny at her side again, loving her, she could conquer anything.

He palmed Mary Elise's back, nudging her forward. She almost charged ahead, then changed her mind. This was Danny's child, too. "Will you bring her to me, please?"

His widening smile, crinkling chocolate-brown eyes, made a hefty reward in exchange for the extra seconds' delay in holding her daughter.

The boys, now stunned silent, stared at the pink blankets with quiet reverence. Mary Elise clutched Trey's and Austin's hands while Danny crossed the small conference room. Stopping in front of the steel-framed wheeled bassinet, he slid broad hands beneath the tiny bundle, cradling her like a pro.

Like a father.

He didn't turn right away, instead standing in profile, gazing down at the tiny face and whispering greetings. A boyish lock of hair fell forward over his brow with familiar regularity. As much as Mary Elise wanted to see her baby, she froze, mesmerized by the glow of love warming her husband's eyes as he met their daughter. An image she would always cherish.

And then he pivoted toward Mary Elise, placed their baby girl into the cradle of her arms as she'd imagined him doing so often.

Her arms filled as quickly as her heart.

How amazing that in a simple second, she couldn't remember a time when this precious little one hadn't been in her life. Mary Elise stroked a knuckle over her daughter's tipped nose, chubby cheek, along the softest skin ever.

"Well, hello, Mary Francis," she crooned her child's name—Mary Francis, after Daniel's father, Franklin, the man who'd given them all a second chance.

She sank to the sofa, Austin and Trey crawling up beside her, Danny kneeling in front of her. His flight suit stretched across his broad, reliable shoulders, almost pulling out the wrinkles she never could seem to iron free. Not that she really wanted to dispense with those creases. Danny suited her just fine as he was, with his rumpled uniforms and knee-melting kisses.

The nurse backed toward the door. "I'll leave y'all alone to get acquainted. Just buzz me when you're ready for her to go back to the nursery."

Mary Elise wasn't sure that time would ever come.

Trey tickled Mary Francis under the chin. "You're named for my dad, Austin's and your daddy's dad, too."

Austin leaned over, closer. "Ooh-rah. Okay? Don't be listening to Trey when he tells ya somethin' else."

Laughter chimed, then faded, smiles remaining as they became acquainted with tiny Mary Francis—her round face with wide eyes, her sprigs of dark hair and the sweet smell of baby.

Daniel cupped the back of Mary Elise's neck, pulled her forward for a kiss, his forehead falling to rest on hers after. "Life is good."

"Yeah, Danny, it sure is." Love swelled, flowed in their old connection, but broader now, binding them in a circle through the family they'd built together.

Years ago, Mary Elise had dreamed of filling her arms with Danny Baker's children. But she never could have envisioned anything quite this perfect.

* * * * *

Watch for a new Wingmen Warrior *story
from Catherine Mann coming in March 2004
from Silhouette Books. Longer and filled
with more action, adventure and romance,*
ANYTHING, ANYWHERE, ANYTIME
is a book you won't want to miss!

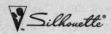

INTIMATE MOMENTS™

Coming in December 2003

The second in

KATHLEEN
CREIGHTON's

miniseries

★★★★★★★★★★★★★

Starrs of the West
Born to shine…

★★★★★★★★★★★★★

The Top Gun's Return
(Silhouette Intimate Moments #1262)

Jessie Bauer was amazed to learn that her "late" husband was on his way back to her—very much alive! But were the ghosts of Tristan's past going to keep him and Jessie from having a future?

And coming in spring 2004, look for another exciting Starr family story, only from Silhouette Intimate Moments.

Available at your favorite retail outlet.

If you enjoyed what you just read,
then we've got an offer you can't resist!

Take 2 bestselling love stories FREE!

Plus get a FREE surprise gift!

✂

Your opinion is important to us! Please take a few moments to share your thoughts with us about your experiences with Harlequin and Silhouette books. Your comments will be very useful in ensuring that we deliver books you love to read.
Please take a few minutes to complete the questionnaire, then send it to us at the address below.

Send your completed questionnaires to:
Harlequin/Silhouette Reader Survey, P.O. Box 9046, Buffalo, NY 14269-9046

---

1. As you may know, there are many different lines under the Harlequin and Silhouette brands. Each of the lines is listed below. Please check the box that most represents your reading habit for each line.

Line	Currently read this line	Do not read this line	Not sure if I read this line
Harlequin American Romance	❏	❏	❏
Harlequin Duets	❏	❏	❏
Harlequin Romance	❏	❏	❏
Harlequin Historicals	❏	❏	❏
Harlequin Superromance	❏	❏	❏
Harlequin Intrigue	❏	❏	❏
Harlequin Presents	❏	❏	❏
Harlequin Temptation	❏	❏	❏
Harlequin Blaze	❏	❏	❏
Silhouette Special Edition	❏	❏	❏
Silhouette Romance	❏	❏	❏
Silhouette Intimate Moments	❏	❏	❏
Silhouette Desire	❏	❏	❏

2. Which of the following best describes why you bought *this book?* One answer only, please.

the picture on the cover	❏	the title	❏
the author	❏	the line is one I read often	❏
part of a miniseries	❏	saw an ad in another book	❏
saw an ad in a magazine/newsletter	❏	a friend told me about it	❏
I borrowed/was given this book	❏	other: _____	❏

3. Where did you buy *this book?* One answer only, please.

at Barnes & Noble	❏	at a grocery store	❏
at Waldenbooks	❏	at a drugstore	❏
at Borders	❏	on eHarlequin.com Web site	❏
at another bookstore	❏	from another Web site	❏
at Wal-Mart	❏	Harlequin/Silhouette Reader	❏
at Target	❏	Service/through the mail	
at Kmart	❏	used books from anywhere	
at another department store or mass merchandiser	❏	I borrowed/was given this book	❏

4. On average, how many Harlequin and Silhouette books do you buy at one time?

I buy _____ books at one time	❏
I rarely buy a book	❏

MRQ403SIM-1A

5. How many times per month do you shop for any *Harlequin and/or Silhouette* books?
One answer only, please.

1 or more times a week	❑	a few times per year	❑
1 to 3 times per month	❑	less often than once a year	❑
1 to 2 times every 3 months	❑	never	❑

6. When you think of your ideal heroine, which *one* statement describes her the best?
One answer only, please.

She's a woman who is strong-willed	❑	She's a desirable woman	❑
She's a woman who is needed by others	❑	She's a powerful woman	❑
She's a woman who is taken care of	❑	She's a passionate woman	❑
She's an adventurous woman	❑	She's a sensitive woman	❑

7. The following statements describe types or genres of books that you may be
interested in reading. Pick *up to 2 types* of books that you are most interested in.

I like to read about truly romantic relationships	❑
I like to read stories that are sexy romances	❑
I like to read romantic comedies	❑
I like to read a romantic mystery/suspense	❑
I like to read about romantic adventures	❑
I like to read romance stories that involve family	❑
I like to read about a romance in times or places that I have never seen	❑
Other: _____	❑

*The following questions help us to group your answers with those readers who are
similar to you. Your answers will remain confidential.*

8. Please record your year of birth below.

19 _____

9. What is your marital status?

single ❑   married ❑   common-law ❑   widowed ❑
divorced/separated ❑

10. Do you have children 18 years of age or younger currently living at home?

yes ❑   no ❑

11. Which of the following best describes your employment status?

employed full-time or part-time ❑   homemaker ❑   student ❑
retired ❑   unemployed ❑

12. Do you have access to the Internet from either home or work?

yes ❑   no ❑

13. Have you ever visited eHarlequin.com?

yes ❑   no ❑

14. What state do you live in?

_____

15. Are you a member of Harlequin/Silhouette Reader Service?

yes ❑   Account # _____   no ❑   MRQ403SIM-1B

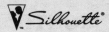
Silhouette®

INTIMATE MOMENTS™

A new miniseries by popular author
RaeAnne Thayne

THE SEARCHERS
Finding family
where they least expected it...

Beginning with
Nowhere To Hide
(Silhouette Intimate Moments #1264)

Single mother Lisa Connors was trying to
protect her little girls. But when she met her
new next-door neighbor, handsome FBI agent
Gage McKinnon, she knew her heart was
in danger, as well....

**And coming soon from Silhouette Intimate
Moments—the rest of the McKinnons' stories.**

*Available December 2003
at your favorite retail outlet.*

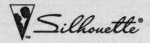
Silhouette®

COMING NEXT MONTH